MARCO

THE COUGARS AND CUBS SERIES BOOK #5

GIGI MEIER

GiGi Meier

Cover Design by GiGi Meier

Developmental Editing by Deep Roots Editing

Editing by Lukas and Leigh Literary Services

Author Photograph by Tara L. Grundemeier

ISBN: 978-1-963625-06-6 (e)

ISBN: 978-1-963625-07-3 (pb)

GiGi Meier Media LLC

GET TWO FREE BOOKS

Sign up for my newsletter to ensure you are the first to know about new releases, sneak peek excerpts, cover reveals, book sales, and author giveaways!

The Cougars and Cubs Series
is steamy, naughty instalust
reverse age gap fun.

DOWNLOAD FOR FREE ON MY WEBSITE
www.gigimeier.com

Paolo and Taylor's story is a duel POV, meet cute,
reverse age gap, workplace romance.

The Cañon Series 🖤

is deliciously dark and intensely traumatic.

DOWNLOAD FOR FREE ON MY WEBSITE

www.gigimeier.com

Dani and Tomlin's story is a single POV, slow burn, enemies-to-lovers, forced proximity romance. Check my website for a list of content and trigger warnings.

DEDICATION

To the hopeless romantics that believe in fate.

MARCO

1

MARCO

As I jog along the winding path of the bayou, the cool breeze is a welcome newcomer, with the edges of summer finally ebbing away. A lifelong resident of Houston, I've learned to coexist with the sweltering heat and oppressive humidity. But that doesn't mean I enjoy it. Most people I know feel the same way.

That's why I choose to run in the early hours of the morning. I once made the mistake of running after work in the sweltering heat, which was torture. If I wanted to endure that kind of pain, I'd work out harder with Giovanni.

With a lone runner passing on my left, I have the entire area to myself to run, breathe, and think. It's my morning meditation. My mind, ever the restless companion, shifts gears from my physical exertion to the digital workspace waiting for me. At the tech startup where I work, we're gearing up to launch a new app designed to help users reduce their carbon footprint by integrating real-time public transit data with their personal schedules.

Our app integrates real-time bus, train, and transit data, along with walking, cycling, and ride-sharing options, to offer users the most efficient routes for their journeys. It provides detailed information on travel times, costs, calories burned, and even CO_2 savings compared to driving a car, helping users make more sustainable choices.

It's an ambitious project. As the lead technology engineer, I ensure the software functions flawlessly and resonates with our environmentally conscious user base. The code needs to be seamless and intuitive. Every second a user struggles is a second closer to giving up the app and our company for this and future initiatives.

The debugging session is scheduled for later today. A persistent glitch in the user interface has been eluding my team, making my hours at work long and my body tight from stress. Running helps, lifting weights is better, but having sex is the best. It's been a long time since that happened. Too long. Sure, I could hit up the bars in Midtown or the Heights, but casual sex hasn't ever been my thing. I much prefer having a woman to call my own.

I glance down at my watch, tracking my pace and speed to see if I'm running too fast. Work frustrations and irritation sometimes cause me to do this.

My exhalation mixes with the sounds of traffic melding beside me as the path curls upward toward the Allen Parkway, past the cemetery, and across from the residential high-rises.

This is one of my favorite routes to run. The views shift from serene nature to bustling city streets, finally ending in the affluent neighborhood of River Oaks, where I dream of building my parents a sustainable and eco-friendly home.

Being the oldest of four kids—my younger siblings are all sisters, with at least thirteen years between them—it's family first. My parents ingrained in me a responsibility to put family above all else. With me being a teenage pregnancy statistic—the result of two horny teens going at it in the back of a Ford Escort—my parents were forced to marry before I was born.

That threw a wrench in many of their plans, but it worked out in the end. My dad finished college and started his career while my mom took care of me. They always wanted a big family. It didn't happen until a lot later—also, not part of their plan. I was just a kid myself when they were having problems getting pregnant.

Not that I understood any of it, but eventually, my sister came along right around my thirteenth birthday. She was an easy baby. I helped as much as I could until the next two came two years apart. By the time I turned eighteen, I was ready to head off to college, but only to my surprise, my parents insisted I stay in town.

Despite having scholarships to pay for school, I knew they couldn't cover the out-of-state living expenses. As the firstborn and only son, I felt obligated to help my parents as much as possible without being a financial burden.

I sailed through my bachelor's and master's degrees, eyeing California for more lucrative offers in greener states. When I discussed my offers out of graduate school with my dad, he said money isn't everything.

It's one of many factors that contributed to my overall decision. As much as I wanted to believe him, I would have preferred making more money and advancing my career, but I couldn't tell my mom and sisters that I was leaving. Thus, here I am, twenty-five years old and still in Houston.

My watch starts pinging wildly from what I assume are exercise alerts until it vibrates with an incoming call from my boss's assistant, which is even more unusual due to the early hour. Slowing to a light jog, my heart racing radically in my chest, I hit the button and shield it with my hand to speak into it.

"Maddie? Everything okay?"

With the honking cars on the roadway beside me, I round

the corner, jogging up a private street to escape the noise as she starts talking.

"No, Preston's losing his shit. Apparently, the venture capitalist group found out about the bug and has been blowing up Preston's phone. They are coming into the office today to see it for themselves."

The panic in her voice and the message she delivers cause my pulse to spike despite its already frantic beating. I slow to a walk, my mind racing through the details of what she's saying.

"Wait, are you at the office?" I remove my hand to check the time, ignoring the metrics from my run. "It's just past 5 AM."

"Yeah, I came in early to handle some filings, thinking I'd be alone, and then this explodes."

A ripple of panic rolls through my body.

"Preston's there with you?" I ask in disbelief while wiping the sweat from my brow.

Preston Walton is the founder and CEO of our startup. We're one of several startups he has, so the likelihood of seeing him once a week is remote, as he's usually at his other companies. The fact that he's in the office is a surprise, but it's an absolute shocker at this early hour, making my stomach turn.

"Yes! That's what I'm telling you! I've tried to calm Preston down, but he's pacing like a caged animal."

Her words break up in the middle, but the stress in her tone is apparent. I turn on my heel, heading back the way I came, and narrowly avoid being hit by a car when I neglect to look both ways. Its red brake lights reflect on my face when it stops at the end of the road to merge into traffic.

"Marco!"

"Yeah, yeah, I'm here."

I round the corner and walk faster, careful not to lose her on my watch's reception, given the tall timbers surrounding me.

"How did they find out?"

"Beats me, but you must get here as soon as possible. This is your launch."

The news is a gut punch. I take a deep breath and transition from a brisk walk to a jog. I need to think and prepare for what awaits me at the office.

"Marco! Did you hear me?"

I shake my thoughts away, focusing on what she's saying while paying attention to the traffic as I cross Shepherd Drive to return to my apartment. My heart is hammering in my chest, but not from my workout.

"Yeah."

Her worry reflects in my tone. I navigate a tight curve in the path, my sneakers slapping the pavement as I push toward the downtown skyline as the streets become more congested with morning commuters.

"Okay, keep Preston occupied until I get there."

"I've been trying, but you know how he gets under pressure," Maddie replies, the sound of papers shuffling in the background painting a vivid picture of the disarray.

"Just tell him to hold tight. I'm less than twenty minutes out on my run. I should be in the office in under an hour. Can you start contacting the team and get them to report their updates? I want everything as soon as I walk in."

I learned to manage crises from my dad, Eduardo, from all the times I was trapped in the car with him, his calls on speakerphone, with no other option but to listen. It annoyed me at the time, especially when he was taking me to school. Now, I am emulating him, and a brief smile crosses my face despite our current situation.

"Got it. Oh, and Marco?" Maddie adds quickly, her voice getting lost in the angry honking of two cars trying to merge and neither wanting to yield. "The lead VC, Mr. Dawson, is personally leading the group coming in. He sounds . . . not happy."

Shit, Dawson is already alerted to this? It's one thing to contain in-house, but having the news hit the venture capitalist guys is worse.

"I'll handle Dawson. Ensure the front desk knows to send them straight to the conference room when they arrive. Order the usual breakfast crap. We need to do everything we can to soften the blow and buy us time until we track down the issue and how they found out about it in the first place."

"Will do. I got to go. Preston's stomping this way. Pray for me."

The words are barely out before he's shouting at her, demanding to know who she's talking to when the line disconnects. I stare at my watch for a few seconds until the face clears and my workout app appears.

Picking up the pace, I dodge a few pedestrians and sprint past a city bus as it groans to a halt. My mind is already shifting gears to how I'll approach the impending confrontation.

Preston will be hot on my heels, demanding answers I don't have and needing to speak to the team. Dawson will be hot on Preston if he gets a hold of him before I do. It's always an interesting triangle between us. Dawson rarely gets face time with Preston.

That's half the problem. Preston defers to me as lead developer, the technical jargon going above his head at times. Dawson hates that, thinking he deserves to only speak to the owner, not the lonely programmer making it all work. Too bad.

I pick up the pace. The physical exertion grounds me as my thoughts plan, plot, and practice what I will say to Dawson and Preston. Maddie's a champ for calling and even more of a champ for being in the office early enough to run interference for me.

She's one of the firm's saving graces, having convinced me to take this position over the lure of a bigger paycheck from the oil and gas companies that dominate this town. Maddie was a year ahead of me at school. We shared the same classes until she downshifted to an easier degree, but we kept up our friendship when she graduated.

By the time I circle back to my starting point, the sun has partially risen over the horizon, casting golden hues over the bayou's water. I feel ready and energized to handle venture capitalists and angry bosses, requiring tact and boldness. I'm prepared to leverage both. After all, it's not just my job on the line but the aspirations of an entire team that believes in what we're building.

My watch buzzes with a text from Maddie.

> Conference room ready. Breakfast ordered.
> Get here FAST!!!

2

VICTORIA

The morning air is crisp, and a gentle breeze flirts with the fallen leaves, creating a soft rustling sound as I step onto the bustling construction site. Towering steel skeletons stretch into the sky, outlining what will soon be one of Houston's most innovative residential complexes. My latest project provides opulent living and redefines sustainability in a town not known for many green building initiatives.

I climb out of my Tesla, my hazel eyes hidden behind my protective shades, clutching my clipboard like a shield. The familiar thrill of staring at my creation—the project I lobbied for within my firm and won out over my male counterparts—is a hefty responsibility, especially as I live my brother's dream. These were his lofty ambitions, which I unexpectedly inherited years ago.

As a child, he watched the Miami skyline transform. Its towering structures of steel and glass, with designs so innovative, made him dream of his name as the architect who designed one. Every day, he studied the progress of the buildings and watched the cranes swirl with building materials as the floors rose higher and higher, all from the confines of his hospital bed.

As they progressed, ascending higher to scrape the sky, he descended into the pits of his illness. Fighting day and night until he finally succumbed to the cancer that ultimately called him home. It's those collective moments and memories, where he would educate me on what and how they were building them, that I carry in my heart as I make my way through the site.

This project, like all my projects, is for him. Not as the architect he once wanted to be but as a project manager, a last-minute switch and a less rigorous degree plan that had me suddenly stepping into his shoes.

I nod and exchange brief pleasantries with the workers, my gaze sweeping over every inch of progress. The project is a dream turning into reality, equipped with solar panels, rainwater harvesting systems, and an advanced HVAC system engineered to minimize environmental impact. Each component is an ode to innovation, but today, my focus narrows on one aspect in particular—the energy systems, the heart of our eco-friendly certification efforts to achieve the coveted LEED certification.

Approaching the central housing where the HVAC systems hum, my expression turns to a frown. These systems, my supposed pièce de résistance, have morphed into a persistent headache. They're failing to mesh with the building's array of smart technologies.

Those crucial communication points, the thermostats stubbornly resist sync with the central system, creating a cascade of inefficiencies that threaten to tarnish the project's green credentials.

Pausing by a large blueprint draped across a makeshift table, I toss my dark brown waves over my shoulder and rub my temples in frustration. Despite rounds of consultations with experts and endless tweaks to the settings, the solution remains elusive, dancing just beyond my grasp. Knowing how much rides on getting this right—not just for the project but for my reputation and, frankly, my sanity—is maddening.

Determined, I scribble my notes on the clipboard, an old-fashioned throwback to the one my brother used in the hospital when documenting the daily changes in the buildings around the hospital that no one else noticed but him.

I begin recording notes, detailing every discrepancy I observe. The meticulous documentation is second nature to me, a practice honed in by years of being a team member on complex projects and their more complicated problems.

"This has to work," I mutter in exasperation.

As the morning progresses, I make my way to each critical junction of the HVAC system, examining connections, reviewing interface settings, and consulting with mechanical engineers who share their observations and frustrations. Each conversation deepens my understanding of the issue and refines my problem-solving approach.

The engineers are skilled, but integrating such advanced systems requires a nuanced understanding of technology and communications. I usually excel in this area, except this time. Having tried all of them, I'm running out of solutions.

Lost in thought, my ears pick up snippets of conversation from a pair of site engineers nearby. They're animatedly discussing a tech startup known for its cutting-edge environmental solutions. They particularly praise their advanced smart thermostats, which promise seamless integration with various systems to boost overall energy efficiency. My interest surges, an unexpected lifeline thrown my way amid the turmoil.

"Excuse me," I interject, stepping towards the engineers with renewed vigor. "Could you repeat the name of that startup? The one with the smart thermostats?"

"Oh, sure. It's Urban Green Innovators. They've been doing some really innovative stuff with adaptive AI for building management systems," an engineer explains, her eyes lighting up with enthusiasm under her white hard hat.

Urban Green Innovators—just the name sounds promising. I jot it down, a flicker of hope igniting within me. Perhaps this is the missing piece, the answer to the puzzle I've been trying to solve.

"Thank you."

My mind races with possibilities as I circle the name several times with my red pen, intending to look them up when I return to my car. The rest of the morning is consumed by cautious optimism that maybe, just maybe, Urban Green Innovators holds the key to the stubborn issues plaguing my project.

As the morning wanes, the construction site quiets for lunch. The clamor of machinery gives way to the softer sounds of the city beyond. I wrap up my final inspection for the day, eager to grab a bite and investigate this new company.

My strides take a brisk pace as I head back to my car, the gravel crunching under my boots where the landscaping will eventually go. Settling into the driver's seat, I waste no time looking up this possible savior to my project and career. With pages full of releases and recognition of the brilliance, the startup part has me frowning. My company is selective with vendors and requires them to undergo a rigorous due diligence process to even make it onto the approved vendor list.

Compliance and legal usually take months to approve a process. If there were a way to fast-track it, I could use it to solve this problem. I've gone through our existing vendor list, meeting with different ones, and come back with more problems than answers at an increased cost that would blow my budget.

With a heavy sigh, I click on their homepage, filled with testimonials, accolades from happy customers, and even a couple of recognizable names. Each click intrigues me further until a particular entry catches my eye—a detailed case study of a recent project like mine carried out with a well-known real estate developer.

The photographs showcase sleek, modern buildings operating seamlessly with integrated, eco-friendly technology solutions from Urban Green Innovators.

It inspires a new wave of optimism and sparks a new strategy. Demonstrating that they have already collaborated with reputable developers might provide the leverage needed to obtain compliance and legal approvals. I quickly screenshot the case study, noting key data highlighting its effectiveness and reliability.

Striking while the iron is hot, I pull up the contact page on their website and dial the number listed. As the phone rings, I rehearse my introduction, ready to explain the urgency and potential fit of their technology with our project. The line connects, and a cheerful voice answers.

"Urban Green Innovators, this is Maddie. How can I help you today?"

"Hi Maddie, my name is Victoria Vega. I came across your company and the work you did for Satterfield's high-rise complex and wondered if you could help," I blurt out far too much information if this is simply the receptionist.

My exuberance to have a possible solution overrides my typically polished and professional demeanor.

"Ah, yes. That building is one of our showcase projects! We're really proud of the work we did there." Her tone brims with pride, garnering an enthusiastic smile from me. "How can we specifically assist with your project, Ms. Vega?"

Realizing I might have gotten ahead of myself, I take a breath to regain my composure.

"I'm leading a sustainable residential complex here in Houston, and we're encountering some integration issues with our current HVAC systems and smart technologies. I believe your smart thermostats could be the solution we need."

"Oh yes, I'd love to connect you with our lead project manager, who can discuss this in detail. Unfortunately, he and the team are behind closed doors now but should be available later this afternoon. Can I take your contact information and have Marco return your call as soon as he's available?"

"Absolutely."

I release a huge breath, relief sinking into every pore of my body while relaying my information.

"Great! I'll make sure to give him the message as soon as possible. Thank you for considering our firm, Victoria. Have a wonderful day!"

After the call concludes, I hang up, and am buzzing with excitement that I might have finally found the company to solve my problems. Not wanting to lose momentum, I open my phone's inbox and draft an email to our compliance officer, attaching the screenshots and highlighting the similarities between the Satterfield project and our own. I emphasize Urban Green Innovators' potential to solve our current problems and elevate our project's sustainability credentials.

"Given the precedent set by their successful collaboration with other esteemed developers, I believe a swift review would be in our best interest," I write, infusing the message with a sense of urgency backed by solid evidence. "Their innovative technology could be the linchpin in achieving our environmental goals and maintaining our project timeline and budget."

With a few more convincing, quasi-pleading sentences, I hit send. Anticipation and anxiety settle over me as I lob the vendor's due diligence ball into their court to get started. To bolster my case further, I decide to reach out to the developer mentioned in the case study. A quick LinkedIn search yields the contact details of the project manager who oversaw the collaboration with Urban Green Innovators. I draft a polite inquiry, requesting a brief conversation about their experience with the startup's technology and services.

As I send off the second email, I sink into my seat, allowing myself a moment to breathe. The next steps are out of my hands, but I've done everything possible to tilt the odds in my favor. With a bit of luck and some bureaucratic agility, they might soon be part of my project, supplying the solutions I desperately need.

"Well, I think I earned myself a long lunch."

I chuckle, slipping on my sunglasses and opening my sunroof to let the breeze caress my skin as I pull out of the parking spot. As I drive away from the site, my thoughts linger on the possibilities ahead.

Today could mark a turning point—the day when a significant challenge morphed into a breakthrough opportunity—all thanks to a serendipitous overhearing and a dash of proactive digging.

3

MARCO

I stagger out of the conference room, feeling every bit as worn as the fraying cuffs on my white shirt. It's been a relentless day—a marathon of technical issues and high-stress meetings. I loosen my tie with a weary sigh, letting the fabric slide between my fingers.

The room is finally quiet, the echoes of raised voices and clattering keyboards lingering in the air. Dawson, the venture capitalist with a fierce, no-nonsense reputation, was the last to storm out. His exit was marked by a door slam and a stern warning to "get this sorted by Monday."

My team, a group of exhausted programmers and engineers, slump over their workstation. Their tired eyes are still fixed on flickering screens.

I run a hand through my hair, catching on the gel I used hours ago. Ever the storm cloud, Preston retreated to his office, leaving a trail of muttered complaints about deadlines and reputational risks.

I reach for my phone, collapsing in my chair to order Chinese food from a place that stays open late. Providing dinner is the least I can do for my team, considering we still have hours of work ahead of us.

Turning to gaze out the window, I stare at the city lights twinkling back at me. My eyes fall to the swimming pool on the hotel's third floor across the street from my building. In the summer, it's a welcome distraction that gets plenty of attention from the programmers when attractive women are out there. In the autumn, the pool temperature is too cold, and the place is usually empty.

It reminds me of life outside the stark, artificial glow of my office. Being disconnected and adrift amid a sea of code and malfunctioning software feels surreal. Our latest fix is holding for now. Testing is underway again, and everyone's silently hoping it sticks.

Maddie's desk is the same wreck we feel from this chaotic day. Abandoned papers are strewn about. Empty coffee cups mark the hours she's been at the office. Long before any of us and dealing with Preston alone. Poor women.

She deserves all the wine she wants to guzzle tonight at her book club meeting. I feel a stab of guilt for all the long hours and early mornings she spent dealing with us lug heads and our egos. She even said as much when rubbing her forehead, complaining of a headache and an overdose of testosterone.

I flash her an apologetic look as I hurry down the hall to my office. Not before she yells for me to return the calls that have piled up for me during the day that aren't critical and related to the problem at hand.

While waiting for the food to arrive and shutting out the view from my window, I start on my inbox. It's overflowing with correspondence from my other projects in various states. My fingertips fly across my keyboard, and I forward reports and metrics from my contractors to necessary parties when Maddie's email about a new prospective client gets my attention.

The information is sparse. It includes a brief explanation of the problem, the company's name, and the contact details of the project manager in charge.

I flip to my browser to investigate the company. Pages upon pages of their projects come up, and I sit forward in my chair. The more I read, the more intrigued I become, realizing the scope and impact of their work, which represents hundreds of millions of dollars in multi-purpose and residential developments.

This could be a substantial opportunity for us. With an unexpected surge of excitement, I want to understand precisely what they do and how we might help them.

Glancing at my watch, I frown and note that it's well past business hours. Concern flickers through me as I debate whether Maddie's phone number is a cell or a work number.

I hesitate, not wanting to risk a late-night call that might be unwelcome or too intrusive if it turns out to be her personal line. The last thing I want to do is jeopardize a potential client relationship by not respecting their time despite having hours worth of more work ahead of me.

Deciding to err on the side of caution, I take a more professional approach and navigate back to the company's website to locate its main contact number. I hope they have a company directory where I can leave a message for her to get on Monday morning. It's probably best anyway, considering how exhausted I am and how blurry my mind is with all that's happened today.

I dial the number, and when the line connects, the automated line guides me through their massive operations to pick her name. Of course, she doesn't answer. I keep the details brief but infuse energy and enthusiasm into the call, which is the opposite of how depleted I am.

After leaving a clear and concise voicemail, I return to my computer, feeling the fatigue tug at the edges of my focus. Despite the long hours and the mental drain, following up with an email will solidify my intent and allow her to reach out this weekend if she so desires.

I navigate to the company's website and head to the "About Us" section to search for her profile. Luckily, the website is well-organized, and I find the information I need quickly. I draft a brief email conveying the same details. As I finish up, my mom's number appears on my screen. She seldom calls, preferring that I call her instead, aware that my hectic job keeps me constantly busy.

My heart races yet again today, but this time for a completely different reason. I answer immediately, rising to my feet, prepared to dash out of the office if it's an emergency.

"Mom, is everything okay?"

Through the phone, the sounds of my family's bustling household fill my ear—the chatter of my sisters and the television blaring in the background so my dad can hear it.

"Yes, mijo. Why wouldn't it be?"

Her voice remains calm and steady, almost drowned out by the surrounding chaos. She makes no attempt to find a quieter place. If anything, it seems she's moving towards the source of the noise.

"It's really loud. I can barely hear you."

"I know. I don't want to bother you because you're always so busy with your big job. But I needed to remind you about tomorrow. Don't forget to pick me up at 8 AM, okay?"

Shit.

I pinch the bridge of my nose. Indeed, I had forgotten about tomorrow. She needs my help setting up at the local farmer's market for a community health awareness event. Usually, my dad and sisters help with this sort of thing, but apparently, the girls ran off last time. My parents panicked until they found them across the parking lot, watching a lady get henna tattoos on her hands.

"Of course, Mom. I'll be there," I assure her, trying to mask the guilt seeping into my voice for forgetting. "Eight sharp, don't worry."

My gaze roams over my desk, covered in schematics and technical notes scribbled on a legal pad. I need more than twenty-four hours in a day and to figure out how to clone myself as I fall helplessly behind on my workload. Taking her to the market is the last thing I have time for.

"Good. You know how important this is to me, and after last time . . . well, I just feel better knowing you'll be there."

Her voice mingles with the increasing volume of the television in the background before she rattles something off to my dad that I didn't quite catch. Hopefully telling him to turn the TV down.

"No worries. We'll get everything set up."

"Thank you." There's a pause, and I can almost picture her nodding, satisfied with my commitment to be there. "You sound tired, Marco."

I absently pick up a stray paperclip, twisting it between my fingers. When I don't respond, she continues, "Are you eating properly and getting enough sleep?"

These two questions are her trademark, posed repeatedly throughout my life, even after I moved out. She asked them in college, even extending the inquiry to my roommates when they fell ill. Her famous healing soup would arrive at my off-campus apartment, much to my dad's chagrin as the delivery man. She accompanied the gallon-size containers with neatly printed cards that detailed how to reheat the soup.

"I'm fine, Mom. It's just been a long day."

I dispel her maternal concerns, not wanting to add to her worries even if I'm not eating or sleeping well. Caring for our family is already tough enough. One less child to look after lightens her load, even if she'll never admit it.

"You always say that, mijo, but remember, your health is

important. You can't do good work if you're run down. Make sure you're taking care of yourself."

Even though she can't see me, I smile and turn away from the window. My gaze lands on the neat rows of engineering and technical books cluttering my small bookshelf, symbolizing all the hours and dollars my parents spent making my dream job possible. There's not enough gratitude in the world to thank them properly, even if I try my hardest to make them proud.

"I will, Mom. I ordered dinner. Just waiting for it to get here."

"Good," she says, a hint of relief in her tone. "Wait, are you still at the office? At this hour?"

I debate for a few seconds about lying, then think otherwise, as she always has a way of knowing, even over the phone.

"Yes, but it's important that I'm here. My team is still working, and I am working alongside them. I can't leave until we're all done."

Her sigh ripples through the phone, even over my sisters' screaming and arguing with each other.

"Oh, I will bake them cookies and give them to you tomorrow. They need more than fast food as a reward."

My mom thinks cookies are a reward at my age, which is hilarious. We could easily have them delivered alongside the food already coming. Equally funny is how she calls restaurant food fast food, as they are distinctly different. Both are lumped together in her book as being loaded with chemicals and bad for me.

Eating out was the gravest of sins growing up. I yearned for McDonalds as a teenager until I had it for the first time. The mystery meat and greasy french fries convinced me she might be right. However, some excellent restaurants rival her cooking, something I'd never admit.

"You don't have to make the guys cookies."

I do little to hide the annoyance in my voice, something she hates, but usually gets the message that she's over-mothering me across.

"Nonsense. I'm making them. End of story."

If the certainty in her tone doesn't drive home her point, it's the last few words. The ones spoken every time she wins an argument with me, my dad, or my siblings. I twist the paperclip even faster, unenthused, by hauling in mandatory cookies tomorrow. The guys will love it, though.

"I'll try."

I manage a weary smile, knowing this is her way of caring from afar. My office line buzzes with a call from the security desk on the first floor, signaling that the food has arrived.

"Mom, I got to run. I'll see you in the morning."

"Bright and early. And get a decent night's sleep. You work too hard."

WITH THE LAST box unloaded and Mom fussing over her tablecloth, I press my thumbs into my back, hearing popping sounds along my spine. The late night, followed by a fitful sleep, has me dragging this morning.

We didn't leave the office until well past midnight, only after confirming that the code and testing had been validated and sending the results to Preston. His immediate response, a clipped "good work," was all we needed to call it a night and head home, weary and blurry-eyed.

Noticing her preoccupation with the tablecloth, which looks perfectly fine to me, I see an opportunity to step away for a moment.

"I'm going to grab some coffee, Mom. Do you want anything?"

She barely glances up, still fussing over the fabric.

"Oh, this darn cloth—I grabbed the shorter one instead of the long one," she mutters, more to herself than to me.

Rather than waiting for her answer, I decide to grab her a cup too. Whether she drinks it or not can be her choice. Walking away, I rub a hand over my tired face and hope they have something good but not too disastrous for my diet plan.

The competitions that Giovanni and I have been doing are on hold for me right now. It should have been cutting season in prep for my next competition, but with the launch of this new app, I pushed all that to next year. Not that I can slack on my meal plan—I won't—it's not in my nature. But with how crazy this week has been and the long hours I've been putting it, a little splurge won't hurt.

Strolling past a few rows of vendors setting up their goods and wares, I pass the row with all the fresh fruits and vegetables brought in by local farmers. It's times like this that I forget how good they are at sourcing farm-to-table. Mom always shops here, but I chose the convenience of the grocery store over the betterment of shopping and supporting locals. When I pass a booth of fresh honey, the vendor still setting up his display, I see a stunning woman further down the way.

Her long chocolate hair tumbles in waves down her back, the edges curling toward the sun as if soaking up its early morning rays. She has sunglasses affixed to the top of her head, laughing with a man as she touches his arm.

It's an intimate touch—one of familiarity that has me clearing my throat in discomfort. The ease and warmth of watching them interact feel like a violation despite being in a very public place on a typically busy Saturday morning.

My eyes drink her in greedily. She's lean with a figure showing long hours and dedication to some sort of physical fitness. Thank God for athleisure wear. I love how it shows off every detail of her body. Her tiny ass is cut high, not overly muscular like the gym girls I see every day, but with a firm roundness that has my cock twitching.

Her waist is trim, and she's on the smallish side from how the long-sleeved workout shirt hugs her body. When she turns to catch a stray strand of hair, her side profile reveals modest breasts, enough to hold in my hands without spillage.

My mouth suddenly goes dry. The attraction is instant and overwhelming. I continue to watch her interact with a guy admiring her assets the same as I am without being overly obvious or creepy. My footsteps fall without thought, guiding me to her as if the morning breeze at my back pushes me.

Before I know it, I'm beside her, listening to them discuss pomegranates. What I couldn't see from afar were the two she is holding in her hands, talking about ripeness or something.

As I stand awkwardly next to them, she turns toward me, her smile wide and radiant, instantly lighting up her face. Her eyes, a striking mix of green and brown, meet mine. My body jolts with attraction. There's something in her gaze that's both inviting and disarming. She's even more gorgeous up close, leaving me momentarily speechless.

"Hi there!" Her voice is melodic, rich, and deeper than I expected. She holds up the fruit, her fingers tracing its leathery skin. "Are you here to buy some? We were just discussing the best way to pick a ripe one."

"Welcome, welcome. Do you need a quick tutorial on pomegranate picking?"

Her companion, the guy I noticed earlier, turns to look at me with an easygoing smile on his face. What I mistook for his attraction to her is his openly welcoming demeanor, as his corny question gets a light laugh out of her.

"I'd say I know my stuff, but then Victoria here knows much more."

The guy tosses her a friendly nod, wiping his hand on his apron before arranging the fruit into a pile on his table.

Victoria.

That's her name. It's my new favorite word. Like clockwork, she extends her hand, introducing herself. Her tongue curls around her name in a smokey accented voice, speaking to a Latin heritage like mine. Her hand is delicate and soft in mine. My callouses from lifting heavy weights are rough against her fragility.

When my fingers wrap around hers, my breath catches, and a million images of her and I doing obscene things with her pomegranate flash through my mind. My body tightens in response to my thoughts, my grip clamping down on hers. She clears her throat when I've held her hand too long. The guy chuckles at her apparent effect on me. Reluctantly, I let go.

"And your name?"

She has to prompt me because, like an idiot, I don't say anything when I shake her hand. I blink away the awkwardness, straighten my shoulders, and blurt out my first name.

"Well, Marco. What brings you to the market today besides pomegranate lessons?"

She holds up the fruit in her hand, a physical representation of her question. I glance briefly at my mother's booth, now fully set up from where I stand, and back at them.

"Actually, I'm helping my mom with her health awareness stall over there."

I point at her, talking to someone with a pamphlet in her hand.

"But I couldn't help but take a walk around with all this amazing local produce."

Her eyes light up at the mere mention of the fruit she is holding. The guy excuses himself from our conversation to move more fruit onto the tables when a lady behind him makes a disapproving sound in her throat.

"That's wonderful! Supporting local vendors and farmers—sounds like you're making a day of it."

A guilty blush creeps over my bronze skin as I recall how fast I abandoned my mom in search of coffee and food. There's no way I'm making a day of this, not with the mountain of work that awaits me at the office, including questions from Preston.

"Yeah, it's definitely a family affair," I lie, hoping she feels the same connection I'm feeling with the ease of our conversation.

Her smile doesn't falter. I'm thankful for the impulsive decision to walk over, guided by curiosity, attraction, or the universe blessing me for being a good son and waking up early when I didn't want to.

Her light and airy laugh fills the space between us as she hands me a pomegranate, which I assume is perfectly ripe by her standards. I accept it, our fingers brushing briefly, sending a spark of electricity through the simple touch.

"Do you want to know what the secret is?"

Secret?

I have no idea what she's talking about, but I'll listen to every secret she has. More than happy to listen to her trauma dump over dinner and drinks. Hear how terrible every man has been to her so I can show her how much better I am and will be.

"You want to look for ones that are deep red and have a bit of a give when you press gently. Too hard, and they're not ripe yet. Too soft, and they might be overripe."

I'll easily give gentle and hard at the same time. She places hers down on the table to wrap her fingers over mine, squeezing my grip to feel for myself. All I can feel is her hand on mine, and I want more.

"Do you feel that?"

Do I feel her soft palm over the top of my hand? Hell yeah! Do I feel the light pressure of her silky fingers intertwined with mine? Absolutely! Do I give a fuck about the fruit? Not a chance in hell.

"Yeah."

My voice is deep, clenched tightly in my throat, which causes her eyes to flash up to mine at the sudden change of tone.

"Sorry, frog in my throat. Do you want to grab a coffee or something?"

I clear the huskiness from my throat. Her hand falls away, and her hazel eyes study me before looking at the sky as if the drifting clouds contain the answer. A crease appears between her perfectly arched eyebrows. With her chin tilted upward, I study how the sun glistens on her hair again, painting the strands orange and yellow.

There's no question that she's stunning. My feet fell of their own accord to meet her, and now that I discovered she's so personable and open, I'm all in on whatever is happening.

"Or a smoothie? Maybe one with a pomegranate in it," I offer when she doesn't immediately accept.

I quickly toss the fruit in the air and place it back on the table. With every passing second, I grow insecure, thinking I overplayed my hand.

She smiles, pleased, her gaze returning to mine.

"A smoothie would be perfect. It's why I adore this farmer's market. Everything blends seamlessly into each other as if it was always meant to be."

Once again, I'm lost in what she's saying about blending. The only thing I focus on is her saying yes. She can explain the rest on our way to find the smoothie stall.

"That's interesting, Victoria. Tell me more."

I shift, turning in the direction we need to walk as she bounces forward on the balls of her feet with an excitement that she doesn't contain. It's adorable, drawing me closer to her.

"It's a little ecosystem. Self-sustaining in that there is almost everything you need right here in this parking lot. It's all interconnected—the local produce, the community, our health.

They say food is fuel, but I think it's much more than that. It brings people together, like these growers and farmers, bringing the fruit of their labor for us to purchase and enjoy with our families. And a place to make new friends."

Friendship is the last thing I want from her.

"Farm to table," I mildly contribute, unwilling to stop her from continuing with the glee on her face and how she's practically skipping beside me. It's obvious she's passionate about this, and I'm passionate about her. It couldn't be more perfect.

"Exactly. But it's more than just that. It's meeting people like yourself or Ross back there with his wife. They have a little farm on the outskirts of town, where he has all these fruit trees for his hobby, but he works at a law firm downtown. Having a community such as this in a big city is neat. People caring about the environment, their carbon footprints and . . ."

She suddenly stops, her hand falling to my arm, and the connection is warm and welcome, at least on my part. Her palm is burning through my skin, imprinting her touch into my memory to the point my cock stirs, wanting more of her touch.

"Sorry, I geek out on this stuff. Just tell me to shut up."

I'd never, ever tell this woman to shut up. She can geek out all she wants if it means I get to spend more time with her.

"No, continue. Geek out. Go nuts," I encourage, about to cover her hand with my own when she removes it to point at something ahead of us.

"You're too nice. Let's pick up a couple of granola bars to go with the smoothies."

Her tone is dismissive, and she moves the conversation onto something trivial, which disappoints me a little. I wanted to talk more about her passion, which I share in many ways.

"Raul is up on the right. He makes the best homemade granola bars and trail mix. It's what I snack on at the office. Trust me, you're going to love it."

I'm all for eating healthy, but loving those two things is not likely to happen. I prefer real food for my macros, not high-caloric, low-protein snacks. She's already striding ahead, leaving me a step or two behind, when I realize a sudden uncomfortableness is rolling off her.

It is as if going into detail about what this place seems to mean to her is too vulnerable or personal to continue sharing. It makes me want to do everything I can to get her to open up again like that.

I catch up with her as she details the various ones she tried, assuring me they are all delicious. She greets him with the same friendliness as that Ross guy with the pomegranates, and I realize it's her personality to be this welcoming person.

We make the briefest introduction while she deliberates over several options. She picks two for us to eat, and I select a couple more that look more appealing. I then pay for everything, much to her surprise.

"You didn't have to do that."

She turns those stunning eyes to me, and man, I'm going to be a goner for her if she's as lovely and sweet as she appears.

"It's the least I could do for the pomegranate tutorial."

I grin, handing her the bag. Her smile returns, brighter than before, easing the slight tension that had crept up moments earlier. The longer we walk and talk, the faster the tiredness dissipates from my body.

"You really are part of this, aren't you?"

I cast her a curious look, trying to piece together why this matters so much.

"I try to be. It's important, you know? To feel connected to the place you live, to contribute somehow. I love it. The people, the food, the atmosphere—it's all just . . ."

She pauses, searching for the right word.

"Home?"

"Yes, exactly. Home."

She beams all the way to the smoothie booth, still bobbing

on her feet. She's making me feel more connected to this place than ever. Watching her enthusiasm for the market and the community it serves rekindles a similar passion in me, one that's been dulled by long hours and too many days spent indoors.

I can't remember the last time I spent a Saturday milling about without an agenda to tackle. She orders some complicated drink with a bunch of ingredients while I order their Saturday special. Typically,

I prefer the protein drink I make at home to the sugar contents of a commercially made smoothie—something I'd never tell her. While we wait, I lean against the counter, watching her interact with a couple of other regulars with an ease and familiarity that speaks volumes about her regular presence here.

Once we have everything, we find a small table away from the busiest paths. She unpacks the bars and offers me the first pick before selecting hers. While she's laying her napkins out, I can't help but feel happy that I helped my mom. Who knows if I ever would have met Victoria had I not come here?

"You said home. Is that how you feel about this place?" she asks before biting into her bar and shredding it into a pile of granola dust on her napkin.

Her pink tongue swipes across her full lips in search of crumbs in the most desirable way possible. The things that tongue could do. I adjust myself under the table, trying to hold back the thoughts of licking granola dust off her lean body.

"Uh, something similar."

"Right?! It reminds me of back home."

"Where is that?"

She grimaces, a look of regret for bringing it up, as she dusts off her fingers and leans forward. Her elbows press into the table, edging closer to me and I couldn't be happier.

"The 305."

"Huh?"

"Miami."

My eyebrows raise in surprise.

"Really?"

"Yeah, my parents run a small restaurant in South Beach. They source their ingredients from local farmers every Wednesday and Saturday morning. Or at least they used to."

Her frown deepens, hinting at something more than just fresh fruits and vegetables.

"Anyway, quality and freshness are important to them and their customers. It's a throwback, the old way of doing things in Cuba."

"Wow, Cuban and from Miami. You must have some stories."

"Uh, sure."

There's a hesitancy—a sudden distance when she looks away, dragging her elbows from the table. I almost regret saying that when she turns her focus back to me, the haunting look disappears. I take the opportunity to dive into my granola bar, which is surprisingly good.

"My papi was buying fresh seafood at the fisherman's market, and a boat goes blazing by, followed by the Coast Guard. It was like a speed boat, and suddenly, it went airborne, crashing into the dock when it didn't make the turn. It was bright red, huge, expensive, and bursting into pieces with the guy being thrown into the water."

Her smoothie goes untouched as she tells the story, her hands gesturing alongside her words. Her arms are wide as she simulates the angle and trajectory of the boat and crash. It's easy to like her. She's gorgeous and sweet, and her Cuban accent makes the details of her adventures adorable.

"That must have been a sight to see," I reply, chasing down the crumbly granola with a sip of the sugary sweet smoothie—

too sweet for my taste as I choke down the contents. "I've never been, but it seems like a fun city with lots to do."

"Miami is so cultured and vibrant."

Her enthusiasm sweeps away any lingering hint of her previous shadowy expression.

"It's such a melting pot, but the Cuban culture stands out. We grew up dancing in the kitchen, music always playing, helping my papi cut and chop while he cooked. Every meal was an event with neighbors and friends coming over to eat, visit, and laugh."

She suddenly looks sad again, her gaze growing distant and looking away, focusing on something over my shoulder.

"And this place reminds you of that?"

I don't want to keep losing her attention to whatever enters her mind. Maybe I should steer the conversation away from her hometown. I lean into her line of sight, her eyes snapping back to mine and bringing her back to reality.

"Sort of. It's that sense of community I feel here when I'm not working."

I nod, deeply impressed by how passionate she is.

"And the art scene—places like Wynwood with street murals and stamped concrete. You walk through the entire district where the walls tell stories."

"I've seen pictures. The artwork looks incredible."

I tear off another piece of the granola and plop it in my mouth. She nods, sipping at her smoothie.

"And we got Messi! Did you see the stadium they are building for him? Incredible."

The words slip past her lips, light and airy, finally vanquishing the drifting gaze and vacant expressions. With that gone, I settle into a more comfortable position, ready to listen to whatever she wants to tell me.

"I did see that. They said he's never come. That America

would never get someone from the European leagues, yet here he is. We have Beckham to thank for that."

Her long fingernails point in my direction before snapping her fingers.

"Did you see their documentary? It tells the whole story. My friend's cousin works in their building. Says they are actually really nice."

"Who? Messi?"

"No, the Beckhams."

Once again, I have no idea whose documentary she is referring to, but it doesn't matter when she launches into another story about Miami.

One story flows into the next until we've both finished our snacks and smoothies. I love getting to know her. Greedily, I want to learn everything about her. That's when I decide I'm going to ask her out.

4

VICTORIA

I'm caught in mid-sentence telling him about U Miami when an older woman makes a beeline for him. With his back to her, he doesn't see her charging forward. Glancing between their faces, I can already tell it's his mom.

Her hand shoots up, frantically waving for me to catch his attention, her other arm clutching a stack of colorful papers. I cut my story short and point behind him. He doesn't have much time to turn around before she's in front of him. Her eyes locked on her son, a bright smile spreading across her face.

Surprise flickers to amusement as he braces for an expected hug. She doesn't disappoint, enveloping him in an enthusiastic embrace that shoves the papers against his face. He's already protesting in her arms while shifting in his chair. She ruffles his hair as if he's still a boy and steps back. With his flustered face and curious side-eye to his mom, she launches into a quick-fire update on the booth's success, her words spilling over as she gestures towards the bustling crowd.

He's still composing himself, running his hands through his perfect hair and trying to get his bearings. She shuffles her pile of colorful papers to the side of her body and sticks her hand out to make introductions.

"Excuse my son for not introducing me."

Her comment brings an instant smile to my face as Marco didn't even have a chance to introduce her. Then again, she reminds me of my mom, who is always in charge, bossing everyone around and then accusing us of being rude. He's left mystified behind her but sits taller when she scowls at him.

"I'm Mrs. Delgado. Marco's mother."

I slip my hand into her warm embrace.

"Victoria Vega. It's a pleasure to meet you."

Marco immediately leans forward, his near black eyebrows shooting up in disbelief.

"Victoria Vega?" he repeats, a slow smile spreading across his face, his eyes lighting up with recognition.

I'm caught off guard, confused about what that look means. Mrs. Delgado watches the exchange with the same curiosity I feel. Her gaze flickers between us as she pieces together the situation.

"Mijo, what is this about?" Her voice laces with a hint of suspicion. "You two know each other already?"

A smirk plays at his lips as if taunting a secret from both of us.

"Actually, we do. I didn't realize—"

He cuts off, shaking his head in amazement. Then, it slowly dawns on me. Marco and Mrs. Delgado . . . He's Marco Delgado, the very man I contacted yesterday, the man I need to help me figure out a solution to my building's problem. Suddenly, my smile mirrors his, and I lock eyes with him in a new twist that couldn't be more perfect on this beautiful sunny morning. This is just another example of the blessing that flows out of this market.

"You're Marco Delgado! I literally just left you a message yesterday." I chuckle, equally amazed. "What a small world!"

His mama looks bewildered, waiting for someone to explain.

"I returned your call. It was late, so I called your company line."

His hand moves forward to grip the table, then balls up his breakfast trash and moves it to the side.

"The projects your firm takes on are massive . . . impressive."

His head still shakes as he shares that he attempted to reach out. Messages collect on my voicemail at work, which I usually clear off on Sunday nights. But seeing as how this is Saturday morning, I wouldn't have checked yet, so I wouldn't have had any idea.

"Marco? Explain," his mama demands, jabbing his shoulder in expectation. His hand gestures at me, but I decide to answer her.

"Mrs. Delgado, some engineers referred me to your son's company for my project."

It is as though the universe is smiling on me, karmically arranging connections to ensure we meet and collaborate on my project. Her eyebrow arches, intrigued.

"They spoke highly of the innovative solutions his company offers, especially in sustainability, which is crucial for the scale of developments we're undertaking."

I gesture around, indicating the bustling market, drawing a parallel.

"Just like this market, it's all about interconnectedness, building something lasting and beneficial to the community."

"That sounds exactly in line with what we strive for. Sustainability isn't just a buzzword for us. It's the backbone of our projects," he adds, scooting his chair closer to me.

His hands nearly collide with mine as I explain the serendipity of this moment and how wonderful it feels. Mrs. Delgado listens, her eyes flitting between us.

"Well, isn't this something?" She chuckles, plastering her

flyers to her chest to clap her hands together in glee. "See, mijo, another reason why you were meant to be here today. To meet this lady!"

Marco rubs the back of his neck, a sheepish grin spreading across his face.

"Seems like it, doesn't it? And to think, I almost didn't want to come today, having worked really late last night." He glances at me while his mama tsks at him. "Kidding, Mom, I'm always happy to help."

Suddenly, her name is called from across the market. The sun blocks my view, preventing me from seeing exactly who it is, but she turns, waves her hand, and then addresses us.

"Well, I'll leave you two to sort out the details then." She shifts the flyers away from her body and into her hand, turning to address me. "Victoria, it was lovely meeting you. Marco, don't forget to visit me before you leave. I have those cookies for your employees!"

Her voice carries the affectionate command only a mama can muster.

"What?" I ask, tilting my head to gaze at him.

"Long story," he mutters, shaking his head and not wanting to get into it. "I'll swing back by Mom."

As she strides away, Marco watches with amusement in his expression. He turns to me, his demeanor more relaxed now.

"So, *Victoria Vega*, tell me about your project."

He sounds eager to explore further, and I'm happy to accommodate him. I retrieve my phone and lean close, pulling up the pictures I took yesterday. He patiently listens as I swipe through my camera roll, explaining my conundrum.

Each schematic represents a crucial part of the development, and his eyes dance with each detail. By how intently he studies the photos, he obviously loves this stuff as much as I do.

Apparently, his company's smart thermostats were an idea he developed with his team. They were the first ones out of college, and after eighteen short months of research, development, and deployment, they've become a staple at his company.

They work so smoothly and with little issue that he's no longer involved in the project, as it was certified and turned over to the sales and services teams to manage.

He points to a specific part of a schematic, raising an eyebrow to ask a technical question. I explain, using my finger to trace the flow of the layout on the screen. Our heads are close enough that I catch a hint of his fresh and woodsy cologne. It's one of many things drawing me to him.

His relentless dark eyes looked directly into my being, intending to know me on a deeper level than just a casual acquaintance. His muscular arms strain against the fabric of his shirt sleeves, and the horseshoe-shaped bulge on the back of his arms indicates how much he works out. His jeans, casual when standing, strain against his strong thighs. The way his smile starts on one side of his mouth before flashing into a toothy grin.

There's no doubt how handsome he is. He is a total package with his perfect skin, immaculately styled hair, dedicated gym body, and solutions-oriented mind.

I'd ask him out if I didn't need him more for my project. But with my steadfast habit of shoving my personal needs aside and prioritizing my career, I ignore the whiff of his cologne and get my head back in the game.

"You see, the issue starts here and ends here."

My fingertip traces the schematics and enlarges the areas so he can see them better. He nods, understanding dawning, and asks more questions. His tone is clearly excited, mirroring mine.

"Give me a second, Victoria."

Suddenly, he stands, collecting the trash from our impromptu breakfast and throwing it away. Then he walks to a booth across from us, chatting with a woman. Laughter bubbles up between them while children dart between the booths, and a dog joyfully barks at a cluster of birds gobbling up fallen food. When he returns with paper and a pencil, I gaze up at him.

"What's that for?"

He flashes me one of those broad smiles, charming and knowing at the same time. I think he likes keeping secrets since this is the same face he had when he figured out who I was.

"I'll show you."

He sketches quick diagrams on the paper, and I watch him work over the crook of his arm. At first, it's all lines and shapes, which do not mean much until he adds some numbers and then code. I follow the first part until he sets the pen down and slides the paper toward me.

"What am I looking at?"

"It's been a while since I worked on this project. Once they are up and running, I'm out of the loop. But I think this might be the solution. Communication is where the issue lies, and this could be solved with coding changes. Naturally, I'd have to see it, and then there would be testing involved, but a preliminary assessment leads me to believe it's this."

He taps the pen on the paper to emphasize his point. Either he's oversimplifying it, or I'm not explaining it fully since he seems to solve my problem on a piece of notebook paper in a minute. We've had the contractor out several times, and communication between the individual units and the master controls still fails to maintain stability.

"Marco, this sounds good, and I'd be delighted if it worked, but there has to be more to it."

He chuckles softly, tapping the paper again.

"There's usually more to it, but sometimes stepping back gives you a clearer view."

He fleshes out more details, his brows furrowing in concentration. His explanations become more intricate as he draws, layering complexity into the simple sketch he started with. The lines connect as his vision takes on a tangible form.

I lean closer, my shoulder pressing into his arm, gaining a lingering look from him before he continues fitting the pieces together for me to understand. He finishes with a flourish, setting the pen down and looking up with a grin that's both proud and a little triumphant.

"How about that?"

His tone suggests he's thrown down a gauntlet, challenging the problem sight unseen with smug expertise.

"Well, I don't know what I'm looking at even after you explain it. Would you come . . . no, never mind. That's asking too much."

I stop myself.

He's here with his mama, helping her, and will probably need to break down when the market closes in a few hours.

"What is asking too much?"

I don't know if it's the way he looks at me or the chance that he could save my ass on this project, but the market around us seems to fade, even the barking dog in the background, until it's only him and I.

"For you to come and look at it. In person. Today," I blurt out, my thoughts as choppy as my words.

His laid-back demeanor instantly changes when he sits up. He moves away from the shared touch, leaving a coolness void of his body heat on my arm. It sends a sweeping chill over my body. I scoot away from him to rest my elbows on the edge of the table.

"Are you kidding? I'd love to see this up close."

His hands flex as if the thought of touching the nonfunctioning systems and troubleshooting them is too much eagerness to contain.

"Can we get in? On the weekend?"

He glances at his watch for what I'm uncertain of.

"Well, yeah. It's my project." I shrug, wondering what he's thinking when he pulls out his phone. "Unless you have prior plans and then we can just . . . reschedule."

His fingertips are already moving across his screen, texting someone. My attraction to him clouds my judgment in assuming he'd drop everything to help me. He stops, his fingers still touching the screen when he looks at me.

"No!" His voice takes on a panicked edge. I'm uncertain if it's because of me or whoever he's texting. "Sorry, I meant I don't have prior plans, just a workout with my buddy that I can move to later."

I raise an eyebrow, skeptical by the urgency of how quickly he was texting someone.

"Are you sure? It looks like you were texting someone important."

A conflicted look appears on his face.

"I mean, I'm supposed to go into the office to work on this project—"

I stand, grabbing the piece of paper, and feel like an idiot for assuming he'd do me a favor when, really, this is business between our two companies. I need to follow the proper protocol for B2B vendor relationships.

"I'm so sorry. I shouldn't have assumed."

I'm collecting my purse when he stands. His hand lands on my arm to stop me. The heat from his palm saturates into my skin, sending desire surging over my body. I ignore it, embarrassed, wanting to rush away.

"Victoria, assume all you want. I just have two things to do today. Go to the gym, which my buddy owns, so that's anytime. And go to the office, which I left about nine hours ago. I'm much more excited to see your project than to go work on mine."

His hand drops from my arm to lock his phone and shove it

in his pocket. He's calm and understanding, explaining as if I have a right to demand his whole day's schedule.

But I see it for what it is, making me feel comfortable while enabling us to go, which is what I want most. I flash him a grateful smile and tuck a strand of hair behind my ear when the wind carries it across my face.

"Great. Then we can take separate cars, and you can continue with your day."

"Perfect, I need to grab those cookies from my mom, but I'll meet you in the parking lot. Sound good?"

"Yes."

My answer is breathier than I intended. He hesitates before strolling in the direction his mama came from. This unexpected meeting feels fortuitous. Fate is working her magic to bring us together. The solution seems simpler now and less daunting.

I'm impressed with his confidence and the apparent logic of his approach. If I can solve this this week, my project will be back on track, which will mean a possible promotion to work on larger projects. I'm so happy I could pinch myself.

The quick drive to the project site does little to calm my racing thoughts. I'm fixated on the possibilities that Marco's solution could unlock. Once we arrive, I wave politely to the guard at the security gate, explaining our need for access.

The guard nods and lifts the barrier, allowing us to drive through. As I pull under the oversized modern entrance of the building, the sleek lines and reflective glass amplify the morning sunlight, casting a hopeful glow over our adventure.

I park and wait for Marco, stealing glances in the rearview mirror. He looks relaxed behind the wheel of his truck, his mirrored sunglasses giving him an air of mystery. It's easy to get caught up in his good looks and calm demeanor.

Part of me wonders if this could be the beginning of a professional partnership and something more personal. If his solution works, then nothing's stopping me from pursuing him. It's a thought I tuck in the back of my mind as he pulls up beside me, and we both step out of our cars.

"Do I need a hard hat or something?"

He hesitates by his door when asking.

"Not at all."

"Cool. Let's see if we can figure this out."

I love how spontaneous this is, but I especially love how passionate he is about troubleshooting, like a true engineer. We walk side by side toward the building, our steps synchronized.

"I've been thinking about your diagram all the way here," I confess, eager to show him. "If your idea holds, this could be a game-changer for the project."

He chuckles.

The sound eases my nerves about being so forward to inviting him here today on his day off. But like he said back at the market, his plans are fluid.

"I hope so. Your project is fascinating."

I'm impressed by his technical acumen and the way he makes complex systems accessible and engaging. As I unlock the door with my set of keys, he quickly catches the doorframe, holding it open for me.

I'm propelled forward with a light touch to the small of my back. My fantasies want to read more about it, but my brain is shutting that down. He's here professionally, nothing more.

The heat from the lobby hits us immediately, and I cringe when I look at him.

"I forgot to tell you it will be hot."

"Being from Houston, I'm used to it. Besides, I figured it would be given the nature of the problem."

His broad smile appears instantly, along with a wink, completely innocent when I want it to be flirtatious.

"Right."

I tug on my long sleeves, dragging them up my arms to relieve myself. I'm tempted to do the same with my leggings if it weren't for him already watching my every move. It's flattering and has me wondering if he thinks I'm attractive.

"So why don't we head up to the electrical room? I can show you where it all comes together."

I'm already hitting the elevator button after we cross the lobby. The building has teams of construction workers on site, but none are working in the areas we'll have access to.

"Lead the way."

When the doors slide open, we enter together, him on one side and me on the other, until I press the button. Then he's suddenly closer, the scent of his cologne hitting me anew. I'm acutely aware of every sound around us.

His quiet breathing, the squeal of the elevator cables above us, obviously needing a work order to address that, and the light ping as we pass floors.

My breath catches when he angles his body to face mine while I face the front of the elevator. He's standing too close to be professional and not near enough to be romantic. My brain can't decide what is happening as I stare straight ahead at our reflection in the steel panels.

"Do you believe in fate, Victoria?"

He rolls the r in my name, a proper pronunciation that gets lost in the everyday annotation of non-Spanish speakers. It's alluring hearing it from him.

"Fate?"

My one-word question is a breathy echo of his, hinting at how his proximity throws me off my game. I tug on the neckline of my shirt, trying to cool down and distract myself from his imploring question.

"Yes, fate, destiny, clandestine meeting."

An electric tension rises between us when I gaze up at him, unwilling to move away as he edges closer. His dark eyes hold mine, unblinking as I stay quiet.

"As if the universe is working to bring us together."

His words are barely louder than the hum of the elevator. Their meaning is meant to blur the lines between professional conduct and more casual meaningfulness.

Fate.

I had the same thought not thirty minutes ago. My mind drifts back to that moment, wondering if I muttered it aloud. I couldn't have. He was already walking away when it popped into my mind.

I lick my lips, aware of his gaze dropping to them. If I were to focus on how good-looking he is, the stretch of his shirt over his muscles, and his irresistible scent wrapping me in a warm embrace, I might launch myself at him and not stop when the doors open.

"Sure," I croak, obviously affected by him.

My heart races. His proximity makes every other sensation more acute—the slight draft from the vent, the elevator slowing, and the fruity scent of smoothie lingering on his breath.

"This meeting." His voice rumbles in the cramped space, somehow vibrating into my body. "I think it was destined."

Destined.

Like the fates of the world bringing us together in this elevator, feeling what I am feeling and gazing up at him to see my desire reflected in his expression. Fated. Like the cheesy romance books I read when lying in bed at night, wishing I could find the one that would cure the feeling of loneliness I've grown accustomed to.

My mouth dries, and my gaze bores into him, trying to figure out what to say.

"Your call yesterday. Meeting today. I think it means something."

It means precisely what he's implying and hinting at it in the overly hot elevator. I wipe the sweat collecting at my hairline, a distraction that catches his eyes momentarily before they return to mine.

His breath is mine for the briefest of seconds, and I want more. I want it fanning my breasts on his journey down to my core. Breathing me in, relishing my taste, and bringing me immense pleasure.

Instead of answering him, I fan myself. Needing relief from the heat of the building, and the heat building between us.

Only when the elevator dings, the doors slide open, and a rush of slightly less hot air rushes into the cab do I finally get my wits about me. Breaking eye contact, I nod at the door, hinting at the need to focus on our task.

"We should . . ."

I leave the rest open to the ethos, the very universe he thinks is bringing us together. He's not wrong about the intrinsic forces at work, but he might also not be right.

"Yeah."

He clears his throat, acknowledging what happened. The agenda he advanced was merely a fleeting and indulgent thought. His footsteps fall quietly back, allowing me to exit first.

The spell is broken as we transition back into our professional roles. Yet, when we exit the elevator, his hand brushes mine, reigniting the spark with a fleeting touch that invites more if I want it.

Our steps sync as we walk down the corridor to the electrical room in silence. The buzz from a moment ago evolves into a charged silence filled with unasked questions and untested boundaries. Seeing the black-and-white plaque affixed to the door, he opens it, allowing me to enter first.

His hand briefly touches the small of my back—the same gesture from downstairs, yet this time, it's packed with so much intention that I slip away from it as quickly as possible.

"Here's the main unit that controls the different sections of the building. As you can see right here, the readings are off with the controls due to a communications issue. Compound that with the software failing when it gets anywhere near max capacity. It glitches when meeting minimum tolerance."

Blurting out the layers of problems to him puts me back in my comfort zone. His face falls into serious contemplation as his dark eyes, which held so much intrigue in the elevator, are steeled on the unit.

"Do you have the specifications handy?"

While he begins to tinker with the unit, familiarizing himself with the controls by ghosting his fingers over it, I retrieve the papers from the top of the steel supply closet.

He doesn't even bother waiting to see them before he opens the control panel and analyzes the motherboard with wires and switches everywhere.

"Yes, I advocated for these, and it's backfiring on me even after I resolved the company's objections to the initial cost of the investment. I assured them it would more than pay for itself with the energy efficiencies the project would enjoy. Savings that are quickly disappearing if I can't get it working properly in all units and common areas."

He hums, absorbed in the motherboard, and then suddenly stops to look at me.

"Don't worry, I'll help you."

Those dark eyes are boring into me again, pinning me where I stand with the earnest truth that he will help me resolve this once and for all. I reward him with a smile, my hand going to touch his, when he suddenly pulls out his cell phone, breaking the moment.

"Let's start slowly and tweak the settings. Document the

results as we go to see what has been tried versus what could work. I wish I still had the original coding on my phone. It would help with the troubleshooting."

He snaps pictures from different angles and then opens his notes app.

"I think we should start with a reroute of partial load to reduce stress on the system and to test what is communicating and what is not. Then move it to peak hours to see what happens."

His suggestion sparks a thought, and I lean closer, our shoulders touching as I open the specs and show him the diagrams. He looks curious before glancing down at where my finger is pointing.

"Okay, we can test the failed units. These are the ones that are operational and have been able to withhold the power surges and failures. If we can integrate a secondary system for load balancing during peak hours, then it might fix the regulations and prevent the primary from hitting max capacity."

He looks up, his eyes alight with pride.

"You really know your stuff."

I blush at how easily he appreciates my knowledge. Something that has gone amiss in the past at my firm. I'm constantly having to prove myself as a woman and a minority in my field.

"I try to."

"It's impressive."

A rush of warmth comes over me, similar to the heat between us in the elevator. We linger, looking at each other until he suddenly breaks it, hunching over the motherboard again.

"That might work, Victoria. Are you ready to give it a shot?"

Give the unit a shot, or give him a shot? Both questions enter my mind, and only one answer exits my mouth.

"Let's do this."

5

MARCO

The team reconvenes for more validation testing to ensure we're prepared with a solid and final solution for Monday morning. My mom's cookies disappear faster than I expected, more appreciated by everyone than anticipated. She'd be so proud and a bit smug knowing I didn't want to bring them. Her point made.

Yet my mind wanders to Victoria, how her floral perfume snaked across my senses, soaking them in pleasure, and how her light, mostly unnecessary touches teased me.

I initially chalked it up to how often she uses her hands when speaking, but the longer we were together in that small, hot electrical closet working on her issues, the more I realized it was mutual attraction.

The chemistry I tagged as a fateful meeting blossomed into full-on flames when she leaned close enough for her breast to graze my arm, leaving it there as my cock tightened in my pants.

I'm usually good at keeping my composure and focusing on the task at hand, especially in critical troubleshooting phases.

Yet, every brush of her fingers, each shared glance that lingered a fraction too long, sparked something more I wanted to explore. This chemistry, this undeniable pull, fuels a growing flame I'm not sure I want—or can—extinguish. It's something I'll explore as soon as I get my work problems resolved.

Now, surrounded by the ambient hum of keyboards testing code and the occasional murmur of my team, apprehension mixes in my gut about what Monday might bring to the office. Preston will be in before Maddie, I assume. Dawson threatened he'd be back for a status report and demonstration. Both must be ready.

A call from my team lead interrupted us on Victoria's project, requiring me to be at the office and cutting my time short with her. I made excuses about being caught up with my mom to my employee, and I made more to Victoria when I had to dash out of the building to get to mine yesterday. Work must come first today, a necessary evil in keeping my job.

My knee bobs restlessly as I pore over the data and double-check each parameter, trying to finish this project so I can see her. The professional in me wants to solve the technical puzzles of her project, bring it to success, and potentially partner with our two firms. But the man in me wants more—to see where this connection might lead and discover if what feels like fate might be just that.

When the tension becomes too much, I toss my pencil on the stack of printouts and let out a frustrated sigh. It's been a while since I've been with a woman, definitely due to my lack of effort, the long hours spent on this project over many months, and my competing in a couple of bodybuilding events earlier in the year.

It's not that I don't want someone in my life. I've just been swamped. With this product launch, I hope to regain some of my life and focus on finding the one who is right for me.

I chug my coffee, pick up my pencil, and start again. The page numbers keep blurring until I see her face. Laughing, joking, serious and concentrating. Like I already know parts of her without really knowing her at all.

It's wild, and that fate comment I made probably scared her off, but I couldn't help it. It didn't feel like déjà vu. Deep in my chest, it's more like a general knowing that this is how things are meant to be.

"What's got you so bothered?"

I startle, my head jolting up to see Maddie in the doorway. A glance at my computer shows it is after noon already. Time is flying by, and I've neglected to order lunch for my team, which I must do as soon as possible.

"What are you doing here?"

Bewildered by her showing up on a Sunday, I shake my head, amazed by her level of commitment. She shrugs, her purse slipping down her arm, which she catches with a slight wobble of her Starbucks cup.

"I always come in on Sundays to get a leg up on you knuckleheads."

Her office keys jingle in her hand as she adjusts her purse back onto her shoulder.

"If I didn't come in on weekends, I'd never get caught up, probably end up killing Preston, or he'd kill me. Either way . . ."

She doesn't finish her thought, choosing to step into my office. The aroma of her fresh coffee makes my stomach growl with hunger.

"Okay."

"How's it going? When I left Friday, it sounded like it was going to be a long weekend." She glances from the coding blanketing my three monitors to the spreadsheets covering my desk. "You make any progress?"

I gesture to the chair across my desk in case she wants to sit.

She shakes her head and takes a drink while watching me intently.

"Yeah, it's been a very long weekend. I'm waiting for the final reports to certify and send to Preston. I want to get his review so we're a unified front when Dawson arrives tomorrow."

I blink, my eyes stinging with fatigue from the intense concentration and analysis.

"Well, that's good. It will make my life a heck of a lot better if you guys can get that thing working. Between fielding those two, I also have the investors calling and demanding updates as if they are entitled to them."

She snorts in annoyance. I can see why Preston depends on her so much. She's the ultimate gatekeeper, only letting out information she wants people to know.

Even I don't get the full story most of the time. Dragging my arms from my desk, I lean back in my chair, my back popping when I clasp my hands behind my head.

"Yeah, I don't envy you."

Although this week feels like a never-ending marathon of work with workouts interspersed, the only bright part is Victoria. When I envision her face in the elevator, flush, unguarded, and full of desire, a knowing smile graces my lips.

"You shouldn't. Now, what is that look for? It can't be about a bunch of codes and crap."

I shake my head, knowing I can trust her as she's a vault for everyone's secrets.

"I don't know. Just something I'm figuring out."

I gaze at her, the room silent as she brushes her short brown hair away from her face and plops down on the chair she declined.

"I thought you said you had all that . . ."

She waves a hand toward the wall I share with the "programming bullpen," as it is called since the team is lumped together in one area for better collaboration.

"Figured out."

"We do. This is something else."

Keeping Maddie in the dark crosses my mind, wondering if it's too early to talk about Victoria. It's probably too early to even think about Victoria, yet I can't keep my mind from wandering back to yesterday. Every interaction is emblazed in my brain, cataloged, and indexed for future recall.

She perks up, leaning forward and setting her coffee on the edge of my desk.

"Oh, this sounds juicy."

Rubbing the back of my neck to ease the tension, I chuckle at her eagerness. The words hover on the tip of my tongue, wondering where to start.

"Come on, spill it," Maddie prompts as she drums her fingers on the desk.

I exhale, deciding to open up a bit.

"I met someone at the farmer's market this weekend. It was . . . unexpected."

Maddie raises an eyebrow, her lips tuck into a smirkish smile.

"At the farmer's market? I didn't even know they had those in a city this size."

Ignoring that comment I've heard many times, I stop rubbing my neck and lean forward for the big reveal.

"You won't believe who it was."

Bewildered, her lips form the word before it even passes her lips.

"Who?"

Like an owl, her eyes widen and fasten on me while inching closer.

"Guess."

Her eagerness slips into disdain at me, keeping her in

suspense. She suddenly falls back in her chair, crossing her arms over her chest to glare at me.

"See, this is why I come in on the weekends because you idiots waste my valuable time with childish guessing games," she scolds but doesn't move a muscle from her chair.

"Alright, alright."

I raise my hands in a truce before spilling the name.

"Victoria Vega."

"Who?"

More bewilderment and a repeat of that single word. I chuckle at her expression, completely confused.

"Is there an owl in here?"

Her face falls into a deeper glare as she shuffles her things around to stand up, ready to swipe her coffee from my desk.

"Marco! Why do I even bother?" She steps back, readying herself to walk out the door when realization dawns. "Wait a minute. That woman from Friday?"

"Yup."

The hope in my chest is hard to ignore, and I don't want to. She's the only bright spot in my weekend.

"Hold up. How did you even know it's the same woman? And how does that even happen? You'll have to break this all down and go slowly. Don't leave anything out."

She's back to perching on the edge of the chair with her bags balanced on her lap, listening. For some reason, I do exactly as she asks. Handing over every detail. The intentional touching.

The brush against my body in the electrical room while working on a solution together. Everything except the closeness and fate talk in the elevator. With the whole story out, she's practically gushing and smiling so big it's unnerving.

"Did you kiss her? Wait, don't tell me."

The long-forgotten keys in her hand jangle when she raises

her fingers in warning. I wouldn't tell anyway. I'm not that kind of guy.

"This was yesterday? What a coincidence!"

I'm not about to dive into the whole clandestine discussion I already had, but basically, yeah. She hit it right on the destiny nail head.

I nod, catching myself grinning like a goof until I clear my voice and straighten up in my chair. Her expression shifts from amusement to concern, sparking a flare of dread.

"But that is a project you need to bring to Preston first. He won't like his lead tech engineer working side hustles for a pretty woman he ran into at the farmer's market. Especially since she called here first, seeking your professional help for our product."

That's one of many things I've been mulling over since I left the job site yesterday.

"Yeah, I know."

The room falls silent again. I'm conflicted about my desire for Victoria and my interest in her project. I want both and will pursue them, with or without Preston's approval.

When her keys slam onto my desk, I blink away my thoughts.

"What's your plan then, Marco? Just going to wing it?"

My hand absentmindedly shuffles the papers on my desk, arranging them in no particular order, distracting me from how she's looking at me, making me feel, and contributing to my dilemma.

"I mean, not exactly. I know I need to handle this delicately. It's a big opportunity for the company to partner with a firm her size. But at the same time, she's not some random encounter."

She tilts her head, suspicion coating her features.

"And the whole personal aspect? That doesn't worry you? Especially with Preston?"

I pause, staring dead at her and considering the right balance of candor.

"It complicates everything. But isn't that always the case with things worth pursuing? Besides, last I saw, Preston had his hands full with two women, one wearing his ring and the other not."

"Oh, no, you didn't!"

Maddie stands from her chair, eager to leave despite being his assistant and fielding his personal calls. She gathers her things and walks to the door.

"You have a point. Just make sure Preston sees it that way, or it's going to be more than just complicated."

I stand, stretching my arms above my head, a brief break from the gravity of the conversation and the debate raging in my head.

"I'll talk to him."

"You do that." She winks as she steps into the hallway. "And keep your head on straight, lover boy."

With a final wave, she exits, her laughter trailing behind her. I sit back down, her implied threat of our boss settling over me, adding to my worries.

Turning back to my screens, the data suddenly seems trivial compared to the potential upheaval brewing beneath the surface of my normally well-ordered life.

The team left hours ago. Two programmers linger in the conference room across from me—the only distraction from the mountain of work that still awaits me. I'm unsure if Maddie is still here. I've been hard at work sending everything to Preston, who has been sending rapid-fire questions before I can even get a reply out for the one before.

My thoughts of Victoria and my dilemma shoved aside to

deal with my workload are now creeping back in as the afternoon sun dips toward the horizon. I should go to the gym, run by the grocery store, and get a little meal prep done before returning here bright and early tomorrow. Yet, none of those things interest me more than the thought of a stunning Cuban and wondering what she's doing.

Her easy smile stays with me.

The casual wave of her hand when I said I had to go to my office. Everything about her is comfortable. Far too comfortable for only having just met her. I've had plenty of time off dating to figure out what I want and what will make me happy—all that culminates in her—Victoria Vega.

I glance at the guys across the hall, engrossed in an animated conversation. With my glass door closed, they wouldn't hear me anyway. Searching for my phone, I find it buried underneath some papers and dial her number—the number she gave Maddie two days ago that I was too hesitant to call. I just hope she picks up and it doesn't go to voicemail.

An edge of nervousness twitches in my stomach while the phone rings. After several rings, I wonder if this is even a good idea. Finally, she picks up.

"Hello?"

Her voice has so much uncertainty that I immediately want to kill it.

"Hi, Victoria, it's Marco."

I pause, then keep talking when my nerves spill out.

"I hope you don't mind me calling on this line. You gave it to Maddie on Friday, so I figured it would be okay."

"Hey! This is a pleasant surprise."

Nerves flutter in my stomach, moving into my chest. A smile breaks across my face as I swirl my chair away from the conference room to gaze out the window.

"How's your Sunday treating you? I mean, despite the problems we worked on yesterday."

"The problems from yesterday live on, but I think your schematics might work. So possibly a light at the end of a very long tunnel."

There's a giggle on her end, a sound that eases the tightness in my shoulders.

"Good. I'm really glad I could help, and I can run by this week if you need me to."

I really can't, not with this launch and Dawson breathing down Preston's neck, who in turn is breathing down mine.

"Thanks, I might take you up on your offer. Besides all that, how's it going on your end testing, I think you said?"

"We're in a lot better position than we were Friday, even better than yesterday. I'm sorry I had to run out of there so fast. I didn't want to, but . . ."

My voice trails off, leaving the rest of my regrets unsaid, until her sigh ripples through the phone to me.

"You're doing important work. It's understandable. But I appreciate your help yesterday."

She worried me for a second, but then her generous praise dissipated my concerns. This is why I already like her. She's easy to get along with and easygoing in general.

"What are you doing this evening?"

Without thinking, I blurt out the question, smacking my forehead for sounding too forward.

"Just pondering the eternal question—what to make for dinner. I'm leaning toward not cooking at all."

She doesn't hesitate to respond, and maybe I didn't fuck it up after all. A smile creeps onto my face, and a plan forms swiftly.

"I can help with that. How about we grab a bite together? My treat, of course, and no cooking is required."

Her brief pause is filled with the subtle sounds of her shifting, perhaps catching her off guard or making her consider the offer. I hold my breath, my fingers tapping against the arm of my chair, waiting for her answer.

"That sounds perfect."

Her breath rushes into the phone, further validating the relief from not having to cook. Being that I meal prep ninety-five percent of the time when not working on a major deadline, I get the boredom and dread that can creep in, especially when cooking for one.

"I know a place."

I rise from my chair, invigorated by the chance to see her despite my body aching from sitting all day when I should be hitting the gym.

"Great. Text me the details so I can meet you there. But keep it casual. I'm even less motivated to put on makeup."

I chuckle.

The thought of her needing makeup is criminal. She's naturally beautiful, and anyone can tell she prioritizes taking care of herself, something we have in common. I hope one day I get to cook for us.

"You don't need make-up, Victoria. Trust me."

There's a huskiness in my voice that matches the stiffening of my cock. Flashes of her laid out underneath me race across my mind. I close my eyes and tilt my head back, trying to calm myself before continuing.

A beat passes before she murmurs, "Thank you," in the silence that follows my compliment.

One day, I'll pick her up from her place and make her my passenger princess. For now, I'll be patient in meeting her, fully understanding why women need to do that these days despite being raised the old-fashioned way by my parents.

"This place is more fun than formal, but I'll send it. Meet you there in twenty minutes?"

"Make it thirty. I need to change clothes."

"Thirty it is."

I'm already standing, gathering my things, and casting a long look at the work, which will have to wait until tomorrow. As I hang up, her soft voice lingers in my ear. I hope it promises that the evening might hold more than just dinner.

I wave goodbye to the guys as I toss my backpack over my shoulder, feeling lighter than I have all day. I don't plan to sleep with her tonight, but I'm making my move. I've dated enough to know that when the chemistry is there, you must take full advantage of it.

"You won't know what hit you, Victoria Vega."

6

VICTORIA

As the rideshare pulls away, I stand on the sidewalk, taking in the revamped Post downtown. The old post office is now a bustling music venue and entertainment hub that I've been meaning to visit but haven't had the chance. I overheard someone saying there's no concert tonight, so it's not as crowded as usual despite all the people streaming into the place.

I smooth the wrinkles from my sundress and straighten the sweater loosely knotted over my shoulders. Then, I scan the front of the building for Marco, and a flutter of anticipation ripples in my stomach.

When I lock eyes with him, he's standing on the steps, casually leaning against the railing, looking relaxed and happy to see me. He's handsomely dressed in dark jeans and a white dress shirt that cuts in at the waist, highlighting the physique I remember all too well from our close encounter in that cramped room yesterday.

It took everything in me not to make a move on him, especially when he started talking about fate bringing us together. I had thought the same thing back at the market. His words were a bit eerie and threw me for a loop.

His hair, which is usually tamed, is a bit unruly tonight, with a hint of a black beard outlining his strong jaw. Dressed the way he is, he must have come from the office or was able to throw this all together in thirty minutes. It's so easy for men to get ready, something I envy.

As I walk toward him, he descends the steps with a broad smile that makes the flutter in my stomach turn into full butterflies.

"Hi."

His voice is rough, matching the dark circles around his eyes that weren't as pronounced yesterday. Before I can respond, he's pulling me into an embrace that has me tightly against his body. His arms are firm around my waist, and his body heat seeps into me.

I'm enveloped in the subtle scent of his cologne—the same intoxicating scent from yesterday. The hug is prolonged. I breathe him in, relishing the feeling of every rugged line of his frame, including a hard cock. Desire pools in my core, a quick response to his innocent touch.

He's tall enough that I can wear my espadrilles and still feel short next to him. My eyes close, and I rest my head against his shoulder, feeling instantly cared for—something I miss. The embrace is grounding and comforting, a feeling I've longed for but haven't found.

He eventually pulls back, leaving his hands resting on my shoulders. His eyes search mine with an intensity that moves the butterflies into my chest.

"I'm really glad you're here."

Every word is infused with meaning, emotion, and something else I can't grasp.

"I'm glad you called."

I reward him with a smile of my own. The buzz from his hands has me craving to be tucked into the side of his body as we ascend the stairs. But I'm not that forward, so I sigh internally when his hands fall to his sides. I swing my purse to my other arm, ensuring no obstructions in case he wants to hold my hand.

"Shall we go inside?"

I'm captivated by him. Our connection is seamless, and our shared interests, his eagerness to help with my work issues, and his kindness toward his mama all accelerate my interest more quickly than I expected. I spent the rest of yesterday at the building, going back and forth with the engineers about his fixes.

Of course, I wanted to call him half a dozen times to talk to him and hear his voice, but I never did get his cellphone number. It didn't even occur to me to ask when he left in a hurry. The guilt of keeping him longer than I intended overshadowed all rational thought.

The guilt quickly turns inward as I grapple with how fast I'm developing feelings for him. The age gap didn't bother me in the past when I dated older men. At thirty-seven, I have the luxury of dating older or younger men. Either way, it's more about their character and personality. If their desires align with mine, I want a promotion and a family for my next life phase.

"Have you been here before?"

His hand brushes the small of my back as we ascend the steps, but it is fleeting and gone by the time we get to the top, much to my disappointment.

"I haven't, but have wanted to ever since they opened."

His face lights up. He steps ahead swiftly to open the door for me, continuing to hold it as a multitude enters behind me. I giggle when he eventually reaches me.

"That was chivalrous of you to hold the door for all those people."

He shrugs, giving me a coy smile. His hand returns to the

small of my back as I take in the remodeled post office. The lobby stretches upwards, grand and spacious, with the original stairway repurposed into a striking centerpiece beyond picture-worthy.

The open staircase transcends three floors, winding up to various entertainment and dining levels. It's an eclectic mix of modern updates and vintage decor that honors the building's historical roots. Something the project manager in me appreciates and admires.

"Wow, this is magnificent. I wonder who did the remodel?"

"I'm not sure, but you haven't seen anything yet."

He guides me left, where another staircase grabs my attention. It's solid white steel, spiraling three stories to the roof and outlined in bright LED lights. Beyond that is the largest food court I've ever seen. People wait in long lines at three different bars and dozens and dozens of varying cuisines.

"Whoa. This is . . ."

His smile is wide as if soaking in my shock and converting it to his own happiness.

"Awesome, huh?"

I was going to say overwhelming. Unwilling to douse his excitement, I nod. My gaze roams the cavernous place, taking it all in. His hand falls away, and his body presses against mine, protecting me from the sea of people milling about.

With loud music piped overhead and a steady pulse of bodies, the place feels like a club rather than a food venue. When someone accidentally bumps into me, I'm knocked into him. My hand splays across his chest for balance, and his arms instantly encircle me for stability. The innocent actions of a random patron catapult us together.

The connection is electrifying and throbs between my legs. When our eyes meet, it's apparent he's feeling the same as his lips drift closer to mine. I'm eager for them to connect, to taste him, and to see how good of a kisser he is.

The chaotic venue and the chatty crowd blur into the background, leaving just him and me. In his arms, enclosed in our bubble, our breaths mingle with shared lust. My heart hammers in my chest, and my brain chants for him to kiss me. His gaze intensifies, a hint of something deeper flickering through his eyes as his arms tighten around me.

"What do you want, Victoria?"

His voice is a low hum, barely audible over the music, yet it resonates within me. What do I want? I've been asking myself this question since he followed me to my project from the farmer's market. Initially, I wanted his help. But now, I think I want him.

"Choose the place."

My thoughts scatter, having delved far deeper than his question intended. I shake my head, my hand tightening into a fist, causing his pectoral muscles to flinch.

"Um, I don't know," I manage to say, though my voice sounds distant.

His body's alignment against mine is distracting, and desire clouds my judgment. His eyes crinkle at the corners when his hands slide down my back, releasing me to look around and decide.

"They have it all. Once you decide, we'll eat on the rooftop. The view there is even better, especially at night."

"I eat almost everything, so maybe it's the one with the shortest line?"

Even that seems impossible since each food vendor has a line of waiting customers.

"I know exactly where to go."

His hand catches mine before weaving through the crowd. His body acts as a shield against the mob of people. Despite its necessity, it's the sexiest thing he could do. We land in front of a place with only a few couples ahead of us. While we wait, I release his hand. A slight downward turn of his lips is the only response to my action.

"Do you always work weekends, Marco?"

Being under the air conditioning vent, the intensity blowing my hair, I brush strands away from my face to look at him.

"I was about to ask you the same question," he murmurs, moving closer to me where my shoulder almost touches his arm.

I chuckle, and he smiles.

"Fair point. You go first."

He sighs.

His shoulders slump forward as if physically preparing for what he's about to unload.

"Not always, but with this project, yes. I'll be glad when it's done."

I roll my lips together, redistributing my lip balm, which doesn't go unnoticed, his gaze lingering on them.

"Why is that?"

"We have a venture capital group that invested and is a lot more hands-on than I realized. That's who I'm more worried about. If they are not confident in our testing and understand that programming glitches are normal when developing a new project, they could delay or even stop funding altogether."

I gasp, wondering if that means he'd be out of a job.

"Do you think that will happen?"

A weary smile passes his lips as the line shuffles forward.

"No, but there are no guarantees in tech. You probably know that. Real estate development can be rocky, from the little I understand about it."

"Sure, but I'm more concerned about your field. Tech in Houston isn't that popular compared to Silicon Valley, so . . ."

My worries trail off as I overstep the boundary of saying his company could collapse. It's a fair assumption I should have kept to myself until I knew him better. Marco glances around, then focuses back on me, his expression more serious.

"I hear you, but I'll be okay."

It's apparent I struck a nerve. Something I hope doesn't damper the rest of our night.

"I'd love to hear more about what you're working on now and what you have coming up."

My offer doesn't chase away his frown, so I let it drop and stay silent. The line shuffles forward, giving us a break from the sudden awkwardness.

"How did everything go after I left? Any luck with the adjustments we discussed?"

He forges on, leaving my misstep behind. A surge of gratitude washes over me at how easily he moves the conversation forward and doesn't dwell. I make a mental note not to bring it up again.

"Actually, yes!"

I clap, unable to hide my excitement at finding a possible solution to a problem that has been plaguing me for weeks.

"I sent your notes over to them. They're going to look at it this week. Fingers crossed."

I cross my fingers, waving them in front of him, eliciting a throaty chuckle that I already love. The relief he must see on my face is mirrored in the tension leaving his shoulders as his posture relaxes. Considering the pressure he's under, our shared win is exactly what he needs.

"That's great to hear."

"Heck, I should be buying you dinner for helping me. It's the least I can do."

His hand covers my crossed fingers, pushing them down to interlace our fingers.

"That, Victoria, will never happen."

I roll my eyes.

The machismo of men is so outdated.

Women can buy meals. We can even split the bill. It's modern dating. When the conversation falls silent, the guilt from earlier rises again, and I want to make it right so there is no discord between us.

"I'm sorry for what I said about Houston having few tech companies. I didn't mean to . . ."

What? Make him feel bad? Make him second guess his life choices? How do I even say that out loud?

As we reach the front of the line, I tilt my head, awaiting an answer. The cashier steps away to fill orders. He exhales and lets go of my hand to run his fingers through his hair, a gesture laden with weariness.

"It's something I've heard before. I understand, but I have reasons for staying in town."

He doesn't divulge those reasons or expand on his answer, so I focus on the menu board in front of us while thinking about him. His willingness to work long hours all weekend, helping me and his mama, and meeting me for dinner showcases his thoughtfulness.

Although we've just met, and I can't fully understand him yet, I'm intrigued by his ability to handle such immense pressure.

"It's nerve-wracking, isn't it? Waiting to see if the work you've put in pays off."

My words float between us, drawing his attention away from the employees working the food counter.

"Exactly. But enough shop talk. Let's order. I'm starving."

He smiles, his hand suddenly stroking down my arm, leaving a trail of tingles in its wake. He orders for us, assuring me I'll love what he selects. Usually, I'm not a fan of a guy ordering for me, but with the sudden awkwardness that I caused, I keep my mouth shut.

He grabs two bottles of sparkling water, pays for everything, and ushers us to the side while we await our food.

"Tell me, Victoria. Have you dated someone my age before?"

His question is so out of the blue I'm caught off guard. He picks up on it immediately and frowns slightly.

"You don't have to answer that if you don't want to."

For some reason, he shifts on his feet while holding both bottles and looks surprisingly nervous. This is the first time I've seen him like this, another thing that surprises me.

The fact that he's asking about dating confirms he's feeling something between us, far more than just professional. I couldn't be happier. To calm his sudden nervousness, I place my hand on his arm. He looks from it to my face with an inquisitive look.

"Seeing as how I have no idea how old you are, I'm afraid I can't answer that."

My words ring with a truthfulness that has him giving me a shy grin.

"Oh, yeah."

He chuckles dryly. Removing my hand, I step closer to stare blankly at him.

"I assume you're younger than me. I could've looked you up online, but I didn't. It didn't occur to me."

His mouth settles into a line as he listens.

"However, I don't care. What matters is compatibility, shared values, and mutual respect. You've shown you respect my work and have gone out of your way to help me solve a tough issue. That speaks volumes over any birthdate."

Marco seems to relax, a smile creeping back over his features.

"Good, because—"

Whatever else he is going to say gets cut off when they call his name and shove a tray overflowing with food toward us. I quickly grab utensils and napkins before taking the water bottles while he handles the tray.

"Alright, let's head up to the roof. They have seating up there."

"I'll follow you."

He turns, cutting through the crowd once again. I hold on to the back of his shirt to avoid being separated and follow him two floors up the winding staircase. The energy between us feels lighter and easier, allowing me to enjoy the night now that I know where he stands.

Marco's broad shoulders block the view as we ascend the last few steps to the rooftop. The fresh autumn air swirls about my shoulders and lifts my sundress slightly, giving the couple behind me an eyeful.

At the top, he steps aside, and the downtown skyline bursts before my eyes. I can't help but gasp, taken aback by the towering skyscrapers and endless city views in every direction. Each building is sharply defined against the night sky, with some outlined by lights that change colors periodically.

"Wow, this is absolutely breathtaking!" I exclaim, my voice tinged with awe.

Marco grins, clearly pleased with my reaction.

"Pretty impressive, isn't it?"

Soft twinkle lights trim the planter boxes while winding pathways and cozy seating areas span the roof. It's welcoming and cozy. I follow him as he hunts for a table closest to the community garden on the far side of the building.

The rooftop is alive with energy. People mingle and laugh while a live band plays classic pop hits on a stage in the middle of the roof. A few couples sway gracefully on the wooden dance floor while children play tag along the curved paths beside the raised flower beds.

"This is an oasis in the middle of the city—no, above the city even," I say, taking in the crowd and the view while he unpacks the tray and prepares the table. He takes the drinks and utensils from my hands, and I beam at him.

"I can't believe I've never been up here before."

"I try to come here at least once a month. Something about it feels inspirational. It's a good place to think and mull over stuff."

The last piece of that statement gets my attention. I sit while he dispenses with the tray. Upon his return, he explains each dish, saying we can share and swap if I don't like something. Since it's family style, he prepares a plate with some of everything and then hands it to me. It's chivalrous, and I like it.

"What type of stuff do you mull over up here?"

A haunted look crosses his face, hinting at another topic that is probably too deep to discuss tonight.

"Everything."

I don't press him when he doesn't elaborate, but I'm deciding to keep the conversation light for now. He hands me the package of utensils, his fingers brushing mine and lingering for a few seconds. His gaze holds mine, the promise of wanting much more in them with the bright lights reflecting on his face.

"Do you feel that?"

His finger strokes mine in mid-air, and neither of us wants to end the contact even though it looks strange. I pull away, breaking the attraction flowing between us.

"I do."

Distracting myself with a bite of food, I wonder if I should admit I felt it back at the market. The way the breeze lifted the edges of his hair caught my attention as he walked toward me. I had hoped he would stop at the booth while I was talking to Ross and was thrilled when he did.

The conversation lightens as we eat. More than once, I laugh so hard my cheeks hurt. The longer we carry on, the more my feelings grow until I'm giddy and utterly silly from the conversation. His stories about childhood escapades, some mimicking my Latin relatives, have me clutching my stomach.

The way he throws his head back in laughter makes him even more endearing.

"As kids, we weren't allowed to speak English at home. Dad insisted on Spanish only," Marco shares, his eyes twinkling with the mischief of memory. "Made for some interesting school presentations when I accidentally slipped into Spanish."

I lean my elbows on the table, and he immediately takes my hand and gives it a light squeeze. His thumb swipes across my knuckles, increasing our closeness.

"My mama was the same, but with her, it was all about manners. 'Victoria,' she'd say, 'how you behave at the table reflects on your entire family.' Made every dinner feel like a state dinner! She'd scold me now if she saw my elbows on the table."

He laughs and launches into another story about his little sisters. Despite their sibling age gap, he seems very close to them, even painting their nails while his mama is busy elsewhere in the house.

Despite the crowded rooftop and children darting around us, the connection, the lights, and getting to know each other better makes it feel more romantic. I find myself staring at his lips longer and longer, wanting to taste them.

He must think the same thing as his story trails off until he's staring at me just as openly. Several long moments pass until the light breeze blows strands of hair across my face, breaking our trance. I look away, fixing my hair and biting my lip to stop the lust racing through my body and pooling at my pussy.

He clears his throat, getting my attention.

"If you're done, why don't we walk around? Take in the view."

"Definitely done."

7

MARCO

I can't keep my hands off this woman and don't want to. There, I said it. Admitting it is the first step for me. Sharing it with her is the next, albeit scary, step. She could reject me for any number of reasons, the least being our age difference, thankfully.

But I'm a fool if I don't shoot my shot with her tonight. It's clear there's something between us. Something that sparks every time I touch her, even asking her for confirmation that I'm not losing my mind.

I've never felt this intense level of chemistry with another woman. It's all I want to explore with her despite the little yawn she stifles when my back is turned, clearing the table of the trash. Walking around is just an excuse to hold her hand, to get closer than the table separating us allows. If I were bold, I'd invite her back to my place and explore every inch of her olive skin.

Fuck her into oblivion and then make her breakfast in the morning before dropping her at home. Not that I think she'd go for that, seeing as how we just met or that we both have work in the morning with critical projects hanging in the balance. Fuck all that. I'm trying anyway. It will always be a no if I don't.

I offer her my hand, surprise flickering across her face for a second before it's replaced with a smile. When she slips her soft palm against mine, I curl my fingers around hers. I like how mine engulfs hers. She comments on her observations, pointing out different things in the city skyline that interest her. I merely hum, watching her enthusiasm and waiting for the chance to kiss her. Needing to test the waters to see how far she'll let me go.

We walk to the roof's edge, the railing high enough to prevent falls without obstructing the views. She breathes in the crisp air with a slight shiver, and I seize the chance to pull her into my arms, shielding her from the breeze.

"Ah, this is very nice," she murmurs, wrapping her arms tightly around my waist.

Instead of gazing up at me as I had hoped so I could kiss her, she tucks her chin and lays her cheek against my chest. It's innocently sexy. She's not overtly hitting on me. No, she's more demure than that. It boosts my ego that she feels protected by me and actively seeks that security. And I like that she is confident enough to be vulnerable with me early on. It turns me on.

Her close proximity, the smell of her clean hair beneath my nose, and the feel of her lean, fit body in my arms are making my cock hard and my balls tight. I squeeze her close. The sudden exhale of air from her chest worries me until she drags her face across my shirt to stare up at me.

Her eyes are dark, not green or hazel, but browner and fuller of desire. The same lust rushes through my veins, causing my muscles to clench with restraint. I want her. There's no doubt in my mind. But seeing it on her face is fucking tearing away at the edge of my resolve to the point I want to blurt out for her to come home with me.

My gaze roams her face, studying every inch before

lowering my lips and watching her eyes close in anticipation. My heart skips a fucking beat seeing her so openly accept me. What I intend to be a soft, introductory kiss changes into a hot and heated demand. My hand slips from her waist, tracing the gentle curve of her tight ass and settling in the center to get a handful. I press her lower body against mine, forcing her to feel the effect she's having on me.

She moans, freeing an arm to wrap around my neck and drawing me into her. Her lips are soft and supple, quickly parting with my tongue and devouring her awaiting mouth. As our tongues intertwine, we both groan. She yanks me closer to her, angling her head to grant me deeper access.

I can't breathe. She consumes my senses. The need to fuck her is so overwhelming that it sends a tremor through my body. My heart races as I imagine the future and what we could have together—a life built on trust, love, and unbridled passion. It's an intoxicating cocktail, and I can't get enough of it.

I thoroughly explore every part of her mouth, craving to feel every bit of her in and around me. My hand kneads her ass while I grind my hard cock against her soft body. She pulls away for air, her hand pushing against my chest to put space between us—completely unnecessary, in my opinion. My lips chase after hers, but she shakes her head, both hands pushing me away.

"There's a kid."

My hold loosens, and I straighten, my hand falling away from her perfect ass. Our breaths come in shallow pants. Her cheeks are flushed, and her lips are swollen from my intense intrusion. She looks up at me with eyes full of desire. I can't help but smile. This moment, so raw and primal, is precisely what I'd hoped for.

I glance over my shoulder to see a small kid staring right at us, unaware of the need for privacy. Yet, it's my fault for getting carried away with her in such a public place. Embarrassed, she turns away, putting her back to me and silently watching the city lights sparkle before us.

My arms move around her body, pulling her into my chest while my hands splay across her stomach. It's still holding her, innocent enough for the nosy kid, but between us, she can feel every inch of my hard cock. The invitation laid out for her to decide where it goes from here.

"I want you, Victoria," I whisper, my voice low and filled with sincerity. "I want you more than I've ever wanted anyone or anything in my life."

Her body tightens, want coiling in her as it has already in me. If I could, I'd lay her down on the engineered grass to my left and make love to her while the stars watched.

"I want to worship between your open legs. Feel your thighs crushing my head, keeping me in place while I make you shout my name."

My head dips, making love to her ears and tracing the shell with the tip of my tongue. Her body is so tightly clenched that I'm unsure if she's breathing. My fingertips tease soft circles into her belly, a pattern I'd repeat over her clit with my tongue.

Her head falls against my shoulder, her fingers grazing mine as they continue torturing her stomach and pushing them slightly lower. Not enough to connect where we both want but close enough to keep her on edge.

"Trail my tongue along your inner thighs until I get to those sweet lips. I'd make you come over and over again until you were throbbing around my fingers, wanting more. Wanting me inside you."

Her breasts rise and fall as she pants, giving me instant feedback on what my words are doing to her. I bet if I were to feel her, she would be as wet as I am hard, painfully so. My fingers slip closer, almost where they want to be when she stops them.

"Marco?"

My lips brush against her hair, and I close my eyes as I breathe her in. My name is a faint question murmured to the universe, fate, and the very forces that have brought us together. Those same forces are looking down on us now under the twinkling stars.

"Yes?"

I open my eyes, nuzzle her temple, and wait. I curl further around her, pressing her into the railing and ensuring no one can see as my fingers find her heated core. Her breath hitches, stopping as her head lulls against my shoulder. Our eyes connect for the briefest of seconds before hers closes.

My touch is soft and teasing, applying just enough pressure to bring her pleasure but not enough to satisfy her. A faint curse word passes her lips, tilting upward in a soft smile. To any outsider or curious kid, it looks as though I'm blanketing her from the cool night air, whereas in actuality, I'm walking her through everything I'm going to do to her when she gives me the word.

"Do you like this?"

I increase the pressure on her pussy, now grinding against my hand and causing her tight ass to stroke my cock simultaneously. It's glorious and torture at the same time. Her words falter. She still hasn't asked whatever question is floating through her mind.

"I like this, Victoria. I want to do more. Much more if you'll let me."

The heat between us is searing. My body is on fire for hers, and my heart beats faster at the possibility of taking her home. To have her in my bed.

To dominate her sexy body in every way imaginable, then falling asleep with her in my arms, to just do it all over again in the morning before work. That'd be the best Monday morning in the history of Monday mornings.

"Yes," she finally answers, opening her eyes to see mine. "But how . . ."

She arches into my hand, her mouth parting rather than completing her sentence. I know she's close, but my truck is parked too far away. Too long of a walk to leave her without a bit of satisfaction.

A devilish plan forms in my mind. I pull back, withdrawing my body to grab her hand and drag her away from the railing. She's completely caught off guard, the lustful haze clearing into wide eyes that stare at me as I quickly lead her across the roof.

"Marco?"

The uncertainty in her voice matches the hesitancy in her steps, yet I don't answer her. Half the fun is not knowing what comes next, and I'm more than ready to surprise her. More than ready to make our first time very memorable if she'll let me.

The more private bathrooms on the far side of the roof are probably meant for employees. They have floor-to-ceiling bathroom doors, not stalls, which is perfect for what I have in mind.

"Come in here."

I'm not asking, nor am I telling. I'm gauging if she's willing to be adventurous. Willing to be a bit wild with me. Either way, I'll eventually have her in my bed. But if I fuck her now and give her what she wants at the same time, both of us will be happy.

"Will we get caught?"

I have no idea how to answer that. We might. We might not. But I'm not letting that ruin this chance since she didn't say no.

"Not if you're quiet."

I'm already pushing open the door, looking inside the bathroom to see all the doors with the green vacant sign above the lock. My hand tightens, shooting her a naughty wink and ushering that tight ass into the last and most secluded stall. She looks anxious, her eyes darting toward the door as I close and lock it.

"I've never done anything like this before."

I don't need her admission. I figured as much with how much she's fidgeting. Without replying, I take her purse, hang it on the hook, and step close to her. Her hands dive into my hair, drawing me close and allowing us to pick up where we left off.

Our lips collide, tongues clashing while I tug her dress up to her hips. I groan when my fingertips touch her silky skin, caressing the curve of her hip and the edge of her panties.

As her fingers comb through my hair and our tongues dance, I can feel her body tense with excitement. Her every move, her every sound, is telling me just how much she wants me. And I want her just as much, if not more.

My cock strains against my boxers and pants, begging to be released. But I hold back, savoring the feel of her lips under mine, her skin beneath my fingertips. This moment is too precious to rush, even though we have little time.

With time ticking away, the threat of being caught roaring in my head, I tug her panties down her legs. My fingers connect with her smooth pussy, overflowing in wetness, causing me to release a tortured groan.

I want to fuck the shit out of her right here and now, knowing it's something we both need. A desperate release from the frenzy I started by the railing.

She tugs painfully on my hair, breaking the kiss and panting hard.

"I . . . need you," she whispers, her voice quivering with desire while her hands move to hold her dress up for me.

"We have to be fast."

The rasp in my voice indicates that I need her, too. I'm met with a curt nod. When her shoulder blades hit the stall door, her stance splaying, I smile. Her sweet scent welcomes me. Her bare lips glisten with her wetness, and I stop to stare, to commit to memory every single moment.

"Beautiful pussy."

Her lips are tight, snug against her body, looking like a small slit, and I lick my lips in anticipation. Gazing at her, desire leaves her eyes half closed but eager.

"But can you be quiet, Marco?"

Her greedy hands move to my pants, grasping the belt buckle and unfastening it. I love how fucking eager she is as I lean away for her to get my pipe out.

Fuck.

Taunting me is fucking insane. I love it, and women rarely do it. When the jingle of my buckle and the zip of my pants is heard, I move her hands away, knowing I'll burst if she touches me.

Her tongue swipes across her lips, her eyes zeroing on my large cock as I unleash it. Her breath locks in her chest, the reaction I'm accustomed to getting.

"I can, *mamita.* But I'm not the one about to be split open."

It's time to expose her to how I like things. It's better to find out the first time than spend time playing Mr. Nice Guy over the next few weeks.

"You want—"

"Turn around and put your hands on the wall."

With my cock exposed to the cool air and the sight of her glistening lips, I'm going to bust a nut before I even slide into the warm, wet pussy. The time for talking and stalling is over. I'm going to fuck her hard and fast, take her home, and fuck her again, slowly and sensually.

"Oooh," she murmurs, slowly turning, causing her panties to fall to the floor.

I swiftly pick them up and tuck them into my pants pocket. Watching her quickly obey my command brings a slight smile to my face. If she complies this easily every time, we will be great together.

Once she turns around, her fingers spread on the stall door. She gazes over her shoulder and waits. This is good—very good for her to learn who will always be in control between us. I catch the edge of her dress, flip it onto her back, and pull her hips closer to me.

"Perfect."

My hand presses against the middle of her back.

"Arch into me, Vic. I want to see your tight ass."

That sexy little thing has the nerve to wiggle it, teasing me with what's to come. I swear under my breath.

"Like this?"

She arches it so deeply that her glutes brush my cock and move in a rhythm that matches her riding my face. I gaze up at the ceiling, exhaling harshly so as to not prematurely blow my load. I let her have her fun as I reach for my wallet and get a condom out.

"Open your mouth."

My voice is rough, my gaze is harsh, and both are no-nonsense, but she immediately complies. I say a silent thank you to the universe that she's this fucking hot and does as she's told. This is going to be a match made in Heaven.

I lift the edge of the wrapper to her teeth, which she grips so I can unbutton my shirt and pull down my pants. Her eyes are glued to my physique, taking in all the long hours of hard work until she sees me working my cock that's going straight into that little slit. Her gaze diverts, and her chin drops, possibly having second thoughts.

I give her a few seconds to think it over while I grab the end of the wrapper, using her teeth to rip it open and fish the condom out to put on. I'm deliberately slow, counting down the time in my head until I can't stall anymore, having given her adequate time to back out if she's concerned about my large cock.

"Good girl for listening to me."

The uncertainty clears from her face. Her eyes return to mine, dazzlingly dark and excited. She spits the wrapper to the floor and shifts to face the door, bracing herself. Without her calling a stop to this, it's full steam ahead. Literally. My hand wraps around the front of her throat, using it as leverage to keep her still as my fist wraps around my cock.

"My cock is hard as fuck for you."

I drag the tip back and forth over her soft folds, teasing her and preparing me. Her body rocks into it, trying to line us up. If I had a free hand, I'd smack her impatient ass. It begs for a handprint on her silky skin.

"Do you feel it?"

I pause at her entrance, not stopping her when she pushes onto me and breaches her tight hole. We both moan at how good it feels already.

"Yesss."

Her breathy word is felt against my palm as my fingers wrap securely around her small neck, keeping track of her wildly beating pulse. It's my barometer for how far I can push her while checking to see if it excites her further.

"Doesn't it feel good?"

I slowly push in, closing my eyes when I hit her cervix and trying to hold back the orgasm, my balls already tingling. She groans, my size a little much for her, which I fucking love. Splitting her open is my new favorite hobby. With her stilled and me holding back, my cock pulses inside her.

Fuck.

Her hips make mini striations, adjusting to the pressure of our connection. Being buried deep in her pussy, to the absolute end of her channel, causes my veins to vibrate with adrenaline. I want to tear into her, take her primally, in an animalistic fashion.

It's difficult holding back the animal in me as I allow her to play with my cock. When her movements become looser, working her pussy back and forth in a larger pattern, I take over.

"You feel so fucking good."

My hand moves to her hip, my fingertips crushing into the bone to hold her still. I don't need nor want her fucking me back. It's not necessary. I drag my cock back slowly, milking those walls into submitting more wetness and slamming into her.

A sharp scream escapes her throat. The sound is far too loud for me, just starting to fuck her. She'll get us caught, thrown out, or worse, charged with indecent exposure.

"Quiet, mamita."

I scold, and her head nods.

Unwilling to take any chances of this ending prematurely. I move my hand from her lovely throat to cover her mouth, which she easily allows. With that precaution in place, my hand holding her in position, I'm free to piston in and out of her.

Muffled exhalations burst from her body at each violent thrust, fanning over my fingers. Knowing I have complete control over her, trapping her screams and forcing her to be quiet unleashes that animal.

I'm rough and jarring, stabbing her repeatedly with my cock. The muscles of her ass ripple at each impact while the door squeaks from the force of my thrusting. Her hand curls into a fist, her forearms flattening on the wood for better leverage.

The hem of her dress falls at the speed of my fucking, getting in the way of my view, and I slow long enough to tuck it into the nape of her neck. The fabric is draped away from her luscious back, and her silky skin begs to be bitten and sucked.

My mouth waters at the sight of her braless back, debating about reaching around and pinching her nipple. Now is not the time. I need to fuck her fast and finish. I'm tempting fate with each obscenely harsh thrust that's drawing louder and louder noises from her.

My body flushes with heat. Her pussy clenches around mine as she orgasms, unexpected and catching me by surprise.

"You're coming, Vic? You like getting fucked hard in the bathroom like a dirty girl?"

I pound my cock into her pussy, punctuating every word, my hand tightening over her mouth as she moans loudly.

"Too fucking loud."

Her back arches further, sinking onto my cock as I continue ramming her cervix. Her body is slumping, and her legs are trembling, taking it as best she can while gazing over her shoulder at me. My hand slips from her mouth at the sight of her lust-induced expression. I could fuck her into oblivion. She's so willing and pliable.

"Oh God."

She moans, her voice barely audible, as her sweaty fist slips on the door.

"You love this. You love my cock rammed into your small pussy."

I growl low and dangerous. Her body shudders with each thrust, her wetness coating my balls and dripping onto the bathroom floor.

"I . . . I do. Yeah . . . love . . . it."

My heart races as she gasps for breath between her words. I can't resist the urge to give her more. My thrusts grow wild and sloppy, my hips smacking against her ass cheeks while the door frame rattles. I'm lost in her, lost in the feeling of her in my hands and around my cock.

Her juices drench my cock and balls. She's so fucking wet it's splashing onto my pelvis after another orgasm has her convulsing and clenching my cock, pulling me closer to my release.

I never want this to end, but the self-control I've had in holding off is quickly waning. Her mouth parts, her breath hitches, and by the look on her face, I wonder if she's in pain until a smile plays at her lips.

My balls are heavy and tingling, my orgasm starting at the base of my spine and ricocheting out of my cock with intense pleasure.

My eyes lock with hers, the heat and desire reflected in her hazel irises as my hand clamps down on her shoulder. She whispers something I miss, my groan drowning out her words.

Her palms are flat against the door, her body twisted to look over her shoulder, wanting a glimpse of getting pounded. It's the sweetest fucking sight until the main bathroom door suddenly squeaks open, and a couple of loud ass women come ranting through the door.

Her eyes widen, a panic-stricken look covering her face. Internally, I'm wrestling with the same reaction. The risk of being caught sky fucking high kills the afterglow of my climax and shrivels my dick to a short stump.

One of them slams the door to the stall next to us, all the while going off about a guy who hit on her or something.

My fingertips lighten from her hip, moving to caress her lower back as I silently pull out of her. The condom is sagging heavily, filled to the top with my ejaculation, which I quietly remove and toss into the toilet.

She and I work in tandem getting dressed, each moving as quietly as possible while the two ladies converse back and forth between the stalls.

She looks nervous, her eyes darting from me to the door separating us from them. I flash her a guilty grin and lean over to gently kiss her lips in assurance. When her hand lands on my chest, I cup it, keeping her in place to rein light pecks over her lips and cheek until I reach her ear.

"Will you come home with me?"

Her breath quickens and then holds, causing me to pull back to look at her. A slow shaking of her head has my gut plummeting. I'm worried that this scared her off. Having sex in public on the first date is too much like a hook-up. It's something I didn't even think about in my lust-filled haze of wanting her.

The regret on her face is sending daggers into my heart as she fidgets with her dress that is already in place despite her underwear still being bunched in my pants pocket.

"Please?" I whisper, raising my hands into a prayer position, jutting my lip out to look as pitiful as possible for her to change her mind.

Her silence is killing the vibe between us. The awkward shifting on her feet and nervous gaze around the space—avoiding mine—is too much.

"Fuck it."

8

VICTORIA

His words barely register before he hastily flushes the toilet with his shoe, then grabs my hand and flings open the bathroom door with open abandonment. His movements are erratic, almost like a tantrum, as he leads us to the sinks, no longer being careful.

It's as if he wants the women to see us or something, maybe an ego thing. Either way, I'm at a loss for the sudden shift in his demeanor at my refusal to go home with him.

The cold water rushes out of the faucet as he turns on the spouts, our hands clasped together under the stream. I can't help but notice how rough and calloused his hands feel against mine, something I loved when they were moving in and out of my body.

There's a sense of intimacy with him washing my hands for me, taking a gentler approach compared to the rigidness of his body and the pulled expression he wears on his face.

Curious about his actions, I let him finish washing and drying my hands before the toilets flush behind me. Startled, my heart beat erratically. As I prepared myself for the exchange of knowing looks and whispered words, Marco suddenly moved his body to block me from their view while tossing the used paper towels in the trash.

"Ladies."

His broad frame shields me completely.

"Enjoying your evening?"

A hesitant voice answers him, and they have a brief exchange before he turns to me.

"I know that food didn't agree with you. Let's get you home."

His hand sweeps down my back, guiding me toward the door and away from their prying eyes. He single-handedly assessed the situation and saved me from any embarrassment. His actions make me think twice about his perceived temper tantrum.

"I'm sorry for rushing you."

His hand remains on the small of my back as we make our way to the staircase.

"I just . . . I didn't want them to bother you. It was my idea to do what we did and where we did it, so I wanted to take responsibility for it, for us."

The venue's noise engulfs us as I descend the winding steps ahead of him. My brain swirls around his explanation. What I mistook for a tantrum was him taking ownership of the situation, worried that the opinions of strangers would affect me. It's caring, especially after going at it like ravenous animals in a public bathroom, of all places.

Never have I done that. It's not on my life bingo card. I'm not sure I'd ever do it again, but damn if it wasn't hot. Flashes of his dark eyes gazing up at me, watching my every move while soaked in my cum—it's making me horny all over again.

The lust-filled haze that had me following him into the bathroom to have sex was shattered when the ladies burst through the door. If it hadn't been for them flooding my brain with mental clarity and sound decision-making skills, I would have readily agreed to go home with Marco. Hopefully, for another round.

My sandals barely hit the bottom steps, so we're not surrounded by the crowd of people that seems to have grown to almost an unmanageable amount.

"Give me your hand."

Marco's command comes a second before he seizes my hand in his, taking the lead in diving through the crowd. Like before, I use his body as a shield, walking in the wake he creates behind him until we are past the food court and walking down the hall toward the multi-story staircase that initially caught my attention.

Expecting to go to the parking lot, he veers to the left, walking past the stairs and into a darkened corner that leads to who knows where. I tug on our joined hands, uncertain about what is happening, when he presses me against the wall. His body shields me from possible onlookers who might pass us.

"I needed to talk to you away from the noise, Victoria."

His voice is low, and his dark eyes are almost black in the shadows cloaked around us.

"I asked you to come home with me tonight because . . . because of what happened between us. I didn't plan for that to happen. And I'm not sorry it did."

Feeling every inch of the cold concrete wall against my back and his warm, hard body against my front, I can scarcely breathe.

"Okay."

His hands move to either side of my shoulders, trapping me in place.

"What we did—I want more of that. I hope tonight, me rushing . . . well, you know. It doesn't change things for me. If anything, it's a chance for more, and I hope you want that too."

I don't know if it's because my body is still buzzing post orgasms or my restraint is slipping, and I want to mount him right now, but I'm not exactly sure what he's saying.

"You want more sex? Marco, I can't—"

"No, Vic."

His voice is almost panicked, and my hands cup his waist. An action that has him adjusting his hand to lean on his forearm to get closer to me. So close that his lips are inches from mine when I gaze up at him.

"I mean, yes, of course. I'd be an idiot to say no. But I want more of you and us, getting to know each other."

"Oh."

"I'm fucking it all up. What I'm trying to say is this wasn't just a booty call. Not for me, at least."

He blows out a frustrated exhalation, his lips drifting closer.

"I want to see where this goes. Dates, go out, stay in, have fun. You know, that kind of stuff. But I want to ensure that what I did upstairs didn't mess that up. That there's still a chance."

Ah, that's what all this is. His jerky actions. His clipped words. The sudden detour to this dark hallway instead of saying goodbye at the curb. He's afraid we'll say goodnight, and I won't respond or, even worse, ghost or decline him next time he calls.

I place my hands gently on his cheeks, and he presses into the warmth of my touch. Lines of worry carve deeper into his forehead as he closes his eyes for a moment, finding solace in the simple gesture.

"Marco, I don't regret what we did either."

His eyes flash open, staring so hard they bore into me.

"I want to see you again. It's just that tonight, I can't. Mondays are a zoo at the office, and I'm sure they are for you."

"Yeah. Tomorrow is going to suck."

His reluctance to share how rough this weekend has been on him is finally seeping through.

"See? So, as much as I'd like to come over and pick up where we left off, I can't. And you can't either."

Not even a breath passes before his lips latch onto mine. His hands collect me from the wall, wrapping around me tightly and trapping my hands against his cheeks. Neither of which bothers us as he thoroughly devours my mouth in unbridled passion.

I moan into his mouth, which increases the intensity with which he kisses me. If upstairs was a preview of how great he fucks, I can't wait until we have more time together. He's going to destroy me, and I'm here for it.

As rushed as it starts, it ends just as abruptly.

"I'm hard as a fucking rock. If I don't stop, I'm going to . . ."

He doesn't finish what he is saying, leaving me to wonder and wanting to test whatever is to come.

"Going to . . ." I prompt, moving my hands off his face when he pulls away.

He cocks an eyebrow, his hands skimming down my body to give my ass a hard squeeze. It feels odd and breezy without my panties, which I assume he still has and something I need to get back.

He doesn't answer, takes me by the hand, and leads us out of the dark hallway to the front of the building.

"Where did you park so I can walk you to your car?"

Puzzled at his assumption since this place is a nightmare for parking, I shrug.

"I took a ride share. If I were to have a drink or two, I didn't want to drive intoxicated." He grins, more goofy than sexy. "What?"

"Then I get to take you home."

"You don't have to, Marco. I can take another car home. It's what I planned on doing."

"Not a chance, mamita."

Mamita.

He said it while he was fucking me. A term of endearment that was soft against the hard ramming I took. It's music to my ears every time it leaves his mouth. With a new bravado about his demeanor, he tightens his grip on my hand as we walk outside.

"I don't trust some random guy taking you home when I can. Besides, you're safer with me."

I've come to expect a certain level of chauvinism with Latin men, my papi being one of the worst offenders that I always chalked up to his age. Marco doing the same has me rolling my eyes.

"I'm more than capable of getting myself home," I protest as we cross the street to a line of cars parallel parked at the curb. "I've been doing it for thirty-seven years now."

He doesn't bother stopping, guiding us to a large silver truck with shiny rims.

"Never said you weren't capable, but if we're going to date, I will pick you up and drop you off every time. I'm not relying on another man to do my job. And don't even think about opening that door yourself."

His tone is unwavering, as are his old-school manners, but his smile is easygoing, charming against the expectations he's laying down. My hand retracts from the silver handle, reaching the truck before him while he fishes out his keys.

"Your true nature is coming out. Very bossy," I accuse, curious how he'll respond. He opens the door, helps me inside, and leans in the open space.

"In some respects, I am, Vic."

Vic.

A shortening of my name, not quite as endearing as mamita, hinting at a closeness we now share. I like it, but not as much as the endearment.

"In the bedroom, I'm very bossy. Outside of that, it's very situational."

His admission is a turn-on, owning who he is when most people don't. I can respect it. My core definitely likes it, clenching tightly, and I hope I'm not dripping a wet spot into the back of my dress.

"Can I have my panties back now?"

His lips curl into a smug grin as he retrieves the items from his pocket. He raises them to his nose, inhaling deeply and savoring my scent—his eyes, heavy with desire, half-close in a look of pure ecstasy.

My body ignites with heat, and my pussy pulses with a renewed desire for him, even after the intense pounding he just gave me. The air around us crackles with anticipation, and I can feel the raw passion radiating between us as I hold out my hand.

"You have to earn them."

His voice is throaty, a groan slipping past his lips when he sniffs them again. His dark eyes glitter with danger, and there is a sudden game in play that I have no experience with.

"Earn them?" I echo, my hand tightening over the purse strap in my lap.

He nods, his eyes never leaving mine as he leans against the truck door, crossing his arms over his chest, fisting the panties. He looks so cocky, so sure of himself that I can't help but feel a rush of adrenaline.

"Yes."

His tone is matter-of-fact, and his stance casual, but the challenge is evident as he doesn't move to get behind the wheel and take me home.

"How?"

"You said you'd come home with me if we didn't have work in the morning."

"Yes, that's true."

"Before I take you home, I want to see you tomorrow night. If you agree to that, you can have them."

He counters by asking me out and letting them dangle from his index finger. The fact that anyone walking by could see us has me trying to snatch them out of his hand, but his reflexes are too fast.

He tsks in mocked displeasure, raising them to his nose once more and inhaling deeply. This should revolt me. I tell myself I am, and yet my pussy pools with more wetness.

"You're going to have to be faster than that, Vic. Or you could say yes, and this will all be over with."

I'm sore from his spontaneity in the bathroom, horny from his current teasing, and completely enthralled with his playfulness.

"And what do I get if I say yes?" I taunt, knowing a game is better when both parties are playing.

His face lights up, lifting off the door and into my personal space. The leather squeaks against his weight, crushing it as he leans heavily against me. His lips brush my ear, his tongue tracing the shell until he nips my earlobe.

"All of me. In, over, and around you. Repeatedly."

His warm breath fans my skin, sending goosebumps down my neck and arm. The fist holding my panties caressing my nipple into a hard and needy point. Visions of his wide tongue working its magic over the peaked crests have me breathing shallowly against his hand.

"Deal."

My voice sounds strange to my ears, barely heard over the pounding of my heart. My hunger for him only grows more desperate. If I didn't have work in the morning, I'd most certainly go home with him. After that dominating performance, I'm curious how things will be in private.

His lips crash onto mine, consuming me whole and making me crave him more. My hands reach up and wrap around his neck, pulling him closer, wanting him deeper. His hand cups the side of my neck, angling my face to shove more of his tongue into my mouth, trying to taste the back of my throat. The more we kiss, the closer we become to not ending this night right now, which I can't have.

My hands slip between us, pushing against his chest and receiving a disapproving groan before he relents and pulls back. His hand covers mine for a second, then pulls it off to drop the lacy panties in my palm.

True to his word, yet they are damp from my wetness. I'd be embarrassed if it wasn't for him inhaling them like a fiend and turning me into an addict myself.

"Let's get you home before I say fuck it and have more sex in the open with you."

I settle into my corner office on Monday morning, clutching my coffee—extra cream, no sugar—as I overlook downtown Houston. The sun casts long, angular shadows across my desk, cluttered with blueprints and digital tablets. I've barely taken my first sip when my phone buzzes, heralding the start of what promises to be a chaotic week.

"Victoria Vega."

"Morning, Victoria. It's Lisa here in Compliance."

This is the call I have been waiting for. Despite the engineers reviewing Marco's illustration and observation, they can't act on them until he's onboard.

Lisa is the first step in that process, and she's very thorough in her vendor assessment. She even refused to approve a couple of vendors I needed on this project when the due diligence didn't pan out.

"Hey Lisa, I know it's preliminary, but what do you think?"

I sip my coffee, needing it a bit more today after an

extended make-out session in his truck last night that ended with us fogging up his windows like two teenagers. It wasn't sex, not by a long shot, but my breasts got a nice introduction to his mouth.

"I'm just going through the vendor submission for Urban Green Innovators. There's a lot to unpack."

I quickly scan the emails I sent this weekend related to his company, prepared to speak to the research I did yesterday.

"Yeah, about that—"

"Can you walk me through the decision? They're not on our usual list of approved vendors, and this looks like a fast-track request."

I push the bridge of my glasses up my nose, wearing them today and giving my weary eyes a break from my contacts. Papers shuffle on her end as I pull up the open tabs, awaiting her call.

"Absolutely, I have my notes right here. Their technology is what our project desperately needs for the HVAC integration. I've observed their systems in action, and it's impressive."

A small but necessary fib. I saw their lead engineer in action, and he's impressive.

"What makes them stand out? And why won't any of our existing vendors suffice?"

I pull up the detailed log of our problems with the current vendors and deluge her into a sea of facts, failure, and false starts. Highlighting the breakdowns internally with resources unable to get them working properly and the existing vendor finger-pointing to the lack of sufficient talent at our company.

"There's a complete breakdown that we haven't surpassed. This company has AI solutions successfully implemented in two pilot projects. I ran into their lead engineer this weekend—a complete fluke—and he was intrigued. Offered a few suggestions that our engineers wanted to hear more about."

Lisa pauses, the line humming with her consideration.

"I see. That's significant. I'll need all the performance data and those pilot project results. And did you say you already met the person you'd be working with?"

Flashes of how his large and veiny cock pushed me to the hilt over and over again until I came repeatedly race to the forefront of my mind. My pussy wept with wetness and wanted more when I pulled my damp panties back on while he drove me home.

"Yeah, one of those smart tech guys who speaks in jargon as if we all understand what they're talking about."

She chuckles, and I blush, unable to get that naughty reply out of my mind.

"Real nerdy type, I see. Just take it easy on him. It sounds like he was trying to impress you."

Nothing about Marco is nerdy. If anyone was impressing anyone, it was him impressing me.

"Perhaps."

"But hey, we each have our part to play in this. Anyway, I need all the performance data and those pilot project results. Send me everything to put together a package for management approval. I'll try to push it through for you, but there are no guarantees. You still need the same five signatures for approval, and one of the guys will be out this week."

Crap.

That will delay this until I figure out a way around it or get the guy who's out to approve it remotely. I jot a quick note to myself and take another drink before setting down my coffee mug.

"You'll have everything within the hour."

"Good, I'll review it then and be back in touch. Thanks, Victoria."

As we wrap up, my other line rings—my boss's secretary. My stomach knots, anxiety racing into my veins, hoping it's not related to the project's delays.

He's been understanding every time I submit my status reports, but that's via email. Rarely does his assistant call. When she does, it's usually not good news, like when we got a complaint about the construction workers blocking the public road with their equipment.

"I have an incoming call I have to grab," I rush out, not bothering to hear her goodbyes as I switch calls. "This is Victoria."

"Good morning, Victoria. Mr. Caldwell would like to see you in his office when you can."

Her voice is cheerful. I would accuse her of being overly cheerful, but it's my paranoia since she uses the same tone with everyone.

"Of course, I'll be right there."

My voice is steady despite the sudden thud of my heart against my ribs. As I hang up, Mr. Caldwell's name fades from my phone's display, stirring a swirl of possibilities in my mind. Could this be about Marco's company and the fast-tracking request?

But that hardly seems severe enough to warrant a personal call. And Lisa didn't sound upset when she called to discuss it. Could it be something else entirely?

I exhale a deep breath. The only remedy I know for sure is to face it head-on. Standing, I smooth my skirt and snatch my notebook from the desk. My heels click sharply on the polished office floor as I make my way to his office, each step sending potential scenarios fleeting through my mind.

His assistant, engrossed in a call about a billing issue, gives nothing away. I knock softly on his door.

"Come in," comes the muted response.

I push open the heavy wood door of his private office and step inside. His expression is unreadable as he sits behind his large desk with one of the city's best views.

"You wanted to see me, sir?"

"Good morning, Victoria," Mr. Caldwell begins, gesturing for me to take a seat as I enter his office. "Thank you for coming in promptly."

"Of course, Mr. Caldwell."

I sit, clutching my notebook in my lap, trying to steady the flutter of nerves in my stomach.

"Is there something urgent?"

He smiles, a reassuring gesture that eases some of my tension.

"Not urgent, but important. I've been reviewing the progress of our ongoing projects and your role in their success. You've shown remarkable leadership and innovation, especially with the challenges on the Westerfield project."

"Thank you, sir." I nod, appreciating the recognition. "I've learned a lot from that project, and I've had great support from the team."

I neglect to mention the HVAC problem plaguing the project, which is being on the precipitous side of a solution this week.

"That's exactly why we're considering you for this new opportunity."

He pushes a bound project proposal across his meticulously organized desk in my direction.

"There's a significant project starting up that aligns perfectly with your expertise—a major redevelopment in Miami. I believe that's your hometown?"

I nod again, unable to find my voice.

"Good. We believe your local knowledge and personal ties could give us a unique advantage."

Miami.

A knife twists in my heart. The thought of returning to a city intertwined with my brother's ambitions is poignant, painful, and tinged with resentment. Each memory of him, etched across the city's skyline, reminds me of the dreams he never realized that I inherited.

Leaving was my escape. I could distance myself geographically and emotionally, pouring myself into my career elsewhere. Advancing professionally was not just for my own sake but in homage to him, building a legacy as a tribute to him.

The prospect of returning to reshape the skyline he dreamed of altering feels nauseating and almost insurmountable. It's a daunting, heart-wrenching thought—not just a return but a confrontation with past hopes and what could have been of my life—the one I designed and then scraped to take over his.

"That sounds like an incredible opportunity."

The words ghost out of my body, an instinctive professional reflex when a boss delivers alleged good news to his subordinate.

"Glad you agree, Victoria. It's not just about leading the project. We're talking about a promotion. A step up to a senior management role. You would have full oversight, from development to execution, and a chance to shape our regional strategy."

My ears absorb the words, churning them into more pain, agony, and anger for my body to absorb, unaware he's solidifying a future that belongs to another—a sweet man entombed in a mausoleum at Miami Memorial Park Cemetery.

"Understandably, this is a lot to consider professionally and personally. I wouldn't rush you into a decision if I didn't think you were ready for this."

I clear my throat, knowing I need to respond somehow.

"Is this the project?"

Knowing it is, I retrieve the proposal from his desk, thumbing through it as the conversation shifts to the project's specifics—the scope, the team I'd be working with, and the board's expectations. Each detail Mr. Caldwell provides makes the role clearer and more unsettling, building dread in the pit of my stomach.

"How soon would you need an answer, sir?"

"By Friday. The project got moved up and is scheduled to kick off next quarter. We must finalize our leadership and mobilize the team in the coming weeks. Take the time you need. Talk it over with your family if that helps."

I nod, my mind racing beyond me to my utterly incapable of being impartial parents. How strained our relationship is and has been since I left. Never returning to their home and my old bedroom housing my wished for life that never came to be.

"It's a career changing opportunity, Victoria. And those don't come around often."

He's right.

It is, and they don't.

This is the culmination of all my years of long hours, hard work, and endless dedication being recognized and rewarded. Everything I had planned for is finally happening. Yet it feels like anything other than a victory.

"I appreciate the confidence in me, Mr. Caldwell. I'll need to think about it and consider all the factors."

While I maintain a composed smile on the outside, inside, I'm unraveling and battling old demons, long kept at bay, threatening to reemerge.

"Of course. We hope you'll accept. Your experience and approach to project management have been invaluable here, and we'd love to see you bring that to Miami."

He stands, extending his hand, and I mindlessly mirror his actions. The bound project smashed against my unopened notebook feels heavy in my hands and on my soul.

Staying in Houston was safe, void of any reminders of my grief, loss, and anger. Miami is putting them front and center, forcing me to work through all the agonizing emotions I shoved down deep, unwilling to address.

"I'll let you know, Mr. Caldwell."

My hand slips from his, my footsteps heavy toward his door, and once through, my mind flashes uncertainty. Miami, a promotion, a new life in my old city. Another factor complicates what should be a straightforward career decision.

Marco.

9

MARCO

I barely noticed when she didn't answer my first text this morning wishing her a great day. I was too consumed with the presentation to Preston, Dawson, a few more guys from his firm, and a couple of key board members. Not that I expected such an audience. I didn't and wasn't happy to have to comb through the details of what occurred, how we fixed it, and how we'll ensure it doesn't happen again.

When mention of the leak arose, I played dumb, failing to look at Preston, who later told me he appreciated my keeping confidences. He also divulged the source of the leak—an employee on another team accidentally included Dawson in an internal email. It's not the conspiracy we originally thought, but more the innocent mistake of someone not double-checking their work before hitting the send button.

A lesson I learned a long time ago from my mom. The less cooks in the kitchen, the better. It always applies in tech, where teams are constructed of hand-selected personnel and no one else.

By the end of the day, I was worried and texted her again. My friends would tell me the dreaded double text was a sign of desperation, but I didn't care. Victoria wasn't the type to play games, or so I thought. Both texts went unanswered, followed by a third when the hours ticked on.

Various scenarios played through my mind. From thinking she was blowing me off because I was too aggressive and took things too far this weekend to being worried she had an accident and was lying unconscious in a hospital somewhere.

I remain at the office, holding out hope while distracting myself with work. It's when my stomach growls and I've plowed through all the healthy snacks that I break down and call her. It goes straight to voicemail, where I leave a considerate message asking her to call me to let me know she's okay regardless of the hour.

As I walk to my truck, disappointment grips me, tightening my chest and muddling my thoughts. My emotions alternate from worry to irritation to discouragement, running in a vicious circle the entire drive home.

By the time I step into the shower, disappointment has morphed into a nagging dread, each unreturned message sending my mind spiraling down different paths.

I pace the length of my living room, pausing now and then to glance at my phone, hoping for any sign of life. Is there any indication that she's just been busy or out of reach?

That she's okay, mad, or for whatever reason, she's ignoring me. Whatever happens, can be talked through, but it takes two, and this silence drives me mad.

The wild, almost manic thought of just showing up at her place crosses my mind, but the last thing I want is to come off as overbearing or intrusive. Considering we just met, concern and respect for her space are delicate. I'd come off as a controlling asshole, indeed ending whatever we've started.

Yet, I've been inside her body, know how her breath catches right when she's about to come and the brownness that eclipses her hazel irises when she wants me as much as I want her.

As the night darkens, the numbers on my phone clicking toward midnight, my plans to take her out for a fun dinner in East Downtown fade. The excitement that bubbled within me this morning, thinking of seeing her, spending time getting to know her, and bringing her back here, turns into a hollow feeling.

I try to distract myself with a home workout, followed by sports reels on social media, but even the sportscaster's commentary prickles at my nerves. My mind keeps circling back to her and us, wondering what it would have been like if she hadn't ghosted me.

The wait is agonizing, and her silence is loud when I lay my head down to sleep. I send one final text, more emotional than the others, mourning the ending of what barely started.

> I don't know what happened. I just want to know that you're safe and okay. If I did something wrong or if last night was too much...

I stop staring at the screen. There are a million different things I want to say, but I keep it straightforward and continue typing.

> I asked you in the elevator if it was fate. You didn't say. I'm convinced it is. I don't want this to end.

> Call me.

> Please.

My finger hovers over the send button, trying to come up with more magic words to get something, anything from her. When my weary, worried brain fails me, I hit send and lock my screen, setting it on my charger to stare up at the ceiling.

The phone buzzes quietly against the nightstand, slicing

through the silence of my room. Glancing at the screen, I see her name light up, and my heart skips, hopeful. The message is there, but it's terse, nothing like her usual warmth, and it cloaks me in dread.

I'm okay.

Let's talk tomorrow.

The screen dims as I'm left staring at those few words, completely puzzled yet grateful she's okay.

My thoughts churn—what does 'tomorrow' mean?

What are we going to talk about?

Is she ending this?

Can she end something I'm not sure we even started?

Her text has left me second-guessing every interaction we've had up until now. I typed out several responses, each deleted, feeling unsure of what to say and scared to say something that would make the situation worse.

I'm walking on a tightrope without a net—a feeling I despise. Finally, I set the phone back down, the unresolved tension coiling tighter inside me as I try to sleep.

USUALLY, I relish Tuesday mornings. The pressure from the start of the week is over. Now that the testing has held up, the team is working on the launch plan for the app, and I'm finally able to focus on my other smaller, less impactful projects. Not to mention when I get my longest weekday run. But not this morning. I hate today already.

My sleep was fitful, eluding me as I stared at the ceiling, the wall, and back to the ceiling. My mind turned over every scenario possible without a conclusion. Operating with little information, I finally concluded that it was not something I did.

More a combination of things I did, all falling under one general thing. I came on too strong. Too eager. I've never been one to play dating games. I don't have the tolerance or bandwidth for that bullshit. I love with my whole heart, always have, and always will. It's not something I should have to apologize for or change about myself. Yet, it completely backfired this time.

I take the long route today, the edge of downtown, past the bars and restaurants in Midtown, and into the regal Museum District. My body is pushed to its limits, clocking a personal best—a victory that should thrill me. But the energy fueling my strides isn't triumph. It's frustration, a desperate need to outpace my racing thoughts.

By the time I push through the doors of my office on the 22nd floor, physically spent and emotionally raw, the absence of a reply from Victoria when I suggest lunch as a pretext to talk, to fix whatever is happening between us. But with each passing moment, the silence grows heavier, and my optimism dims.

Usually, my phone is stowed away in my backpack during focused work. Today, it sits prominently in the middle of my desk, with no lock screen and the ringer volume on high. Nothing will prevent me from missing her call or text if she decides to reach out.

I plow through my work, my eyes darting too many fucking times to my phone, silently hoping to hear from her. When lunch rolls around and I'm still working and wishing, Maddie pops her head in.

"You've been awfully quiet today, considering you saved the world yesterday."

I chuckle, the sound hollow, not quite ringing true.

"World-saving's easy. It's the personal stuff that's tricky."

Maddie steps in, leaning against the door with that all-too-familiar smirk that says she's caught the scent of something more.

"Oh? Trouble in paradise for our superhero?"

I hesitate, the truth on my tongue, but it's Maddie—she'll ferret it out anyway. I shrug, a non-committal gesture that invites more than it dismisses.

"Let's just say not all superheroes get a parade," I manage, the words laced with more bitterness than intended.

Her smirk deepens, her arms crossing as she makes herself more comfortable.

"This wouldn't have anything to do with a certain lady from the farmer's market, would it?"

I frown, knowing my silence speaks volumes. Maddie's not one to drop her line of questions, especially if it's juicy or salacious.

"What happened, lover boy? Your excess amount of cologne turned her off already?"

She fans the air, which has me sniffing myself. Her laughter rings out loud, and she is annoyed at having gotten me since I forgot to put on cologne today. I am too absentminded in my worrisome thoughts.

"She's not really responding. It's like talking to a wall."

I run a frustrated hand through my hair, my eyes looking down at my phone for the millionth time, all under her watchful eye.

"But wait, didn't you just see each other like Saturday?"

"Well, yes. And I took her to dinner Sunday night."

To my ears, I sound needy and desperate. But I'm not about to divulge what we did and how that deepened our connection.

"We had plans to see each other last night. She ghosted me until it was too late to take her out."

Maddie's smirk widens, her eyes twinkling with mischief.

"And just like that, the mighty Marco is down for the count?"

I can't help but grimace, shifting uneasily in my chair.

"It's not like that. I thought things were going well."

"Isn't that what they all think?"

She leans back, propping herself against the doorframe. Her teasing is relentless, but a hint of sympathy in her tone tells me she's not just here to make fun.

I let out a heavy sigh, looking away. The quiet hum of the office buzzes in the background, an annoying contrast to the storm brewing in my mind.

"I don't know. I might've come on too strong. Or maybe it was too much too soon."

She pushes off from the wall, taking a few steps into the room, her expression turning serious.

"Or maybe she's just busy, you know? That whole problem you were helping her with. Maybe she had a nightmare day like you had Friday?"

She gestures toward the boardroom, making too much sense, raising my hopes that she's right.

"Besides, not everyone's glued to their phone."

My fingers drum against my desk, and I need to expel this negative energy. What I really need to do is hit the gym over lunch or jerk off in the bathroom, something to relieve the pressure that is about to boil over.

"But she always answered quickly before."

Maddie tucks a brown curl behind her ear before shrugging.

"You did what felt right at the time. If she's worth it, she'll see that. If not, maybe she's not the right one for you."

I instantly hate what she's saying. Her logic should prevail over my emotions, yet it does little to comfort me. It's a harsh reality I've mulled over many times and immediately discarded.

Fate proved we were meant to be together. If we weren't meant to be, why would the universe put her at the market while I was there? It's too fleeting to be explained any other way. This . . . this sudden silence is a small bump in the road to the journey she and I are on.

"Besides, you've got plenty here to keep you busy. Don't let her ghosting get you down."

Her smile returns as she heads for the door, the usual spark in her step.

"And if she does, you're still a hero in Preston's book."

"He's not my type."

She laughs, unaffected by my personal misery.

"Go back to saving the world, Marco."

She waves a dismissive hand toward my phone, then points to my computer as if I haven't been chained to my desk, using work as a distraction. An afterthought question blurts from my mouth.

"Do I seriously wear too much cologne?"

She laughs again, only louder and more obnoxious, disappearing down the hallway without answering me. Yet her words echo in my mind. She always has a way of cutting through the noise, leaving me with clarity, whether I wanted it or not.

Maybe all hope isn't lost.

Focusing on what Maddie said, maybe Victoria had a day like my Friday, which left no room for personal matters. It was all hands on deck, and there was barely time to eat or go to the bathroom.

"I sure hope that's it."

10

VICTORIA

Death and darkness haunt me. I'm tumbling into the abyss I've avoided for years, where achieving his dreams now threatens the fragile peace I've built in a city that knows nothing of my family or past.

The demons I locked away in the darkest corner of my closet have broken free, overwhelming me too quickly to resist, dragging me back to a place filled with anguish, gloom, and devastation.

I battled the deep depression that followed his passing. Sought help for it and learned my triggers, the city being one of them. The shadows of my past in Miami loom larger with each avoidance, reinforcing the barriers I've built against returning. My parents grew accustomed to my excuses, no longer questioning my absences—resigned to the fact their grief and actions after the funeral pushed me away.

This avoidance has become my armor, shielding me from the raw, unresolved emotions that city holds. As the offer to lead a major project there beckons, I'm forced to confront these long-buried feelings, weighing the professional gains against the personal upheavals it would undoubtedly trigger.

The allure of career advancement tests my resolve to maintain distance, presenting a crossroads between the safety of emotional distance and the risks of confronting my past head-on.

Standing at the tracks of my past was bound to happen eventually. That speeding train of memory and emotion will never stop until I finally confront the unresolved issues—the how and why—all questions that live naggingly in the back of my mind, waiting patiently for their turn to be addressed.

Yesterday was a blur. Going through the motions without actual awareness of them, as if split into two selves. The career-driven Victoria managed tasks with practiced ease while a part of me—the mourning teenager clutching her dead brother's cold hand—remained curled up in the corner of my soul, weeping silently.

This duality exhausted me to the point that I intentionally didn't respond to Marco in all the ways he reached out. He's blameless in my actions. Standing at the precipitous of the tracks, the train's relentless charge, blowing the whistle with each jarring thought of how I'd return to this city and confidently take on a new project and promotion, is beyond me.

In fairness to him, I sent a curt text. Grateful he didn't push or demand more, as I have nothing to give. When I received his offer for lunch today, I knew immediately I couldn't sit in a public place and unpack all this.

Unsure that it's even right to do it privately. How much do I tell someone I just met and am developing feelings for? Someone I will have to leave in a few weeks or months, depending on how quickly the team is scheduled to assemble.

I ignored it. Ignored him. Getting swept up in another day of robotic actions by Victoria, the business professional, until my teenager could break free tonight, like she did last night in crying, throwing things, and asking the universe why, of all the places in the country, it had to be Miami.

When a dozen long-stem roses arrived, I knew instantly who they were from. Their fragrance filled my office. My female colleagues oohed and ahhed over them, admiring their grace and beauty while nudging me to share the suitor's name and story. Finally, I broke.

I'm sorry.

I hadn't even set my phone down before his text came through.

Don't be.

Are you okay?

I hold my breath. Mentally flipping through different answers to his simple question until finally settling on one.

No, I'm not.

Are you hurt? Do you need help?

Are you home or at the office?

His questions are rapid-fire, pinging my phone until I silence the ringer.

Tell me where you're at.

I'll come right now.

No

Guilt seeps into my consciousness at his concern. His readiness to drop everything and come to my aid underscores his character—a man of genuine concern and generosity.

. . .

Vic. Please.

I'm going out of my mind with worry. Call me?!

LIKE HIS LUNCH OFFER, I can't and won't get into everything at the office.

It's a long story.

I can talk tonight if you want.

Dinner?

There's a new place on Gray Street in Midtown.

I hesitate before replying, each second stretching longer than the last. My fingers tremble slightly over the keyboard.

I prefer to stay in.

Feeling as though I should explain more to him, I don't get the chance when his next message comes in immediately.

I'll bring over dinner.

What time?

He's already blown past any need for reasoning. It lifts the edge of my lips into a slight smile. A tidal wave of emotions wells up, threatening to overflow onto my work, which is the last thing I need.

Sure. 7 pm

Perfect.

Vic, don't apologize.

I'm glad you texted.

My gaze moves from the screen to his beautiful flowers, meant to evoke our text exchange. Despite how it happened, I'm glad he kept reaching out. I return my attention to my phone, sending him one last message before returning to work.

Thanks for the flowers.

They are lovely.

Their fragrance is calming, aromatically pleasing, and visually eye-catching.

Not nearly as beautiful as you. I can't wait to see you tonight.

I want to forewarn him because he has the wrong impression of what tonight will bring. I want to intentionally prepare him for what's to come, and it's not good.

It won't be like Sunday night.

Things have changed.

The last part of that text is ominous and probably harsh, but he must know the fun and games are over for us now that I have come to a decision. The three circles appear and then fade. My heart rises and falls in anticipation of how he'll receive my foreshadowed words—a long second passes before his message pops up on the screen.

I understand.

Just getting a chance to talk means a lot.

See you soon.

His response settles in my chest, heavier than expected. The anticipation of tonight's meeting is charged with more gravity than I had anticipated. What was meant to lighten my guilt does the opposite. A sinking feeling settles over me. I sigh, put the phone aside, and refocus on my work. The roses are a bittersweet reminder on the edge of my vision.

My townhouse, usually a sanctuary adorned with cream colors and soft lighting, feels too vast and too quiet. Its view of Memorial Park, the tall timber canopy dominating my large bay window, casts long golden shadows over the floor. Anxiously, I pace the room, wringing my hands and rehearsing what I will say.

When his truck pulls into the driveway, my heart skips despite my resolve. The headlights sweep across the front of the house, illuminating everything and exposing me as I wait for him. I run a nervous hand over my clothes, an instinctive action to steady my nerves.

He knocks—a simple thud that resonates deeper than intended. Opening the door, I'm met with his expectant smile, dimming slightly as he registers my apprehensive stance. He holds up a bag smelling richly of garlic and basil—an offering.

"It smells amazing," I manage, stepping aside to let him in.

Surprisingly, he moves closer, folding me into a comforting embrace. His face buries into my hair, his nose nudging my ear while his lips find my neck. It's a lingering kiss. Relief seeps from him as he exhales quietly against my skin.

"Thank God you're okay."

His words are pressed in my flesh, heard in my ear, and felt in my heart.

"When I didn't hear from you, my mind went to terrible . . ."

I wrap my arms around his waist, pulling him closer, my hands moving up to stroke his back. It's a mutual comfort, a shared need for reassurance, and I nuzzle into him.

We stand there for a moment in the silence of the foyer, our breathing syncing in the quiet. Slowly, he pulls back, eyes searching mine for any sign of the turmoil I've been feeling.

"I wanted to explain—"

My voice is as shaky as my body, but he cuts me off with a reassuring kiss.

"Victoria, breathe. We don't need to rush this, okay?"

His understanding threads around me, lowering my defenses.

"Let's just enjoy the meal, talk about your day, how the project is going . . . anything other than the serious stuff."

Having estimated that my news or decision would surprise him, he must have surmised this was bad news from our text messages. Not that I can blame him. As disarming as his suggestion is, I find it more stressful than alleviating.

His hand loosens from my waist, and he sweeps an appreciative look over my casual sundress when he steps away.

"Now, where is the kitchen so I can unpack all this? I forgot to ask what you wanted, so I got spaghetti and meatballs, chicken alfredo, and if all else fails, a Caesar salad with salmon."

He's already moving down the hallway, searching for the kitchen, finding it on the right, opposite the staircase. I'm left trailing behind him after closing the front door.

Pulling his wallet and phone out of his pocket and setting them on my counter speaks to a familiarity we haven't established. I move behind him, preparing to get plates and everything we need to sit in the dining room.

"I'll grab some plates."

"Don't worry about it. They gave us all that stuff. We just

need drinks. Whatever you want."

His back is toward me when I glimpse him dishing up a bit of all three on both plates. He's taken charge in a way that comforts me, yet the simplicity of the evening underlines the complexities of communicating my decision.

"Wine, okay?" I ask, selecting a red.

"Perfect."

I head to the dining room with the bottle and glasses in hand. He follows with heaping plates of food, far too much for me to eat. Once I get the wine open and poured, I hand him a glass. Our fingers brush briefly, bringing a smile to his face.

A true gentleman, he pulls out my chair for me. Once I'm comfortably seated, he settles into his seat across from me.

"Tell me about your day. The light stuff before the heavy."

I sigh, wondering how to separate the light from the heavy because they are so intertwined. Or at least my current situation and my future are a tangled mess in my mind. He digs into his plate, gesturing for me to start. I pick up my fork and stab at the food while we dance around the real reason he's here.

"Well, your company got approved today."

His eyes flicker from his plate, studying me, and he sets his fork down.

"Why doesn't that sound like good news?"

There's a quiet sigh that escapes me, knowing small talk isn't going to work. Not when what I say weighs so heavily on my mind and soul.

"Marco, I can't do this. I can sit here and pretend everything is all right when it's not."

I place my utensil in the middle of my plate, unsure if I'll eat anything. My stomach has been upset with the back-and-forth about Miami. At moments, I'm sure to turn it down, but other times, I'd be an idiot for not taking the promotion and transfer.

"Okay."

His expression changes to immediate concern, hands bracing on the table as if to steady himself against whatever is coming.

"Tell me what's wrong so I can fix it."

And there it is—the crux of it all. It's not for him to fix. It's not even fixable. Nor is it his burden to bear, even though I appreciate his willingness to dive in and make it his.

"Marco—"

"Please, Victoria. I'll do anything you want. I just need you to talk to me."

Marco reaches across the table, his fingers brushing mine, attempting to connect and bridge the gap my words instantly create. I glance at his hand, then up at his face, finding a somber resolve in his eyes.

"They offered me a promotion."

His eyes light up, and his wide smile eases the tension across his handsome features. His hand crushes over mine, needing to touch and share what should be good news.

"That's wonderful! Congratulations!"

My teeth clench, my sides steel.

"In *Miami*."

Realization and disappointment befall his face. For his part, he recovers quickly, and the slight lessening of his smile is the only indication of his disappointment.

"Back home? That's even better. Your family must be so excited."

His head shakes, slowly processing the limited information I've shared.

"Thing is, I haven't told them."

My chest aches, and I feel like I have heartburn, even though I haven't had a bite to eat yet. The feeling has lingered since my boss dropped the news on me yesterday morning.

"What?"

He shifts in his chair, loosening his grip. I slip my hand

from his to rest in my lap. He instantly frowns.

"Why not?"

"Marco, I . . ."

I reach for my wine, taking a longer-than-normal drink before setting the glass down. Usually, I'd savor the taste, but with the last twenty-four hours of driving myself into near madness, it only tastes bitter.

"If you're worried about us, yeah, sure, it changes things. But it doesn't have to mean the end."

He moves his chair next to mine, itching to get closer.

"I mean, we couldn't see each other during the week, but weekends and stuff. It's only about a two-hour flight."

His face is so earnest, nearly convincing. I tamp down the hope that he or we could actually do a long-distance romance with how busy he already is. With my promotion, I'll work long hours and leverage weekends to learn. I don't see how it will be possible to date.

"Marco."

"Don't, Vic. Don't end this before we've even started."

He leans in, finding my hand to hold while appealing to me.

"I don't know what it is about you, but I've never felt like this. And don't say it's too fast because I already know that."

My chuckle is hollow and bitter, as that was exactly what I'd been thinking when I cataloged all the reasons to consider staying or leaving.

"It is fast. I'm not even sure what we're doing."

He grimaces, hurt by my words, and hints at ending us if there is an us.

"Look."

His dark eyes lock with mine, beckoning me to see beyond the present moment.

"Maybe it is fast, maybe it's crazy. But sometimes, that's how the best things start."

His thumb gently strokes the back of my hand, his touch

warm and surprisingly calming. My breath catches a little at his sincerity. The determination and vulnerability in his expression are heart-wrenching.

He's all in. That much is clear. And here I am, on the brink, unsure if I can match his leap with one of my own. I can't help but feel a flicker of hope, even as realism gnaws at the edges of my thoughts.

"I don't know if I believe that."

The words tumble out with an honesty that scares me. I'm pushing away what seems to be a great catch. For what? Fear? Doubt?

"But moving back to Miami, starting a new project . . . it's a lot. Not to mention dragging you into this mess of long-distance dating, flights, and weekends."

He squeezes my hand a little, interrupting my spiraling thoughts, which are well supported by other, more difficult concerns.

"You're not dragging me anywhere I don't want to go. Because whatever this is, it feels worth figuring out."

His reassurance is firm. Almost stubborn, as if he's made up his mind and nothing I say could convince him otherwise. I let out a long breath, my other hand tracing the stem of my wine glass, gathering courage.

"Us aside. I'm not even sure I want to take it," I murmur, tiptoeing into the more daunting reasons tormenting me. The room seems to shift, closing in on me and darkening.

His jaw drops, eyes widening in disbelief as he fixes his gaze on me.

"Why not? This is a huge opportunity."

I look away from the intensity of his disbelief as it calls to my apprehension. Making fast friends of the negative emotions ruminating every thought related to this decision.

His thumb swipes across my knuckles, meant to comfort me, but it's suddenly too much. Too much to unpack over this lovely dinner he brought. Maybe he was right in discussing the light before the dark. It buys me time while I figure out how much of my past I want to share.

My gaze returns to his with a slight frown.

"I'd want to finish my project here. You were supposed to be a part of that. Joining our firms together and such."

My excuse is hollow, knowing that his firm doesn't need my company in the least. When I looked them up online, I saw that they have a pipeline of projects that stretch years into the future.

The least of which is my project's malfunctions to add more stress and weekend work that already monopolizes too much of his time.

"Mamita, if it comes down to a choice between being with you or working with you, you know what I'd choose."

The firm set of his jaw and the intensity in his eyes cut through the air, leaving no room for ambiguity. He leans closer, the warmth of his breath mingling with mine—a tangible conviction of the seriousness of his declaration.

"I'd choose you, every single time, without hesitation."

With targeted determination, he's torpedoing my excuses and blowing them up as fast as I'm putting them down until I'm left with only the tragic ones.

His lips brush mine, once, then twice, convincing me that this will work between us. Its assurances are as fleeting as his lips when he angles back, reading my face.

"There's something else, isn't there?"

"I can't go back to Miami," I blurt out despite having practiced different ways I could tell him.

He'll understand since he's so family-oriented. Or at least, he will since he's always been calm and understanding with everything we've discussed.

His gaze softens, the firmness giving way to confusion and concern.

"Why can't you? What's holding you back?"

Pausing, the words lodge in my throat. How do I explain that Miami isn't just a city to me but a landscape of past sorrows and unresolved bitterness? Where dreams went to die, and the graveyard that holds them threatens to let the tormented souls out to haunt me anew.

"It's . . . it involves my brother . . . Victor."

My words falter, a sob catching in my throat. Saying his name aloud feels like a violation, as though I'm betraying my carefully guarded memories of him.

No one in my adopted town of Houston knows about him. Not the very few friends I've made here nor any passing relationship. He's too precious to speak of in any other light than reverence. Sharing him is not only difficult but necessary despite how painful it is.

Tears well faster than I can control until Marco is a watery blur. He quickly dabs my cheeks with a napkin while reaching for me. Snuggled into the side of his body, I cry.

Crying about the immense responsibility of succeeding in a project that was Victor's dream. The crushing fear of failing, of not living up to the legacy he had wanted for himself. I could make mistakes in this town and cut my teeth on other less critical projects.

But in Miami, I'd have to be perfect. The project would have to go perfectly. If they don't like the architectural design or if it doesn't meet all the environmental and sustainability initiatives we published, it could face public backlash. Not to mention, I have faced internal and external scrutiny for being one of the youngest project managers, which compounds the pressure.

Facing my company and my brother's disappointment, even in memory, would destroy my career and me. Then there is the bitterness and resentment of having to travel a road I didn't intend, a path to dreams opposite my own.

As I cry, nestled against Marco, his murmured words of

encouragement silence the roar of my insecurities. With my forehead resting in the crook of his body, my tears fall into his lap, unnoticed by him.

"This is his dream, not mine. He was the one that wanted to change the Miami skyline. Leave a lasting impression with the buildings he erected. And then . . . he just didn't get the chance. He died in the hospital, surrounded by sketches of the skyline, the buildings he was going to build, the specifications of those skyscrapers he could see from his bed while gazing out the window."

My voice cracks with the pain of the memories, resonating with Marco, who squeezes me tighter into his body. His arms steel around my sides, collecting me slowly until I'm sitting in his lap, weeping.

"Vic . . . I'm truly sorry."

His voice is thick with emotion, and he gently rocks me, comforting me with his sympathetic strength.

"What if I fail, Marco? I'm not only letting my company down. I'm letting him down. Letting down everything I've strived for to make his legacy come true via me. How do I live with myself if that happens?"

Whispering my darkest fears out loud intensifies them. It makes them a reality and not just a haunting inclination of knowing. Failing him is failing me, the teenage girl who wanted to be something and someone else.

"What if it's not, mamita? What if what you build becomes a lasting symbol of his legacy, a true homage to him? The *el tiro de gracia* of Miami? Imagine it as a resounding success, where the building's dedication is to him. You could even inscribe his name into the foundation as a blessing over the entire project."

His idea weaves through my storm of doubts, planting a seed of possibility. A gentle finger hooks my chin, lifting it until his lips are a breath away.

"It would be a beautiful gift. One only you can give. Maybe

that's what this is really about?"

Listening intently, his eyes are rimmed with a sad sincerity. His presence is a pillar of quiet strength and patient understanding.

"Perhaps your brother, God rest his soul, orchestrated it all from above? Putting the plan in motion from the start?

He's probing the depths of my grief, carefully stepping through the landmines of heartbreak and devastation to find the only remaining flower in the field. Its blooms are wilted but still alive, with slight charring to the edges.

My mind spins at this sudden paradigm shift, and I am unable to fully absorb it as true because the pain of mourning has had a strong hold on my heart.

"You share a name. You share his dream. But couldn't it be possible for him to live through you? Excelling with you every time you ascend to the next level. You're holding his hand, helping him climb the mountain. Miami is the summit. Imagine the view from the top of the building that you both built. It'll be breathtaking."

My hand covers my mouth, and fresh tears roll in and stream down my cheeks. I shake my head in amazement, then nestle my face against his neck.

The truth in his message breaks through the sorrowful, saturated storm cloud of my soul, sending a gentle golden light to bask upon the little flower until its petals rise to the sky.

I'm so overcome with emotion that I'm utterly speechless. This decision, which I have wrestled with, vacillating between fear and logic, heartbreak and acceptance, is laid out so clearly. From his viewpoint, he opened my heart, saw the blackness of mourning that refuses to heal, and somehow repaired part of it. Marco stuck a beautiful bandage on it to stop the hemorrhaging.

"Vic, the way I see it. How can you say no?"

11

MARCO

I'd be lying if I said my heart wasn't ripped out of my chest at this accomplished woman shredded with grief and doubt. The weight of her lithe frame curled against my body, and sobbing is wrecking me.

The swirling thoughts that kept me awake most of the night have evaporated. She's trying to end us, but not for the reasons I assumed. Moreover, she worries about preserving my feelings from being hurt when her world is turning upside down.

My lips press into the crown of her hair. Her head is buried into my shoulder, shutting off her beautiful face and those stunning hazel eyes. The tears streaming down her face wet my skin, dripping past my shirt collar.

I could never have guessed why she stood me up last night—not that I hold it against her. I feel awful, thinking she believed shutting me out was her best option instead of opening up as she had tonight. Given that we've just met, her hesitancy makes sense, but I seize the chance to clarify that she's mine. Here. In Miami. Wherever.

"Vic?" I repeat with a softness, needing a response. Something to let me know she won't pass up this opportunity. "Please talk to me."

Her chin raises. A sad sigh loosens from her chest as she tries to regulate her emotions. My hand at her waist slides up her body, rubbing comforting circles across her back.

The golden flecks circle her pupils, nearly glowing in the shimmer of tears rimming her lids before spilling over. Even upset, she's stunning. Seeing her this vulnerable stirs a fierce need to help her. To figure this out and be the shoulder she cries on at this pivotal time and decision in her life.

"What do you want me to say?"

The curve of her body, slumping in defeat, pushes against my hand at her spine. She reaches for a napkin, dabbing her cheeks and wiping her nose. When her gaze returns to mine, she seeks answers—confirmation or validation of what to do.

"I want you to say that you'll take it. Despite being sad, having doubts, and a little fear that you'll do it."

"A lot of fear."

Her challenge to my words brings a smile to my face. She's not completely lost in her sorrows, and that's good. This version of her right now is a far cry from the passionate and powerful woman I met this weekend.

Both sides stir my desire for her. When she can be brave and battle the world, leading major projects, and then come home to sit in my lap and let me cuddle her against the cruel twists of fate, I will be happy.

"Then you'll do it?"

I press her, gently moving us forward even though I have no idea how I will make Miami and us work. If she's correct and my company has been approved to work with hers, that will be an immediate project added to my already heavy workload.

Her long fingers trail up the stubbly hair of my arm until her palm rests on my chest.

"And you're sure about us? The long-distance thing?"

I close the distance between us, connecting with her lips and tasting the fruity red wine on her tongue. She wiggles on my lap, my cock springing to life and wanting to slide right into her. It would be so easy with only the denim of my jeans and her sundress separating me from where I want to be.

Her arm winds around my neck, demanding more from me than I think this moment warrants. I have half a mind to fuck her against that front window, show the world how beautiful and powerful she is if it would convince her.

My tongue slips around her mouth, and my hand tangles into her hair to hold her in place. The silkiness of her skin as my fingers trail up her leg makes my balls tingle with lust. I already jerked off this morning in the shower to her. Her scent and sounds are permanently imprinted on me. The aggressiveness radiating from her sloppy kisses and grinding hips has me groaning in restraint.

I end the kiss abruptly and push her back to watch a few reactions ripple across her face.

"Vic, I'd fuck you naked against that window, but now's not the time."

Her breaths are coming in light pants. Either from our kissing or the feeling we are fighting—tearing into each other.

"We need to finish talking about this."

"I'm done talking."

Suddenly, she stands, her hazel eyes getting darker. A mischievous grin tugs at the corners of her lips. She shimmies out of her sundress and quickly tosses it to the floor.

"*Chinga madre.*"

I greedily drink her in, moving to the edge of my seat to touch her when she steps just out of range.

"Mamita, are you sure?"

I've never asked that in my life. Yet a few seconds ago, she was crying in my arms, now a naked vixen with miles of silky skin begging for my mouth. I don't give her much time to respond before I fall to my knees in front of her. Level with her tiny slit, my hands circle her curves, caressing her leg slowly and tantalizingly.

"Definitely."

One word.

Full steam ahead.

Her skin is flawless and soft, something I could caress and stroke every morning and night. I inch forward, her aroma hitting my senses and making me instantly drunk. Needing a hit of the most potent drug—her cunt.

"I've thought about you all day. Fucking my fist to you," I mutter before burying my face into her delicate flesh.

Her fingers weave into my hair, pushing me harder into her folds. She tugs on the strands, sending a sting of pain into my conscious that is instantly erased by the pleasure of drinking her in. She's so fucking wet, so ready, that I'm surprised. Perhaps the visceral reaction to this big decision causes other places to be just as sensitive and delicate.

"Oh . . . Marco."

Her hips grind, her pussy rubs against my face, and I'm fucking about to lose my mind with how much I want her. By the time my hands reach her ass, her wetness is dripping from my chin and making a sexy mess on the floor.

Reluctantly, I pull away from her heated core to gaze up at those brown, lust-filled eyes, the golden flakes gone for now.

"You're so fucking wet. Did you come today?"

I blow on her clit. Goosebumps break out over her skin, and she tugs on my hair to bring me back to her.

"Did you rub your pretty clit and think of me?"

Her breath is shallow and ragged with need. Her small breasts with their tight pink nipples arching toward the ceiling in need. If I had more hands, they'd be on her breasts, pinching and squeezing while I separate those delicate lips, weeping wetness into my hands.

"No."

"Why not?"

Her stance widens with need. With my mouth talking, she's using my stroking fingers to get friction between us and attempting to satisfy her raging need to come.

"I . . . I just . . . Marco, please."

The panic edge in her voice is music to my ears. Even more, she saved my pleasure. Something I'll easily demand when I fly to Miami to see her. Not that she'll ever need to touch herself. I'll keep her so freshly fucked, she'll be sore all the time. Remembering every time she sits in her fancy glass office—*Chinga madre.*

"I want to watch you get off. Watch how you touch her. Give me one orgasm."

The pressure of my fingers increases, sliding from her slit to her pussy and back again. I continue watching her stare down at me. Her hand is still clutching my hair while she pants with need.

If I were to wager, she's probably not comfortable, but for me, this is educational. I want to learn what she likes and how she gets off so I can do it better. Blow her fucking mind when giving oral.

"What's it going to be, Victoria?"

I give her a few savory licks, my fingers stroking in long lengths until it includes her taint and asshole, causing her to squirm. Teasing and testing boundaries is part of the fun. When she doesn't stop and moves in rhythm with me, I know more things are on the table. Possibilities light up my mind.

My cock is blistering hard. Stays hard with her now in my life. Even the faintest thought of her has my balls tightening. It doesn't help that I haven't been to the gym in several days, which usually helps burn off this energy. But tonight, I won't be gentle if she wants to continue. I can't be with how badly I need to fuck her.

Her hand loosens from my hair while the other skims down her stomach, fingers splaying until she reaches her folds and spreads them.

"Chinga madre," I growl at the sight of her exposed clit, harder and more engorged than I thought.

It's impossible to resist sucking on it. My mouth descends, my eyes closing and groaning in pleasure. She gasps, the hand on my head drops to my shoulder as her body tilts into me. With my stroking fingers refusing to penetrate her, she's not getting what she wants. Little whimpers of protest fill the space between us.

"I need . . . it. I need you. Please. Please."

Her legs tremble, her pussy gyrating against every part we're touching until her hand fists my hair again. She's pumping harder, grinding harder against my face.

My nose is buried in her sensual scent, and my mouth is filled with her tangy flavor. Wetness pours from her pussy, overflowing my fingers to the point she's a slick mess. With the tightness of her clenched body, the need to consume her coiling inside my body, I slip two fingers inside her.

"Yes . . . Oh . . . right there."

Her voice trembles with desperation and need. Her fingers tug at my hair to the point of becoming painful. It's all sensory play for both of us.

My eyes close, shutting off the vision of her melting into me, lost to the blackness. It heightens my hearing. Her gasps and moans louder as she climbs closer to the orgasm I'm giving her.

My fingers shove in and out of her pussy, a placeholder for what's to come. With devious intent, I grab her cheek, squeezing and pulling it hard.

Not painfully like her grip, but enough to provide a bit of room for my ring finger to press against her puckered hole. She doesn't flinch, instead giving into the taboo by spreading her legs and allowing me access.

Knowing she is willing to let me play with both her holes has heat surging through my body, and my brain explodes with lust. Sending jolts straight to my cock that have it leaking uncomfortably in my underwear. I'm going to get her off, then sink into her and take her fast again.

"Make me come, Marco."

I know exactly what she needs right now, and it's not just an orgasm. It's the knowledge that she belongs to me that I can give her anything she desires, anytime I want. However, I want. It's fucking me up mentally, wanting to do everything to her all at once. But for now, I'll give her what she asks for.

I tug on her ass cheek, giving her little time to prepare for my finger breaching her tight hole. I groan, the sound vibrating her clit as she's impaled on three fingers, grinding against me until she screams my name.

Her body jerks, convulsions overtaking her control as her hand slips from my head. Opening my eyes, I gaze up at her. She's breathtaking. Her face falls into ecstasy, her dazed eyes unfocused, looking down at me and then closing.

Her head falls back, her body relaxes, and the full weight sags into my fingers, pushing them further, which elicits a long moan from her.

Fully surrendering to me, she's putty in my hands. Allowing me to take her intimately and cross a new line that I wasn't sure she'd be into. Her breathing is ragged.

Her chest rises and falls rapidly as the anticipation of release abates with her climax. Her hips slowly grind to a stop, and before any reasonable thought enters her mind, I drag my fingers and face from her body, ready for my release.

She's surprised, her eyes suddenly focusing when I stand, knees popping to reach for my wallet. I drag out a strip of condoms, rip one off, and toss the rest on our uneaten dinner.

"Open."

Like before, I place the edge of the condom between her teeth. Her hazel eyes are blown out to brown and full of lust. Fingering and eating her was a precursor to what was next.

Visions of her being fucked fast and hard race through my mind as a preview, bringing a smirk to my face.

I run my arm across my face, collecting as much of her wetness and my saliva as I can before undoing my pants. My cock is hard, the tip almost purple from the pressure surging out of my balls.

"This is going to be hard and fast, Vic."

The husk in my voice matches the lust coursing through my veins, bringing a slight tremor to my hands as I jerky on the wrapper. She blows it to the ground once I fish the condom out and secure it over my cock.

"Aren't you going to take off your clothes?"

"Not a chance."

The dynamic of me being clothed and her not is a mind fuck. It inflates my ego and strokes the primal thought of her being open and available for the taking.

Although my clothes contain heat and sweat, it would probably be far more comfortable to feel her skin sliding against mine. I can't help this version. Her feeling the rough fabric of my jeans, the buttons pressing into her delicate flesh as I fuck her, is too much.

I squat, scoop her up with a surprised yelp, and she wraps her arms around my neck. The need for her to secure herself as I lift her into my arms is useless. I bench, squat, and hip thrust far more than she weighs, and the very reason I lift is so I can fuck in this position.

Her legs wrap around my waist, and my hands lightly cup her ass, leaving her feeling unstable while lining the engorged head of my cock against her slippery lips.

Letting gravity take over, my fingers aggressively spread her until she's sinking onto me. We groan in unison. Her hot channel engulfs my cock until she's fully impaled.

"You feel fucking amazing. So wet for me."

She kisses my face, chasing my lips just out of reach. Now is not the time to make out, even though I love the idea of her tasting herself on my tongue.

I walk with her pussy bobbing on my cock, the movement eliciting a hiss from her. I glance into those brown eyes, full of lust and needing this just as much as I do.

I pause in the hallway, lifting her slightly to fuck her tight hole. Wetness spills from her. She loves this as much as I do. Her arms clench across my nape, leveraging her weight to slam herself down on my cock in a violent attempt to get what I promised.

"Trust me, mamita. I'm going to fuck the shit out of you."

With that spoken promise, she switches to grinding against me as I resume walking. Like at the Post, she's not asking what I will do, and I love it.

Her being so eager to let me lead, to fuck her how I want, not only fucks with my cock, but it also fucks with my mind. She teases at the carnal desires I have for her without even knowing it.

"You better. I'd hate to have to use my toy afterward."

"Chinga madre."

That taunting little minx. Now that I know she's into ass play, I might just use that toy in her ass while I fuck her pussy. There are so many possibilities that I will burst—anticipation slides down my spine, my body on fire and sweating underneath my clothes.

Her pussy clenches my cock, nearly pulling the cum out of me. She does it repeatedly until we're in her living room, her back and ass about to be pressed against the window for all the world to see.

I fucking love the idea of her getting fucked hard and fast in public. Something she unleashed in me that I didn't even know I liked or needed until her.

"Do you like that?"

"Keep it up, Vic. We'll see how it works out for you."

Meeting her challenge, I press her against the cool window. The shock registers in her eyes as they widen, the white visible around her irises.

"Marco, we can't. What if someone sees?"

Panic raises her voice as she attempts to twist and turns to look over her shoulder. With her position flat against the panels, the evening sun long set behind us, she's not as visible as she thinks, but I'm not going to let her know that. She's going to feel exposed, vulnerable, and as desperate as I am to get a release.

"Let them watch. Let them see you getting fucked good and hard by me."

I don't give her a second to respond when my fingers dig into her ass, lifting her higher and slamming her down onto my cock. She screams, surprise and pleasure mixing into it. No longer is she twisting and turning in my grasp.

She's accepting her fate.

The one that will bring her to new heights of passion. My cock repeatedly stabs her, having a mind of its own and chasing a release that's been building all damn day.

"You fucking love this, Vic. You naughty little thing. You love getting fucked in public."

She's panting now, her breathing ragged and desperate. Her head lolls back to rest against the glass, exposing the delicate curve of her neck, which sends a shockwave of need to the pit of my stomach.

I lean down to nibble on it, the sensation of her squirming beneath me sending more lust through me.

"Admit it."

With each word murmured into her skin, I punctuate her

pussy. Demanding to hear what I already know. Her arms slacken, letting the full weight of her body rest on my thrusting cock.

She's taking it, good and hard, letting me fuck her with wild abandonment. Her screams echo in my ear, fueling my pace and speed to give her all I've got.

"I . . . I . . ."

She's getting it so good she can't even form a response.

Perfect.

"That's it," I growl into her skin. "You want this. Want my cock buried in your tight slit while the world watches."

"Yesss," she purrs, "I love everything you do to me."

Fuck.

She's going to really get it now. Her body arches into mine, and I can feel her muscles clenching around my cock. She's so fucking wet, dripping past my fingers, making her slippery. I adjust my hold, using the window as leverage to slip my arms under her legs and stretch her further than before.

"Too . . . much. It. . ."

I move my head back, her eyes glazed and half closed, with her head shaking side to side. I slow down, measuring what she's saying. The increased weight on her pussy, the apex where we join, and the feverous pace of my cock thrusting into her repeatedly is not too much, judging by her lack of action to lift herself off me.

It's sensory overload, taking her past the boundary of comfort and pushing her body harder.

"It's not too much, Vic."

My voice is thick like my pipe. Her only response is a teasing smile and arching further into me. A sign she wants and needs more, and I can't wait any longer.

"That's a good girl. Take me deep. Let that tight pussy suck me in."

I pick up pace, thrusting into her with an uncontrollable

recklessness. My heart is pounding in my ears as I slam into her repeatedly. She moans with each thrust, still grinding against my cock until she screams my name, long and breathy.

Needing her to be fully consumed, I press my lips against hers, our tongues dancing with fervor as I continue to fuck her against the window that squeaks from the pressure of our actions.

She's grinding against me so much that I can feel her hard clit against my pelvis and her wetness soak the edge of my jeans.

Her pussy clamps down on my cock, sending pulsating ringlets of pleasure deep into my balls, making me nearly lose it. I get her saying it's too much. We're too much together. She clutches my shirt, her legs tighten over my arms, and she fucks me back.

"Yeah, fuck yourself, mamita. Use my big dick to get off."

With her using me to orgasm again, I can't hold off. My legs tremble with need, my balls tighten, and my cock explodes. I'm a goner, emptying ropes of cum into my condom and assuming it's spilling out the top with such volume.

I don't care.

I need us.

I need *her*.

Damn, Miami and her transfer. I'm making this shitty long-distance thing work.

With renewed vigor, I fuck her past the point of pleasure, my cock slacking after such a powerful release to almost painful. I pull away, ending the kiss that leaves us both panting for air.

"Oh God."

Her body convulses in pleasure. Her eyes are wide and glassy. I can tell she's reaching her peak, and it's only a matter of moments before she comes again.

"Fuck me!"

I know what she wants, what she needs. It's written all over her face, how her eyes dart from side to side as though searching for something more. More of me and us. My hips pump with all the strength I have left after my fantastic ejaculation.

"Be a good girl. Come on, my cock."

My demand comes out of my own need to stop, to give my sensitive cock a break from the overwhelming sensations flooding into my pelvis.

She whimpers again, her breath hitching as she clings to me tightly. The sight of her like this, so vulnerable and needy, is too much. I need to feel her come once last time.

"Right there... don't... ahhh."

Her body shudders violently, the sounds of her pleasure filling the air around us. Our combined scent fills the air, an intoxicating aroma that has me needing to taste her, to fill my mouth with her soft lips and tangy flavor.

I cut her orgasm short with my selfish desire to feel her pulsating pussy on my tongue. I squat, moving my arm down to release one leg to the floor, where she slightly sways, still clutching onto my clothes.

I move her other leg over my shoulder and greedily shove my face into her pussy. I'm smothered in her scent, her cum overflowing onto her inner tights.

She gasps, her hand pushing against my head and away from her pussy.

"Too... too sensitive."

Her words are lost in her breath. Her body gyrates at the pleasure coursing through it as I lap at her lips, nibbling, sucking, and gently biting until she violently pushes me away.

My lower face is drenched, and I am gazing up at her. She smiles and then closes her eyes to lean her head against the glass. She radiates with the streetlight from the park, shining like a halo by her head.

I memorize every detail about her right here and right now, knowing I'll replay this a dozen more times at home when I fuck my fist.

"That was . . ."

"Perfect."

Like her.

She's perfect.

Perfect for me.

Her hand releases the fist of cloth to push her hair out of her face. Opening her eyes, she gazes down at me. The moment fills with so much emotion between her and me that I don't know what to say. I simply stare.

"You said you want to see where this goes."

"I do."

"Good."

She smiles, her hand stroking through my hair, collecting sweat as she goes and seeming unbothered by it. Unable to resist, I swipe my tongue across her clit, and she jolts away.

It's hard to say goodbye to what is fast becoming one of my favorite parts about her. But even I need a break to recover, possibly recharge for round two if she lets me.

With a trail of kisses to her inner thigh, I gently remove her leg from my shoulder and help steady her before standing. She leans forward, expecting a kiss, when all I want to do is hold her. I take her into my arms, wrapping her in a tight embrace and burying my face into her hair.

She sighs, the weight of her problems ebbing away as quickly as our orgasms. We'll be okay. We'll figure this out, and that's all I can ask for. The thought makes me grounded, knowing we won't end as quickly as this started.

She rustles a bit, her arms slipping around my waist and her cheek flattening against my chest. As much as I like to fuck her, I realize she needs comfort just as much. To be honest, so do I. We both need the same assurances.

"I hope no one saw us."

Her words are muffled against the starched fabric of my button-down shirt. My head rises, my gaze locking eyes with a guy walking his dog and zeroing in on us.

He drinks in her naked form, half hidden by hands blocking her ass from his view. The thrill of being seen fucking her ends abruptly as a possessive streak washes over me. Suddenly, I don't want anyone to see her naked and vulnerable like this.

The idea is revolting.

My hands clench into fists at the man's smug smirk. Without missing a beat, I adjust our positions, moving my body against the window and blocking her bare form from view.

He'll only see her arms anchored around me if he's still looking. Claiming me as hers and hers as mine.

I'll never do that again. Never have her on display for others. This beautiful body is only for my eyes and pleasure, no one else's. I squeeze her tightly, lowering my forehead to rest on her shoulder and breathing her faded fragrance in. It's calming and unravels the knot in my stomach of having almost lost her.

"You're okay, mamita. We're okay."

Saying it more for me than her.

"Here. Miami. Wherever."

12

VICTORIA

The morning sun, not yet overtaken by the burgeoning Houston skyline, casts long, slanting shadows across the glossy floors of my office as I step inside, latte in hand. Today crackles with the energy of new beginnings, pulsing with the potential of choices we discussed last night before Marco wholly owned my body.

After such an emotional day, his relief in seeing me, wanting to swim in the depth of my sorrow and grief to sort it out for me, solidifies my feelings. His words are an anchor in the swirling storm around me.

Here. Miami. Wherever.

Meant to assure me about us, yet it did more. It assured me about my ability to lead this project. To take a gigantic promotion, one I've longed for while also feeling unprepared and unqualified. All my fears in the past few years are suddenly silenced by his conviction and unbreakable belief in me.

His assurance that I am not just choosing a location but also choosing myself and my dreams over the ghosts of my past. It quieted so many things I've been struggling with and let me lean on him, the only person in this world that I've truly opened up to like this in such a short amount of time.

He commented on fate bringing us together, a recurring thought in my mind. We've been so perfect so far. It's exhilarating and a little overwhelming. I didn't intend to start crying, but my mind and body broke. I needed a release from all the stress and tension that had built since the offer came.

He held me, let me cry like a big baby, and then kissed away my worries. He believed in me more than I did myself. It was too much and not enough.

Desire overflowed, needing to get closer to him, needing his assurance in other areas. The way his warm brown eyes cloud with lust every time he sees me, it's clear he's as enthralled with me as I am with him. I needed him in my body, needed the satisfaction of being wanted, needed him to consume me as completely as my thoughts had done.

His pounding me against the windows, their squeak with the repeated impact a reminder of his ferocious fucking. One I desperately needed to clear my brain and only feel. Feel where we meet, feel his cock growing harden inside me, and feel every brutal thrust until I came over and over again.

As I sip my coffee and sink into my chair, my pussy throbs with soreness and my body is achy. He stayed clothed as we ate dinner and asked me to stay naked. A power play. An indulgence I granted despite my pussy weeping into the towel I put down to protect the chair.

Temptation and lust teetered between us while the conversation remained on Miami, the few details of the project, and possible parts of town I'd live in. His eyes would drag over my body, listening intently as we slowly ate.

I had barely set my fork down before he was on me, scooping me up and taking me to the couch for me to ride him.

My phone trills, pulling me from heated memories when I see his name. Instantly answering it.

"Good morning, sunshine."

"Mmm, I could get used to that."

His thick voice pulls through the phone, and my pussy clenches, wanting to go with him.

"How are you feeling? How's my favorite slit?"

Slit.

I chuckle at his phrasing.

"We're fine. Sore, but that's to be expected."

He grunts his satisfaction.

"Good. I want you to feel me every day, especially when we're apart."

I'm quickly discovering that he has an ego like most Latin men. It's more discreet, not as obvious, but when he proclaimed no more public sex, I knew something was up.

He didn't answer my question when I asked why. Just thrusted up into me and pinched my nipples, bringing me to another orgasm as I ground onto his cock.

"Why am I not surprised."

"I did love you being naked through dinner. I think we need a no clothes rule from now on."

The smile on my face, unseen from him, is evident in my voice.

"That goes for you too?"

"I'd be more than happy to follow a no-clothes rule."

He chuckles, and the amusement in his voice widens my smile. I can almost picture him smirking on the other end of the line.

"But I'll have to see how well you follow it before I commit. After all, you were quite the good girl last night. Obeyed without saying a word."

"Obeyed?"

Such an odd word. I hadn't thought of it outside of a dog obeying its owner.

"You need to rephrase that."

A hint of mischief creeps into my voice. I don't hate the word, but I'm uncomfortable with it.

"Let's just say you're very good at following instructions. Something I'd like to do more of."

The thought of spending every moment with him naked makes my heart race. The images flooding my head at following more instructions, "obeying" him makes my body heat and my pussy wet. I realize just how much I desire this man, not only physically but also emotionally.

"I'd like that too."

I can't help but blush at the thought of more fun to come with him. He brings out my inner sex kitten. The way his eyes devour me, his mouth sucks the soul from my clit, and his cock shoves into my pussy, makes me squirm with want. This feeling has been missing for so long, and having him in my life has brought it back with a vengeance.

"Good, mamita. Now tell me what time you're talking to him?"

It's safe that he moves the conversation to work. Getting all hot and horny before seeing my boss is not the best idea, especially when I need a clear mind to ask a few follow-up questions.

"8:30 am. It was scheduled for later, but his assistant texted me this morning that he's leaving the office around lunch."

I lean forward, tapping on my keyboard to check the appointment time on my schedule even though I have it committed to memory.

"Knock it out. I like it. Call me when you're done. I want to hear how it goes."

The authority in his voice makes my core clench with desire. I nod despite him not being able to see me.

"And Victoria, everything will work out. You'll see."

The nerves swimming in my stomach while getting ready this morning come roaring back. Dwelling on thoughts of us last night and the security he brings chased them away temporarily.

Now that I glance at the clock, my stomach is fluttering. The coffee I cherish every morning is now rough in my stomach, and I push it out of reach as I remind myself not to drink it absently.

"I appreciate that. I don't know why I'm so nervous, but I am."

Voicing those words out loud amplifies the flutter, and I press a hand into my midsection to stop it.

"Because it's a big deal. But you're an even bigger deal. All you have to do is say yes, Vic."

Strong conviction ripples through the receiver, Marco doing what he does best, calming me.

"Let him do most of the talking if that helps. Otherwise, you've got this."

I blow out a long breath, wishing I had gone to yoga this week. The movement and meditation always ground me. Marco is quickly becoming my yoga replacement.

"I got this. They want me, not the other way around."

"That's my girl."

His tone softens. Everything about those words feels right. Feels good in my soul.

"Now get ready for your meeting and call me when you can. I've got a busy day with the launch this week, but I'll call you right back if I miss you."

"Okay."

As I disconnect the call, I can't help but smile. Taking a moment, I stare off, thinking about how the long-distance thing will work. It only exacerbates my fluttering stomach, so I quickly switch gears and tackle my overflowing inbox. This will burn up time until the meeting and keep my nerves at bay.

An hour passes quickly. Interrupted with an incoming call from Lisa.

"Good morning, Lisa. What can I do for you?"

My voice is smooth and polished, ever the professional, even with my knee bouncing as I countdown the clock to the big meeting.

"Well, I just had an interesting call from the lead engineer on your project. Apparently, he's been going back and forth with some specs or designs. I don't know which exactly, but someone at the company you want to onboard."

I look at the phone display, my brain rattling over the details she's telling me.

"He's singing the guy's praises over there as a genius or something because he called me to get them onboarded too. Have you spoken to your team lead on this?"

I shake my head, trying to combine two and two, but I am still missing pieces.

"Wait, I'm not exactly sure what you're talking about."

"Do you know a Marco Delgado?"

My heart leaps in my chest, beating radically as my personal and work worlds collide without my knowledge. Privately, they had already collided into the biggest bang of my romantic life, but no one knew that. I seriously doubt Marco would divulge that, either.

"I do. He's the lead software engineer I listed as the contact on the due diligence I sent you."

"Right, right, of course."

She hums as if forgetting despite it being only days ago.

"Anyway, he's been discussing a solution with your engineering team, which appears to be working. They called to sing his praises, saying they could use him on other projects within the company. They wanted to recruit him to work here, but that's above my pay grade."

Marco working here? With me?

My pulse races faster, and my knee bobs at the same rate. A cold chill slides down my spine. Marco can't work here. We have a no-fraternizing policy, and we also have that with vendors, but I needed his help with this project.

I want to get it up and running and deliver a successful project worthy of this promotion. However, the security I felt from Marco's early call is slipping away quickly, leaving me grasping for a lifeline.

"What . . . what did he say?"

The anxiety surging through my veins ripples out into my voice, which I hope she doesn't pick up on. If he works here, my career is over, taking my budding relationship with it.

"Basically, no thanks. He was humbled and told our guy that he's flattered but enjoys his company."

Relief loosened my body, my knee stopped bouncing, and a ripple of thanks to Marco rose in my mind.

"Said he was just glad that his ideas helped. Seems like a nice guy. All that said, his company is approved. I contacted them to set up invoicing, and a lady named Maddie answered, saying Mr. Delgado was tied up but did the work pro bono. He said he was paying it forward, but I don't know what that means since he's new to everyone here. Odd, right?"

I beam, genuinely captivated by Marco's generosity and the smoothness of how he handled this entire situation. Especially after I hid away from him for a couple of days and then almost ended it with him last night. He's good to me in ways I didn't even know about until now.

"Odd, maybe. I wouldn't give it much thought."

I downplay all her suspicions, needing to play it cool like Marco had.

"I'm just glad they are approved. Thanks for all your help! And thanks for the favor in fast tracking it."

Papers shuffle on her end, and then a door creaks closed.

"If you keep finding good vendors like this, I'll be happy to help you. Anyway, I'm late to a meeting. Just wanted to share the good news."

The line goes dead before I can ask her about Marco collaborating with my team. With only a few minutes left before taking my own important meeting, I place the receiver on the cradle and pick up my cell phone to ask.

I just had the most interesting call.

Have you been working with my colleagues?

My fingernails tap the chair of my arm, not out of annoyance, but rather releasing some nervous energy. Going to the bathroom beforehand would be a good idea, as would checking my make-up and ensuring I'm presentable. His text comes through while I reach for my lipstick in my purse.

Yes, is that an issue?

Before I can assure him it's not, I'm more curious about when and how it happened, and he follows up.

They reached out on Monday. I was going to tell you, but then...

But then I ghosted him and didn't call or reach out until yesterday. Yeah, that's on me.

I hope I didn't mess up.

Not at all.

I was just pleasantly surprised.

With my eyes drifting back to the time as I reapply my lipstick, I can't really get into this with him.

Good. I wanted to help.

Still want to help.

Those guys are nice. I'm glad you're not mad.

I heart his message, running out of time to hit the ladies room.

Hey, don't you have to go?

I do. I'll text you later.

No, call me. I want to hear your voice.

Good luck.

The nerves attempting to reappear are temporarily doused because of Marco's goodness. His calm, level-headed approach makes everything easy between us. Right now, I need easy. This promotion and transfer are hard enough, and the thought of returning home is even harder. That's why I haven't told my parents, but I will have to soon since I'm saying yes to the transfer.

Oh well, let's get this over with.

I slip the sleek tube back into my purse and stand, smoothing my hands over my red suit—a color of power and allure. At the very least, I'll look fantastic if my boss rescinds the offer.

With quiet steps and subtle waves to my colleagues, as I pass their glass office, I let out a long, deep breath while clutching my portfolio—using it as a shield of protection while also coming prepared for note-taking.

"He's waiting for you. Go on in," his assistant says in hushed tones, her hand covering the receiver of her phone while waving me forward.

Stepping through the slightly ajar door of Mr. Caldwell's

office, I catch the tail end of his phone conversation, his tone pleasant yet firm. He waves me in with a nod, signaling the end of his call as he sets down the receiver.

For a moment, I wonder if they are talking to each other, but then I quickly dismiss it as none of my business.

"Victoria, come in, please. Have a seat."

He gestures towards the plush chairs across from his massive desk. He watches me settle in, a speculative look on his face as he adjusts his tie to drape down his starched shirt. His suit jacket lies across the chair beside me, ready for him to dash out the door with.

"I understand you've had time to consider our offer?"

His voice is even and businesslike, yet there's a hint of anticipation in his tone, contrasting with the relaxed way he leans back in his chair. I nod, clasping my hands around the portfolio in my lap to keep them from trembling.

"Yes, Mr. Caldwell, I've given it a lot of thought."

His fingers intertwined when he regards me over the rims of his glasses.

"And? Will we be seeing you take the lead back in Miami?"

I swallow the lump in my throat, my answer ready despite the flutters in my stomach.

"Yes, I've decided to accept the position. I believe it's a great opportunity to advance my career and contribute to the company in a significant way."

His smile is quick and pleased.

"Excellent, Victoria! I had no doubts. Your expertise and connection to Miami make you the perfect fit for this role. It's an ambitious project that can make your career. I'm confident you will handle it with the same dedication and skill you've shown here."

He pauses, allowing his words to sink in before continuing.

"Now, regarding the transition, we'll need to start planning immediately. There's a lot to prepare, and I'd like you to be on the ground there within the next month. We'll arrange for your relocation, buy out any time you have on your lease, and ensure you have everything you need to hit the ground running. Human Resources will be the lead on that, so I'll have Helene contact you to gather the details."

The speed of it all sends a jolt of anxiety through me, making my stomach flutter even more. I knew it would be quick. He already mentioned that when he made the offer. His confidence is reassuring, even if mine is not.

"Of course, Mr. Caldwell. I'll begin preparing right away and coordinate with the teams here and in Miami to ensure a smooth transition."

"Good, good."

He nods, his expression turning thoughtful.

"I know this is a big move, Victoria, but I'm convinced it's the right one. And, of course, the Board is fully supportive. They're excited to see this expansion into a new market."

The Board of Directors?

I want to vomit.

Bile rises from the anxiety-laden pit, having drowned out the butterflies. I grip the leather fabric in my lap even tighter before standing, needing a break from the reality of all this crashing down on me. He suddenly stands, and I immediately follow suit.

"You're not just going to work on a project. You're going to build something lasting, something you can be proud of."

His hand juts across the desk, offering his congratulations when our hands join.

"Welcome to Miami, Victoria."

His encouragement somewhat fortifies me. His blistering smile and confidence bolsters my resolve. I return his grin, withdrawing my hand to clutch my folio again.

"Thank you, sir. I won't let you down."

"I know you won't, Victoria. Now go make this a landmark project for Caldwell Enterprises."

As I leave his office, the weight of his expectations and my aspirations settles on my shoulders—not as a burden and not quite a victory. It is more of a mantle pushing me out of my comfort zone while propelling me to greater heights where my demons lie in wait.

It would be a beautiful gift. One only you can give.

Marco's sentiments float through my mind on the walk back to my office. This is my chance to forge ahead, on my terms, in a place filled with painful memories and potential for new beginnings.

To deliver a gift that only I can give to the city in honor of my brother. By the time I sink into my office chair and close the glass door, shutting out the rest of the office, I do the one thing I've dreaded and avoided the most—calling home.

I type out the telephone number I've known my whole life, Mama writing it on my arm every time I rode my bike to school until I could finally remember it. As the phone rings, I brace myself for the conversation ahead, ready to share the news.

"Hello?"

Her voice is cheerful, unaware of the turmoil on my end.

"Mama, it's Victoria."

Dread coils tightly in my stomach as I wait for her reaction.

"Victoria! What a surprise. Is everything okay?"

There's a palpable pause, the silence stretching out as I pick up my pen to tap nervously on the top of my desk.

"I have some news to share."

I pause, taking a deep breath, my hand gripping the phone tighter.

"I'm up for a promotion."

"*Mija,* that's most excellent news!"

The thrill in her voice is unmistakable. If my papi is there, she's almost certainly calling him over to listen.

"Wait, let me get your papi."

She hollers out his name, barely covering the phone and blasting my ear. I'm careful to put my phone on speaker to avoid it happening again when she yells his name a second time.

"I don't know where he went. He was here a minute ago, but you know your papi, he slips away to tinker on things."

The pen taps faster, wanting to get this over with. Her hollering for him only heightens my anxiety.

"It's okay, Mama. I'll tell you, and you can share it with him later."

I lean closer to the phone, staring at their number on my display and keeping my voice down so my colleagues do not overhear it.

"Well, I want him to hear it from you, not me. It's your news to share."

As much as I appreciate this, I just want to get it over with. Ignoring her hollering for him a third time, I pick up the phone and yell over her.

"I'm moving back to Miami!"

The pen slips from my hand, and I turn my chair to look out the window. At the buildings surrounding mine and the sun sending rays of light to cascade the sidewalk below.

"What? Mija?" She sputters as shocked to hear it as I was earlier this week. "What did you say?"

"You heard me."

I tread lightly, caution edging my tone while tempering the anger that always rises when speaking to her.

"The promotion is in Miami."

"Here?"

Dread coils in my stomach again, heavy and unrelenting. It's one thing to confront my past and the pain of losing my brother.

It's another to bear the crushing weight of my parents'

transferred expectations, their unspoken demand that I somehow fill the void he left behind—a resentment that festers no matter how hard I try to let it go. The line is quiet, and I take a second to compose myself since I just snapped at her.

"It's our first entry into the market, and they want me to head up a new project in Brickell. It's the culmination of all my years of hard work, long hours, and dedication to the company. It's both a promotion and a transfer. Back home."

I don't know why I added that last part. Although I'm obviously moving back home, I'm still grappling with the prospect.

"Back home?"

The words ghost across the line, questioning and near disbelief, the same as they did when repeating the city. It's been well over a decade since I left, making it clear I was never coming back, not on my own accord.

Yet here I am, moving home and still not really on my own accord. I'm sure she doesn't know what to make of it either.

I ignore her heavy sigh and explain how it came about. My current project in Houston, the projects before that, and my loyalty to the company. The Board and my boss selected me, rooting for and supporting me in this new endeavor.

They believe I can change the Miami skyline with a skyscraper of my own. I boast, the ego of my achievements overriding the resentment and bitterness collecting in my throat.

"Just like Victor."

And there it is. The elephant in the room. The dark shadow that has haunted us ever since I watched his casket lower into the ground that blistering hot day to the wails of my parents. Sounds no child should ever have to hear. The kind of grief that settles into a family, cold and unyielding, breaks them apart long after the dirt settles and the flowers wilt.

"Yeah, just like him."

My crisp, cynical words rumble over the phone. Guilt and

anger gnaw at me. I'm living his dream—the one he told everyone about, including hospital staff and anyone who entered his room and saw his sketches.

My dream was more frivolous and fanciful—studying ceramics and earning a Bachelor of Fine Arts from California College of Arts. Owning my studio with an attached gallery where patrons would celebrate my works was all I envisioned until the day that dreaded diagnosis came.

My parents' attention and focus converged upon him, battling the relentless illness that ravaged his body. My aspirations disintegrated, reduced to the same hazardous silica dust that erodes the lungs—just as cancer had eroded my brother and our family.

"Well, someone has to earn your acceptance since he's too dead to do it."

It's a sickening harshness, even for me. Crossing lines I hadn't and didn't intend to cross. Yet the pressure of this week, my boss, this promotion, and everything else is forcing them out and wanting to hurt her as she's always hurt me.

There's a sharp intake of air, followed by a broken sob. Tears well in my eyes, and I quickly wipe them away as they fall.

"Mija."

That one word is filled with so much emotion, expectation, and disappointment. She doesn't need to say anything else. I feel the stabbing in my heart once again.

Her favorite died, leaving her with the spare—the problematic, free-spirited child who challenged her at every turn. I don't even recognize that person, the young lady I used to be.

Somehow, over all the years, I morphed into the version of me they always wanted, the female version of my brother. It's the God's honest truth. And in places too dark in my soul to admit as true, I hate them for it.

"I have to go. I'm at work, and they are calling me."

It's a lie, maybe not known to her. Yet, she's always seen through my lies, so many she knows the truth this time.

"Please tell Papi for me. It will be easier since I will be swamped setting things into motion over the next several days."

My word vomit comes to an end. Being on the offense, I don't have to deal with her emotions or mine. Shoving them back behind the wall that surrounds my heart, where grief, disappointment, and hurt run amuck on the playground of my soul, I blink back any remaining tears.

"We are proud of you, Victoria. We always have been."

Her words come too late, not by a fraction but several years. Well over a decade too late. Pulling back my shoulders and straightening my spine, I turn away from the window.

Composed and polished, ready for the rest of the workday, I wrap things up without my colleagues knowing the secrets I carry carved on my being.

"I'll be in touch."

I don't bother waiting for her reply. I need self-preservation more than anything else, especially in a professional work environment where emotional outbursts are unwelcome and warranted.

Renewed guilt surges forward, and I do my best to tamp it down by taking a drink of my long-forgotten coffee and turning my attention to my overflowing email inbox.

"Proud my ass. Where were you and Papi when I needed you both the most?"

13

MARCO

The bullpen of programmers is a frenzy of activity and an area of the floor most everyone stays away from, even Preston. It's a perfect place to hide away and get work done as the team pushes through the last checks before our app's soft launch. Triple monitors cast a bluish glow across the dark room, with my screens cast on the wall for the team at the front of the room in preparation for going live.

The air is thick with caffeine and concentration, often punctuated by a sharp exclamation of triumph or a muttered curse. Perched on a table at the front of the room, my laptop balancing on my thighs, I take last-minute notes for Preston before our final meeting later today. I also draft talking points for him to share with Dawson after Monday's argument and misunderstanding that had him storming out of Preston's office.

From my vantage point, I can scan the team and see who's still working, up and about, shoulder surfing, and collaborating on different coding tweaks. It's my job to keep this ship steady and navigate the choppy waters of pre-launch jitters and the associated pressure, yet my mind wanders to Victoria.

Last night was full of surprises, the pendulum swinging

from emotion and needing my comfort to wanting to be fucked again after taking her in front of the window. She was loading the wine glasses in the dishwasher, naked, I might add, and intentionally bending over, flashing her tight slit at me between her trim thighs.

What's a guy to do but lick the candy offered? She yelped in surprise and bent further, her way of permitting me to continue.

Chinga madre.

It's been a long time since I've felt this good, this alive. And it's all because of her. She's the one who brings out this animalistic side of me. Limp to loaded in seconds. I can't get enough of it. Enough of her. My cock rallies every time I think of her. It's a problem, especially now when I'm about to signal my team to release the app.

My gaze flitters to the clock on the wall for the millionth time, seeing it's just past 9 am when she's supposed to be with her boss. It will be a bit before she calls me, but at least I got to talk to her this morning, which left a lingering smile on my face.

Maddie busted me with it and just murmured, "Hey, lover boy," in passing. It didn't even get a rise out of me nor wipe the smile from my face.

I'm taking her advice and meeting with Preston at Victoria's company, especially since the conversation with her construction team has progressed to the point that they want me on hand over there as they work. Something Preston will need to know about and approve since it sort of conflicts with this launch.

But if it will help Victoria out, I'll be there. And even though my boss doesn't think anyone on my team is as capable as me, several talented programmers can take over for me if needed.

I resume my exhaustive email to Preston, partly for his

knowledge but mostly for my documentation to include in my technical papers. The alarm chimes across the room, and heads jolt up, glancing at the clock.

A couple grimace while a few finish typing before turning to face the front. I hit send on my email and then set my laptop on the table beside me, ready for the final briefing.

"Okay, team, let's sync up!"

"First things first, let's go through the deployment checklist one more time."

I point to the team's administrative assistant to drive my slide deck on the screen while I present. Taking each bullet point separately sparks a brief discussion, technical jargon flying fast and furious as the assigned team members double-check every detail.

"Backend servers?"

I glance at Jenna, our lead backend developer.

"Green across the board."

She taps her keyboard to display the latest server stats and moves out of the way to make her screens visible to the room. The green lines on her screen are a good omen.

"Good work." I nod at her and continue to the next bullet point. "Front-end functionality, any issues?"

My eyes find Tom, who's been debugging since sunrise. He pushes his glasses up the bridge of his bridge and stands to address the group.

"A couple of minor alignment issues on mobile, but it'll be fixed in the next few minutes."

He immediately sits, fingers flying over his keyboard to deal with said issues.

"Lisa, how's the user flow holding up under stress tests?"

Satisfied, I glance to the corner where Lisa, our UX designer, is poring over user feedback from our in-house company beta testers. She looks up and leans back in her chair, which swivels side to side.

"We're good. No crashes, and navigation is intuitive for new users. I've got some tweaks for the onboarding process. You know, making buttons bigger and cleaning up the font, but they're not launch blockers."

"Alright, people, let's get this to the finish line. We go live with the soft launch in two hours."

I clap my hands together, a sharp sound that slices through the low-level noise.

"Remember, today is about ironing out kinks and smoothing the user experience. We need this app to be bullet-proof in time for full release on Friday. Don't forget to document anything you find on the central issues log on the shared drive or just kick it over to Jeanine, and she'll do it."

I gesture my head toward the assistant and she's already giving me a thumbs up.

"They have. It's all updated, so we're golden."

As the team turns back to their workstations, I stand and stretch my back, needing a good long run after work to unleash the pent-up stress. I'd prefer my cardio with a certain brunette getting pounded underneath me, but we agreed to take the night off with both of our stressful days.

In hindsight, I wish I hadn't. I'd lay into her all night and use coffee to keep me awake tomorrow. Isn't that what it's for?

I flop into a chair by the table, my makeshift command station today, and pull out my phone. When I don't see a missed call or text, I reach out to her and think how lucky I am that she doesn't play the text-for-text game. Nor does she mind my double and triple texts, something doing the same thing herself.

On a quick break, thinking of you and hoping everything is going well.

I debate typing more about my work and how the app soft launch is going, but refrain. Today is already stressful for her, and I don't want to inadvertently add my job stuff to the mix. There's plenty of time to discuss it tomorrow or this weekend.

Which reminds me, I need to ask her out for Saturday. It would make me happy as fuck if she could spend the night and we could see each other the whole weekend. Assuming the launch goes well, the team and I don't have to work another long weekend. Finger crossed.

Knowing I won't hear from her right away, the pressure of the soft launch takes hold. I lock my phone, put it away, and dive back into the whirlwind of last-minute preparations. Two hours till launch speeds into post-launch activities, issues, and documenting fixes while pushing more updates out to the initial users.

Delivered lunch blurs into afternoon vending machine snacks and into another delivered dinner as we fix, refine, and optimize. Time evaporates until Preston pops into the bullpen, his gaze roaming over the dark room, where overhead lights are never turned on, the glow of the computer monitors preferred.

"Marco, a word?"

His words barely float over the rhythmic clacking of keyboards. He waves me over with a casual but urgent gesture, indicating that I should follow him out of the bullpen.

I stride wordlessly behind him, catching the door he holds open and following him into my office, where he avoids taking a chair. If his serious expression indicates the importance of this meeting, I remain standing as well.

"I've been reviewing the emails from this morning and all the updates throughout the day. Are we solid for the launch in two days?"

Preston doesn't waste a moment, arms folded across his chest, and strain lines are wearing on his face. I round my desk, sitting to log onto my workstation mirrored in here from the laptop still in use in the bullpen.

"Everything's lined up. The team's managing the soft launch

seamlessly, and we've tackled every critical issue that's popped up. We're set."

I turn my screen toward him, showcasing a dashboard glowing with green status indicators and real-time analytics. He leans over my cluttered desk, scrutinizes the data, and his eyes dart across the graphs and metrics, absorbing the pulse of our project.

"Good, good. Just make sure this holds. A single hiccup could derail us. I don't have to remind you of the stakes here."

He shifts away from the screens and tightens his tie, which hangs loosely from his neck as if pulling himself together. His words hang between us—a tangible reminder that this app could define our company's trajectory and, more importantly, my career.

"Understood," I respond, my resolve echoing his intensity. "I'm on it. The team is dialed in, and I'm right there with them."

Preston's demeanor shifts as he processes my assurance, his posture relaxing slightly, an implicit trust in his nod.

"I'm counting on you, Marco. Keep me updated. If anything, and I mean anything, starts looking off, I want to be the first to know."

"Absolutely," I confirm, turning the monitor back to me when I remember the other project—Victoria's project. "Oh hey, there is this project that sort of fell in my lap. It's not related to this or our other initiatives. It's partnering with a local real estate developer."

"Real estate? We're a tech company," he says flatly, unimpressed.

"It's with Caldwell Enterprises. I'm certain you've heard of them."

His eyebrows raise, his interest piqued with a contemplative look.

"Go on."

"I've started some exploratory discussions with them, a sort of pro bono collaboration on their Westerfeld project, to be precise. They ran into an issue, and I was able to help this weekend. Initially, I didn't think anything would come of it as I wasn't certain my solutions would work for their system control issues. It turns out it did, and they want to work with me on correcting that and a few other bugs they are encountering. It's small stuff we're testing but could lead to larger scale projects with more tech demands for our company."

I hope to illustrate the potential benefits beyond the set forth quarter strategic plan.

His posture shifts, stroking his chin in thought.

"Pro bono? Not on company time? Why am I just now hearing about this?"

Because I'm in a budding relationship with the project manager.

"I wasn't sure if anything would come of it."

That statement was true at the time for both the project and my hope that Victoria would like me back. But we're past those concerns now that both are on track for success.

"Fair, but I'm not happy to hear of the moonlighting, especially with this launch looming over us."

He thumbs the adjoining wall to the programmers, a frown hanging from his lips.

"Don't worry, I didn't let it interfere. It was more of a palette cleanser from the app when we waited to see if the patches would hold overnight."

Going in for the kill and not leaving him any room to negotiate further.

"We're testing our tech with their systems on a small scale to evaluate compatibility. Not to mention custom billing, which would get Dawson off both our backs with a consistent revenue stream coming in."

By bringing home the irritation of Dawson sulking around here all week, much to my boss's dislike, I will reinforce the point with consistent revenue to repay the equity investors ahead of schedule. I also hope to illustrate the potential benefits beyond our one app development and deployment business line.

He percolates on the idea, his jaw tightening at the mention of his nemesis whom he's in bed with.

"Interesting, but our primary focus remains on the app launch. Make sure that goes off without a hitch. Once stable, we can consider expanding resources towards this Caldwell project if your initial tests show real promise."

That's a green light if I ever heard one.

"Of course. The soft launch is going well. It's fascinating to watch how users are interacting with it. I can take you back there and show you what we're looking at if you'd like."

He waves a dismissive hand in the air, unwilling to be bothered by that granular experience.

"No need. I trust you to get it done. If that's all, I'm heading out to a late dinner with a client."

Another straightening of his tie as he walks to the doorway. We both know it's not a client dinner but time with his mistress. But hey, that's none of my business.

"Enjoy your night."

"I intend to."

His words linger in my office long after he walks down the hall, bringing flashes of Victoria naked, fisting my hair as she explodes into my mouth. My cock twitches, wanting a repeat of last night. Realizing I left my phone in the other room and haven't heard from her all day, I drag my weary body from my chair and go to retrieve it.

The urge to tell her everything about this day is overwhelming, but I know her day is far more important—life-changing—than mine. I push through the bullpen's double doors, past the hum of collaboration happening in clusters around the floor, and snatch my phone off the table to return to my office.

I glance at my watch, seeing it's well past 8 pm and knowing her cell is the best number to call her. A wave of mental fatigue washes over me as I fall back into my chair. My ass is numb from so much sitting on it today.

By the third ring, she answers, breathless, and my balls tighten. That breathlessness pressed against my ear as I push into her is one of my favorite sounds coming out of that hot body.

There are so many more I love, such as when I fuck her hard, racing toward my release, and when she's most pliable. She's usually spent from multiple orgasms, gripping my body tightly and muttering Spanish curse words to encourage me to finish. It's hot as fuck and sending heat through my body.

"Hey, Marco. How's everything going?"

Her voice lightens with more life. But the fact that she's asking about me first makes me smile. Caring is at the forefront of her mind when it should be on herself.

"Mamita, I didn't call to talk about me. I want to hear how everything went with you. I'm sorry I couldn't call sooner. It's been a long day."

I don't hide my tiredness, and that's the beauty of being with someone older. No games, only truths.

"Oh, well, I blew it out of proportion."

She chuckles, the relief evident in how airy it sounds.

"I did meet with Human Resources, and my head is swimming with how fast this is progressing."

"Everything went well with your boss, then?"

I wish I could be with her, holding her as she tells me about her day. A flash of us in a high-rise in Miami flashes through my mind. She comes through the door, kicks off her heels, and dumps her bags on the table before joining me in the kitchen, where I make a delicious dinner. It gives me an unexpected pull in my chest, a longing I didn't know I had until now.

"Yes, of course. He made it very easy, and like you said last night, I didn't have to say much. That helped."

Her words shake me from my daydream, leaving me confused and hopeful.

"That's wonderful, Vic. I'm glad everything went smoothly for you."

My words lack the emotion they should evoke. My brain still processes what happened and why I suddenly feel weird.

"It's just a lot to take in, all the paperwork, the benefits, and the relocation details. But it's all good, really good actually."

She doesn't seem to notice my hesitation, thankfully.

"And I already discussed it with my parents."

There's something in her voice when she mentions that last part. A downward turn of her voice, as if disgusted, but that's too strong of a word for the subtle inflection. Picking up on it, I press her for more details. She didn't mention them much last night.

"That's good."

I realize my question came out more as a statement and I immediately correct myself.

"Isn't it?"

A beat goes by, and then another before she breathes into the phone.

"Sure."

"Victoria?"

Another silence.

"It's a long story, Marco."

The exhaustion in her voice spans years and years, not just a couple of sleepless nights she's experienced this week. Judging by the hesitancy and clipped response, there is far more than a long story there that I should probably mind my own business.

"You don't have to tell me if you don't want to."

I offer her an out before turning away from my open door when a programmer walks out of the bullpen and passes my office with a brief nod of acknowledgment.

"Honestly, I'm not sure where to start or even if I should . . ."

She trails off, and I almost hear her wrestling with the words.

"If it's too much right now, that's okay."

I lean back in my chair, staring at the ceiling as if I might find the right words there.

"But if talking about it helps, even a little, I'm here."

There's a sigh from her end, not of relief, but resignation—a sound that tugs at something deep inside me.

"My parents . . . there are a lot of unresolved issues. I feel as though I'll never measure up. After Victor died, everything . . . shifted. It's like I had to step into his shoes, but no one asked if I wanted to. They just assumed. I gave up on my dreams, which everyone always thought were silly at the time. They never took me seriously because, well, I didn't take myself seriously back then."

I pause, letting her words sink in, trying to offer silence as a space for her to continue.

"I was the wild one, you know? Always been an artist, dreaming of my own studio and gallery. I planned to go to school in California to study ceramics but never got the chance. Everything changed. I dropped all that to become what he was supposed to be. And my parents . . . they just went along with it. They never said anything. They acted like it was what I wanted. They seemed relieved when I told them I would follow in Victor's footsteps and go to his alma mater. My mama didn't bat one eyelash at the sudden change of heart. Instead, she embraced me and whispered, "That will make us proud." But damn, Marco, didn't I already make them proud just by being alive? Shouldn't parents be proud of their kids without having to take over their dead sibling's legacy?"

Her voice cracks with emotion from confession, and I can hear the years of built-up pain, frustration, and sadness. My chest tightens. Her hurt becomes my hurt, and it's too fucking much being this far apart. She gutted me in the worst way by telling me over the phone.

"*Mamita—*"

"They never even asked, Marco. I was just expected to take over his dreams like they were mine. And now, going back . . . I don't even know if I'm doing it for me or just continuing something that was never mine to start with. And then I'm the selfish asshole that is sitting here whining about promotions and transfers when almost everyone in the company would kill for this. I've received congratulations from colleagues all day once word got out. And I've caught a few envious looks when they did."

I'm at a loss for words.

The pain in her voice echoes through me.

With half a mind to leave this place and drive to her so I can wipe away the tears that must be running down her face by the sound of her voice, I blow out a harsh breath instead. Preston would kill me if I left my team. Hell, I'd be pissed at myself if I bailed on them. But both need me, and I feel so torn.

"And, of course, I can't tell them this because I sound ungrateful. I am ungrateful. I should keep my mouth shut and tamper it all down like I have been. But you know, sometimes it's hard to go it alone. Even though I've been strong and don't need the support of anyone, it would be . . . would be nice if . . ."

Sobs are breaking up her words, driving a fucking dagger into my chest as I lean forward, catch my head in my hands and stare at the carpet.

"Vic, I'm so sorry you've been carrying this around."

My hand tightens over the phone, trying to make this right from afar.

"I wish I was there right now. I want to hold you and take away all this pain."

"I wish that, too."

She sounds so tiny, vulnerable, and torn apart by her past.

Much more than the grief and loss of a loved one but of the resentment and anger at being forced into something and someone she's not.

"It's okay not to be okay. But you have me, Victoria. I'll be strong for you, *with you*. You don't have to go it alone anymore. *I'm* your support. You got me now, mamita."

My voice holds steady, pushing through the speakers with every ounce of strength I can muster.

"Remember what I said when we first met? It was fate that brought us together. I'm convinced of it. You know it too. I saw the way you looked at me. You felt it. You still feel it."

"I do."

There it is.

This is an acknowledgment that we're on the same page. It wasn't just her job that needed me. She needed me as much as I was coming to need her. Fate brought us together. Connection, chemistry, support, and eventual love will keep us together.

"I wish I could do more from here."

I lean back, the chair creaking under my shifting weight while sniffing, taking over from the previous sobs.

"I can see you after this wraps up. I don't know what time that will be. Maybe pretty late but I'll come so you're not alone."

I once joked that I'd swim in the trauma caused by other men to show her I was different. I had no idea it hit far closer to home. Yet, I'm still not backing out. She needs me, and I'm there for her. I want to be there for her in every way I can. The pull between us is unexplainable. I call it fate, yet it feels like so much more.

"I can't ask that of you. It's been a longer day for you than me."

Her voice cracks, woven with weariness and a sense of relief from my words. It sounds like the act of sharing the burden has eased it, if only slightly. My chest feels strange, aching for her hurt, and proud that she's leaning on me to help her through all this, even if it's temporary.

"I don't care about that. I want to see you. I want to kiss you and hold you. Take away all your pain and make you feel good."

A long breath filters through the phone, and she laughs—a slight, choked sound, but it's laughter all the same.

"I'm not sure I'm up for sex tonight."

The inference is distasteful, and I need to clarify.

"No, Vic, I'd never ask that or assume you'd have to do that. I didn't mean sex at all. I'd hold you in my arms, kiss away your pain as you fell asleep protected, supported, and cared for."

"I appreciate that, I really do. But I think I will have a glass of wine, draw a bubble bath, and head to bed early. I hope you understand."

Chinga madre.

The thought of all that delicious skin covered in shiny bubbles makes my limp cock load up immediately. Clusters of the white stuff trapped between her fantastic tits and tight thighs have me blowing out a harsh breath. I'm going to jerk off to that vision tonight. But now it's not the time for all that.

"I completely understand. You do what you need to. But tomorrow night, let me take you out. Celebrate properly."

"I'd like that. And Marco, thank you for listening. It's more than I've had in a long time."

"Always, Vic. Just keep talking to me, okay? Whatever you need, whenever you need it. I'm here. Always."

The words are firm, a lifeline thrown across the miles.

"And I won't turn it down if you want to send me a picture of your bubble-covered body.

She laughs, the mood instantly lightening.

"I'd never do that. But tomorrow, if you want to see it covered in bubbles, we can repeat tonight."

"Chinga madre."

"I'll take that as a yes."

"Consider it required. Now call me if you need anything. Otherwise, I'll be handling business in the company bathroom."

"Good luck!"

She sends a kiss through the phone before hanging up, leaving me rock hard and staring at my darkening screen.

"She's going to get it tomorrow. Celebratory or not."

14

VICTORIA

Excitement buzzes through me as I adjust my body-hugging red dress one last time while the doorbell chimes through my house. Marco's timing is impeccable, arriving seconds after I finish applying my matching lipstick. Taking a deep breath, I open the door, and there he is—handsome as can be in a tailored black suit that accentuates his broad shoulders and tapers down to his trim waist.

The crisp black shirt underneath and silver tie would make him look more intimidating without his genuine smile. Wetness collects in my panties, wanting to reenact the other night when he was fully dressed and I was naked. I'd quickly get on my knees, with his help in this dress, and blow him. He's that gorgeous with his appreciative gaze and bouquet of red roses.

"Wow, you look stunning."

His head is shaking slowly, unable to believe what he's seeing.

"Absolutely beautiful."

He steps across the threshold, enveloping me in a tight hug and dropping his head toward my neck. I expect a gentle kiss, with my skin exposed on that side and my curls swept into a hairpin behind my ear.

"I'm the luckiest man alive to have you as mine."

His words are thick with lust, the same feeling heating my body and making me want to forgo dinner altogether. The actual celebration is what will happen later in my bedroom.

I lean my cheek into his face, avoiding getting my lipstick on his face.

"Yeah, you are."

The boldness in my declaration has him suddenly licking and sucking on my neck, a taste of what's to come.

"Behave, or else I'll show you how lucky you are."

He grinds his hard erection against my core for effect, and I'm swooning at it. We're both on the same page, and I could burst from the attraction. He calls it fate. Maybe it is destiny. Either way, I haven't felt this electric energy from a man in a long time. It's as intoxicating as it is tantalizing.

"Then show me."

My tongue traces the shell of his ear until I reach his lobe and sink my teeth into the soft flesh. He groans, his arm tightening around me to the point I'm nearly breathless. His hips grind teasingly slow, and his hand travels up my back to clutch the back of my neck, pulling my teeth away to gaze into my eyes.

"Is that what you want, mamita? You want to forgo dinner downtown to get fucked?"

His question hangs in the air, heavy with anticipation. I look into his intense eyes, feeling the heat of his desire and the promise of pleasure that lies ahead. It takes a few seconds to decide I can have dinner delivered, but this right here, what I'm feeling, how he looks, and his fucking hot words. No, I can't make it through a charade of dinner only to countdown what I want. Him.

"Nothing would make me happier to give you what you

want. If that's dinner, we leave now. If it's hours of pleasure, then put these flowers in the water while I get condoms out of my truck."

A slow, sultry smile crosses my face as I slip from his tight embrace, reaching for the flowers. They are barely in my fingers before he plucks them out, tosses them on my hall table, and spins me around. Before I realize what's happening, I'm pressed into the wall, his hand on my throat and the other on my hip. It's powerful, primal, and utterly delicious.

"Are you sure about this, Vic? I had a nice evening planned for us."

My palms flatten against the plastered wall, and my makeup probably leaves an imprint that I'll worry about tomorrow. I arch my back, pushing my ass out until it connects with his body. He growls, his fingers tightening over both parts of my body.

"Yes, sir," I purr, knowing he'll respond aggressively.

It's just his nature to call the shots with me as he does at work. It's one of the many things I like about it. I'm already so busy at work, in charge of various teams, that it's nice to relinquish control to someone who enjoys playing that role.

"Chinga madre."

Making good on his threat, his hand leaves my throat, planting on my hip to pull my ass further from the wall. He slaps it once and twice, causing surges of want straight into my core. My pussy clenches in anticipation, my breath shallow as I eye him over my shoulder. His face returns to mine, leaving a gentle lingering kiss on my cheek. The tenderness is unmatched by the hard clench of his fingertips into my flesh.

"I'll be right back. Stay just like this."

Ignoring his command, I catch his wrist, twisting away from the wall when he begins to pull away.

"Don't. I'm not with anyone but you. If that's how it is for you . . ."

I leave the rest in the suffocating air between us. His stare is blistering, long, dark, and intense despite the pink tongue swiping across his lips.

"You're it for me, Victoria. There isn't anyone else. There won't be."

Heat emanates from his body, a fierce, primal energy that ignites something within me. I take a step forward, my body pressing against his once more. The desire raging between us is undeniable, and I know he will not back down from my offer.

"Then what are you waiting for?"

My words are a tease and a threat, goading him to be that aggressive lover I'm quickly becoming addicted to.

His hands move with urgency, putting me back against the wall like I was and crushing his body to mine.

"Nothing."

His lips crash into mine with a hunger that sets my entire body on fire. His hand grips the back of my neck, forcing me to twist toward him. His tongue claims my mouth in a way that leaves no doubt of his dominance. I feel his erection against my hip, threatening me with a good time.

I moan as our kiss intensifies. His hand skims across my ass, finding the high slit of my dress and following the curve to slip under my skirt, searching for the wetness he knows he's caused between my legs.

His fingers brush against my damp panties, groaning at how ready I am for him. He tugs the fabric aside to stroke my soaked folds, sending shivers down my spine as I grind into his touch.

"You want this just as much as I do," he murmurs against my lips, pulling away slightly to look into my eyes.

"Admit it. You need to be fucked. Needy and horny for me. Only me."

"Yes."

My core throbs with a need or want, both perhaps. I'll take whatever he's offering or giving. Willing to do anything to get a release from the stress of my life, especially the last two days. I went from being sexless for a long time to becoming addicted to his touch, needing it more than I want to admit.

More than he's demanding, I admit. If he could fuck me every day, fuck away the tension, worries, and stress of this promotion, and move back home, I'd feel better, more balanced, and ready to make this change.

"I need you. Only you."

He doesn't let me say anything else, crashing his lips to mine as a second finger joins the stroking. Whimpers of need seep out of me as I clutch his shoulders, attempting to keep him where I want him. Asserting my dominance from a place of wanting to submit, wanting to fall into my feminine energy and receive what this beautifully masculine man is giving me.

He breaks the kiss, leaving me panting as he puts me against the wall for a third time. The hem of my fabric is tugged up, the coolness of the room's temperature hitting my core when I arch my back.

It's a divine sensation when he tugs my panties down my legs, tapping the heel of my pumps to widen my stance. My fingers splay against the textured plaster, and my breasts dip toward the floor when he pulls my hips toward him.

"You're stunning like this. Spread out, your pussy glistening and this tiny hole winking at me."

His fingers stroke delicately from my clit to my lips, collecting fluids to circle my tight hole. I gasp, the feeling usurpingly good, intimate, and vulnerable.

Yet I trust Marco.

He'd never hurt or push me farther than I want. For that, I'm further endeared to him.

"You're stalling so much. I'm beginning to think you don't want this."

I smirk over my shoulder at him, his eyes glued to my

body, mesmerized as he watches what he's doing to it—my ass shakes, sassy and expected, which garners me a sharp spank.

But thankfully, he rips through his belt and pants, unfastening them at record speed before pulling out his thick and dripping cock. It's not even a second before he's pushing into me, forcing a loud groan from both of us.

"Fuck, I don't want to bust a nut yet, but damn that mouth of yours and this view."

He's struggling, filling me up, and staring at the ceiling to keep from coming. It's another compliment—one that has me smiling internally. Being with him, as he finds me so desirable that he's trying to keep it together, is all I need to know about how he feels.

I move my ass, needing some sort of friction to get this started.

"Don't."

He groans softly, his pelvis shoving into my ass, forcing his cock deep against my cervix and filling me completely.

It's perfect.

Everything about us is perfect.

Exactly what I've needed for so long.

I never expected it from a guy so much younger than me. He is mature beyond his years and equal in what we both want.

His teeth sink into his lower lip, eyes clenched shut as he wrestles with himself to gain control.

"Fill me up. Make me yours."

I can't help but purr seductively, feeling my pussy spasming around him, more and more eager for his possession. Just like him, it won't take much to push me over the edge, but I need more than being impaled on his thick cock.

Taking my words as another challenge, he slowly pulls back, dragging his length over my swollen folds before slamming it back into me. The force of it causes me to cry out in pleasure. Every nerve ending is alive under his touch, and I need so much more.

With each thrust that follows, I feel myself melting further into his hold, melting into the hand at the back of my neck, keeping me in place against the wall. His fingertips curl into my hip bone, steadying my body with each violent shove into my dripping pussy until all I can feel is his raw desire.

"*Fuck.*"

He curses under his breath as he slams himself into me once again, this time with such ferocity that I know there's no turning back. His pumping becomes more frantic, his body pounding against me in an unyielding rhythm. My moans mix with his deep grunts, the sound echoing the effort to hold himself back while getting me off.

His cock pulsates with every beat of my heart, the tip brushing against my sensitive G-spot with each stroke. It feels like he's trying to brand me, claiming me as his own.

Without the protection he usually wears, I feel every hot, dripping inch of his cock, dragging up and down my walls and pulling mini orgasms out of me on the climb to the big one. It's fucking fantastic having no barrier between us, having nothing to block how we feel about each other.

"Oh . . . yes . . . *Marco.*"

I gasp at the intensity when he nails my G spot straight on, the pleasure twinging with a bit of sweet pain. The combination is too much, sending me spiraling into the dark abyss of ecstasy. I can barely hold on.

My fingers curl into fists against the wall, and my eyes close to revel in the overwhelming sensation bursting over my body. I come for what feels like forever, screaming for more while he consistently hammers into me. It's so perfect. My pussy clenches, my thighs quake, and blood rushes into my head.

The pain is there, but it's nothing compared to the pleasure that comes with it. Each impact sends waves of ecstasy coursing through me, heating spreading over me as I sweat in my nice dress.

His pace quickens and his thrusts become far more erratic until he suddenly stops. My eyes fly open as I gaze over my shoulder at him. It's a stunning sight. His dark eyes bore into mine, and his mouth slacks as his jaw relaxes. An expression of awe washed over his face.

He's quiet this time. There is no dirty talking, no possessive words spilling from his full lips, just free-falling into the abyss with me.

Beads of sweat collect at his temple, evidence of his effort. Otherwise, his suit is perfect, his tie tight against his bobbing Adam's apple as he pants from his fast fucking. I'll remember this moment forever.

His hand on my neck lightens, and his fingers sweep my hair over my shoulder, wiping away the perspiration that collects under his grip. A light smile eases the tension on my face. My hand unfurls, moving from the wall to intertwine with the one still digging into my hip.

"Victoria."

My name is a groan. A lust-filled confirmation of what we are to each other.

Colleagues.

Lovers.

Soulmates.

In that moment, I feel a surge of recognition, a powerful connection that leaves me breathless. This man, this powerful figure with the eyes of a predator and the soul of a poet, he sees me, truly sees me, and it unravels me.

My hand tightens around his, pulling him closer as our bodies remain one. His lips find my neck, nipping gently at the sensitive skin, causing goosebumps to break out.

"Victoria," he murmurs once more, now with a soft plea in his voice, pulling me into another kiss.

This one is gentle and filled with love and longing. We hold each other tightly, our bodies moving gently in sync with the rhythm that consumes us. Finally, he pulls away, his dark eyes filled with a look of pure bliss.

"I don't know what is happening, but I've never felt this way. Please say you feel it too."

His confession is vulnerable and scary. Saying what I'm thinking, knowing there's no going back from what's happening between us.

"I do. I feel it, Marco."

My heart pounds, and a flutter of nerves in my stomach as I confirm it's mutual. My worries from this week dissolve into nothing so long as I have him. Nothing else matters. His fingers tighten over mine, almost painfully with the intensity we're both feeling.

"Chinga madre."

He shifts back, his fingers loosening over my mind to slowly pump into me. His cock is still rock hard, teasing and testing to see if he—we—can go another round as we are.

"I don't want to stop."

"I don't want you to either."

Releasing his hand, I place it back on the wall, pushing my ass further and adjusting my stance as an open invitation to continue. He shuffles back, dragging me with him to allow more space for my body without his cock leaving my pussy.

His mini striations are lazy and lingering, opposite the fast and almost angry pace he set a moment ago. My body tightens, the edges of pleasure curling around his thick shaft as he withdraws slowly and pushes back just the same.

"I want to see you naked. In just your stilettos."

His fingers are already fumbling with the zipper on the back of my dress, pulling it down and exposing me to the room's cool temperature. The fabric rushes against my skin as it is peeled away, bringing a nice sense of relief and a renewed desire.

"I want to taste you, Marco."

"Fuck, Vic."

He pulls his cock from me, leaving a strange hollow feeling behind that I want to be filled again. I turn in his grasp, his hand instantly out to help steady me as I get rid of my dress, standing only in the requested stilettos and my chandelier earrings that dust my shoulders.

"Damn, I'm lucky."

He gasps, his eyes devouring the place his cock just was, seeing the glistening of our combined release sticking to my inner thigh. The compliments that pour out of him with ease add to my boldness, wanting to pleasure him as much as he pleasures me.

"You're about to get even luckier."

His hand tightens over mine, carefully steadying me as I sink to my knees on the tile floor before him. When I gaze up at him, his cock full hard, poking through his dress pants with a huge wet spot on the front of them, he groans from the back of his throat. It's both a plea and a thank you.

"Just when I think you can't get prettier, I see this. Damn, mamita."

His hand cups my chin, his thumb pressing against my lips and smearing my perfectly coated lipstick onto my lower cheek.

"I want to make a mess of you. To live out my fantasy of you sucking my cock, but I want something else."

His brown eyes are nearly black, glittering with intent, arranging me as he's only seen in his eyes. I'm curious and thrilled, eager to find out more about how he fantasizes about me in the quiet of his bedroom. It makes my blood pump, my pussy pulse, and my heart race.

"Whatever you want."

A dark smirk curls up one lip as he continues making said

mess of my makeup. He guides my head towards his straining erection, his hand never leaving my chin.

His dark eyes bore into me, the tip of his cock swiping across my mouth as his thumb had. My tongue darts out, licking it as he spreads my saliva onto my cheeks with his dick. It's hot and teasing—the saltiness of our releases combined on my lips and tongue.

Gazing up at him, naked and objectified, is a role I am eager to play. One that has him licking his lips until I end his toying with a tight fist to the base of his cock. I suck that tight mushroom head, releasing him with a pop only to do it again and again until his fingers tighten over my lower jaw, guiding me to stay on him.

"Naked on your knees . . . worshipping my cock . . . fuck, Vic. It's so much better than my dreams."

His words are thick, throaty, and deep as if he's struggling to match his fantasy with reality. Not knowing what he envisioned, I twist my hand, connecting it to my mouth in a longer channel for his thick cock. He mutters under his break, something in Spanish that I can only translate a couple of words, the rest lost to his growling husk.

His hand never leaves my face, gently angling it how he wants, letting him control me like a fucking doll. It's making my body flush, my pussy pulsing with need. I'm convinced there will be a puddle on the floor underneath me when this is over.

"My perfect mamita. You love this."

His hips begin a slow thrust, meeting the back of my throat as I savor the taste and feel of his cock sliding in and out of my warm, wet mouth. Each time he shoves forward, it causes him to moan deeply from the back of his throat.

"Take it all."

He tugs on my chin. His pelvis pushes beyond where he was before, leaving me choking. It's a couple of seconds, testing how much of him I can fit in my mouth and down my throat while still enjoying this sensation. My nose is buried in his closely trimmed pubic hair that smells like his cologne, my hand cupping his balls once he takes over control.

His thumb swipes into my mouth, pulling at the corner and dragging saliva out to smooth across my cheek. I breathe through my nose, then slowly back off his cock when another gag consumes me. It's turning me on, making me wetter the longer we play like this.

"Good mamita."

His compliment is rough, jagged as he pulls his cock entirely from my mouth. His hand at my chin remains while he bends down to kiss me long and hard, exploring my mouth and our combined tastes.

My moan is met with a satisfied groan rumbling into my body. The fingertips from his other hand dance across my skin, catching under my arm to help me to my feet without breaking the kiss.

He continues claiming my mouth, marked by his domination and my surrender. His tongue tangles with me, exploring every inch and tasting us until I'm breathless and pushing at his chest.

"Chinga madre"

A smile at his favorite phrase. The inner vixen in me wants to be just that. Wild, free, and willing to burn it down between us. I want to take this to the next level, get crazy, and see how far we can go.

"Wanna fuck against the window again? Or in the garden where the neighbors could see, will definitely hear?"

A wrinkle of something passes through his expression, and I don't know what it means. But the slow shake of his head confuses me, offering things outside my comfort zone and more in his, which seems fitting—a natural progression between us.

"No, I don't want the world to see what is mine. Your moans, your cries for more, my name spilling from these lips . . ."

His thumb swipes over the bruised flesh, rhythmically and entrancing me when he doesn't stop.

"It's only for me."

This sudden possessiveness is new and exciting. Intimate and sexual. Flipping from public voyeurism to intimate and soul-baring sex is turning me on even more. The wetness drips onto my thighs with how ready I am for whatever he has in mind.

"And yours for me."

I stake my claim, equal to his, by gripping his wrist and dragging his hand away from my chin. A deliciously dark smile ghosts across his lips, feeling his pulse throb against my palm.

"Of course."

"But why didn't you let me finish you off?"

I tilt my head up, wanting to understand him better. Every guy loves their dick being sucked, a few preferring it to sex. He flips my hold on his hand, suddenly raising my hand to his lips, kissing the palm before sucking on my first two fingers.

"Because I want to watch *you* get off."

His teeth gently tug at the tip of my finger before moving it to my core. I'm left speechless and staring. I open my mouth to just close it again. My mind bursts.

Get off?

Here?

With him?

"Um, you want to do oral on me?" I ask with so much uncertainty that I'm going back and forth about whether I will or not once, he clarifies.

He steps back, allowing a gust of cool air conditioning blocked by his body to tickle my heated skin.

"No, I don't want to do oral."

His taunting eyes are locked to mine, challenging and hopeful. With his fingers over mine, continuing their rubbing my clit into a horny tizzy, he's making it super clear.

"I want to watch you get yourself off. Show me how you like it."

His fingertips leave mine, skimming lower to stroke my pussy too lightly to be anything but coaxing. My breath catches, my pussy clenches, and I chant for him to do it, to slip a couple fingers in and help. I can work my clit, expertly, I might add, but I'd love to grind on his fingers while doing it. Maybe drape my leg over his elbow to allow his deeper access.

"I don't..."

Perfect strokes at a tantalizing pressure have me gripping his wrist and holding it in place. His gaze drops from mine to his fingers, separating, caressing, and teasing my core that's getting wetter in response.

"But you do, mamita. You touch this little slit far more than I do. I want to see it. I need to see how you touch yourself so when I lie in bed at night, I will think of you. Dream of this night."

His hand plants on my shoulder, walking me backward without breaking contact with my needy pussy. When my back hits the wall, his hand moves to the side of my head, angling it up to look at him.

"Do this for me, and I'll fuck you however you want, but not outside and not for the neighbors to hear. Can you do that for me?"

Chinga madre.

To borrow his phrase. If he keeps asking me slowly and quietly as he just did while softly stroking my aching core, I'll do just about anything he asks.

"Yeah."

I inhale the word while inhaling his scent. The masculine cologne seeps so far into his clothing that his pubic hair smells like it. He reeks of it in the most tantalizing way possible.

With a stroke of boldness, I push against his chest, and he obeys, stepping back until he's out of fingertip reach. His cock is rock hard, ready to watch as well, and glistening under my hall light. He looks dangerously dark, intimidating as hell, when he glares into my eyes before raising an expectant eyebrow.

With a long breath in, my tits rise, catching his attention until I drag my fingers into my mouth, collecting saliva to rub sloppily against my lips before circling each nipple.

If he's going to watch me get off, I'm going to put on the best damn show possible. His body clenches, the muscles across his chest tightening when I pluck them into hard nubs.

"Do you like this? Like watching me?"

He doesn't answer, his greedy gaze eating up everything I'm throwing at him. My fingers go back in my mouth, intending to mark trails all over my body that I want his tongue to eventually follow.

He swears under his breath again, loosening his tie and dragging it from his neck. As if he's rewarding me with a strip tease of his own or getting ready to make good on his promise to fuck me however I want. I cannot decide, but both have a great outcome.

I make a ridiculous sound of gagging myself, the way I had around his cock. His chest rises and falls as he struggles out of his jacket, tossing it on the floor alongside his tie.

Once I've collected more spit than I need, I drag it down my body, skimming past my clit to wet both sides of my already soaked lips. My shoulder blades dig into the wall when I angle my body outward, widening my stance to give him a better view.

"Fuck, mamita"

Fuck is right when I spread my pussy lips apart, exposing my tight clit. His cock looks ready to explode, dripping steadily onto the floor and mixing with the puddle of my fluid. How he's able to maintain control is a marvel, awarding winning once I plunge two fingers into my pussy and moan.

"Oooh, so hot and soft."

His hand flies to his cock to tug on it violently, painfully hard to either come and get it over with or to stave off his orgasm. My slow and gentle exploratory strokes are counter to his harsh pulls, grunting loudly each time.

"So ready to be filled up. Ready to milk that thick cock of all its cum."

A solitary finger swirls over my clit, ensuring I don't block the view as the other two dive in and out, drawing strings of wetness that I show him before plunging back inside.

That sends him over the edge, suddenly, the front of his shirt off. Buttons fly in the air to land in droplets all over the floor before he squats to capture my legs in his air and shoves into me.

"Marco!"

His name is a shriek of surprise and delight. His cock, on the other hand, is an assault on my delicate pussy, shoving in with one thrust and hammering away like a madman.

My legs dangle uselessly over his elbows, almost like I fantasized, as I clutch his sweaty shoulders to hold on for leverage. With the wall at my back and the beast of a wild man at my front, I'm not at risk of falling. I let gravity work for me, my body weight sinking further onto his cock and getting a combined moan from both of us.

"You drive me mad."

He grunts in my ear, his breath heavy against my neck as he fucks me harder and faster than before. My teasing has unleashed the fury by how he's consuming me.

There's nothing gentle or playful about this. He's straight-up fucking as if both our lives depend on it. I'm convinced they do. For us, all of humanity, and definitely my neighbors, who've got to hear my screams of passion roaring out of my body.

"Oh please, Marco . . . please!"

I gasp, my legs quivering from the intensity. My nails dig

into the flesh of his broad shoulders as I beg for more. Each plea draws him further into his animalistic state.

The intensity of our fucking is borderline violent, yet I thrive in the ferocity of it. My body craves the friction, needing to be filled by his manhood in every possible way. The slap of our bodies connecting, the wetness that escapes from deep within me, and the slurping sound we make drives me insane with lust.

"I'm coming! I'm. . .ahhh."

The familiar tightening in my core is blistering and overwhelming, throwing me over the edge with a rapidness I'm unprepared for. His name leaves my lips once more, bouncing on his cock to meet his thrusts in desperate need as I spill all over him.

His hands grip my ass roughly, his fingers digging into my soft flesh as he shoves into me. The crudeness of his touch heightens my orgasm.

"I'm coming," he growls, his voice rough with exertion and need.

I can feel it in the way his body shudders, with each thrust getting reckless and loose. The wall behind me trembles with each violent impact, the rawness of our primal urges echoing through the room, marking our territory as we fuck with abandon and as we peak together.

His face moves out, inches from mine, to see the sweat pouring down his temples. It's sexy seeing how hard he's working to please me, to get off to our passionate fucking.

But the look in his dark eyes, the reflection of myself, muzzled and sated, catches me by surprise. The corners of my mouth lift in a slight smile until he kisses me softly, gently, and almost apologetically.

My arms loosen around his neck, slick with sweat, as his skin glistens under the shine of the overhead light. His hips continue pumping, slower and lingering, riding out both our climaxes while we catch our breath.

"Was I too rough? I don't know what came over me, I just had t—"

I cup both sides of his defined cheeks in my hands, my thumbs stroking the wet skin until one rests on his lips, which he kisses.

"That was perfect."

He gives me a shy grin.

"Congratulations on your promotion, mamita."

15

MARCO

The sky is a muted grey, hinting at a storm brewing in the coming hours. It adds to the anxious edge I woke up with after coming home exceptionally late from Victoria's place. I tossed and turned in the few hours that remained until I said fuck it and decided to come in earlier than planned.

My truck's headlights cast long shadows across the empty parking garage as I turn off the ignition and gather my things. Stepping out and slinging my backpack over one shoulder, the crisp morning air nips at my skin, contrasting with the warm cocoon of the car. The quiet of the predawn hour lends a surreal feeling to the start of what I know will be a hectic day.

Heading across the garage and into my building, the elevator pings with a loudness I usually never notice. The empty corridors echo with the soft click of my dress shoes, a sound usually lost in the noisy environment that always bustles with activity. It's the calm before the storm, both literally and figuratively. It's the official launch day for our new app, months in the making that has consumed countless hours of my life for the better part of the year.

Bypassing the deserted break room where I usually grab my first coffee of the day, I decide against it. My stomach is already tight with nerves, and caffeine won't help. Instead, I crave the clear-headedness that the morning's quiet offers a few moments before the rest of the team arrives and the day kicks into high gear.

Once in my office, I power up my computer and dive straight into last night's updates. The team made several last-minute tweaks in response to feedback from Wednesday's soft launch, and it's my job to ensure that all these changes are meticulously documented.

The software and documentation must be flawless and crystal clear to avoid any hitches during today's broader rollout. The records are also critical for auditors to review why specific changes were made.

As I update the files, my thoughts drift to Victoria. Last night was supposed to be a fancy celebration at Mastro's for her promotion. However, true to her spontaneous nature, Victoria had other ideas.

Chinga madre.

Did she have other ideas.

My cock twitches as I relive last night in my head, the same as I did when lying in bed, staring at the ceiling and willing sleep to come. It was warranted. The intensity released tension both of us collected from a difficult workweek. That red dress and red lipstick, *fuck.*

If she had it out, I would have drawn it on my dick and made her lick it off. She's so sexual, stunning, and provocative that all I want to do is stick my cock in her warm, wet hole the second I see her.

With her, there is not only the promise of a voracious sexual appetite to keep up with me but a mischievousness in her actions and a grounding of something more in her eyes. It's an intoxicating combination. The fact that she loves to role-play and loves to submit to me is icing on the fucking cake.

She has yet to tell me no, seemingly game for anything I want to do and try. How the fuck did I get so lucky? After going another round in her bedroom, she splayed out on her bed wearing her make-up and silver heels—I couldn't help myself.

In my post nut clarity, I was quick to lock her up this weekend. Spewing out plans for tonight and this weekend—how much fun we're going to have together.

Fuck, my dick is at full staff under my desk. With no one else in the office yet, I could handle business in the bathroom, something I never do.

"Hey, lover boy."

"Jesus."

I jump in my seat, my heart racing and my hands clenching into fists, when I look up to see a sneaky Maddie standing in the doorway of my office.

"Warn a guy next time."

She shrugs, her arms loaded with her personal belongings, which seem like an unnecessary number of bags. Even her oversized coat and scarf around her neck seem excessive for the cooler temperatures outside.

"Whatever. You ready for today?"

The cheer in her voice suddenly grates against my nerves, and I'm not exactly sure why. Maybe it's because I have a hard-on I'm trying to hide, or perhaps because she interrupted my daydreaming about Victoria. Either way, I'm annoyed.

"I don't know, Maddie. What could be so special about today? I wonder." I let the sarcasm fly, payback for scaring the shit out of me. "Of course, we're ready."

"What crawled up your ass and died? Are things going bad with our vendor? You know the conflict of interest you haven't told our boss about."

Her emphasis on certain words is as unnecessary as her armful of crap rattling when she does finger quotes.

"He knows. I told him already."

I respond with a smug smile. Also, grateful that this whole conversation, also unnecessary, is making my cock shrivel up. Her face twists into suspicion, unwilling to let this drop despite it being super fucking early, and I'm trying to forgo coffee, which now seems like a terrible decision.

"You did not!" she accuses, seemingly ready to threaten me again if I don't tell him.

I already did, just not the part I'm involved with said vendor. If that happened, then I'd have to bring up the mistress he has, and it would go downhill from there.

"I did."

"When did you tell him?"

Her eyes narrow, casting daggers as I chuckle.

"Wednesday night."

I lean back in my chair now that my erection is completely gone, inverted into my body at this rate. My hands thread behind my head, watching the emotions change on her face.

"When he was heading out for a later dinner with you know who."

She gasps and looks away down the hallway before stepping into my office.

"Are you sure?" she whispers as though there was someone else on the floor who could hear us gossiping.

"Pretty sure."

"Well, if you're right, they are back together."

She glances over her shoulder, yet another unnecessary action.

"Do you know she called Wednesday? She was screaming at him on the phone. I could hear everything."

I raise an eyebrow at her, feigning ignorance. Unwilling to

add anything more since I don't know and don't care what my boss does outside the office.

"Marco, don't you see? If he was going to see her that night, they're not broken up like she threatened, and I must continue hiding everything from his wife."

There's a tremor in her voice. Suddenly, everything makes sense. She comes in early to finish her work, but not because of us knuckleheads, as she said before, but because she has to play referee all day between the two women.

"That sucks."

I cut her some slack. That's too much nonsense for her to deal with, regardless of what he pays her. That kind of stress and drama is why I prefer my office to be right by the bullpen. We're insulated from the politics.

No one likes talking to the engineers and programmers since we tend to speak in technicalities far above their heads. The trivial crap like this doesn't hold our interest the way testing results do.

Maddie huffs, shaking her head.

"Yeah, it does," she mutters, turning away from me and heading towards the door. "Anyway, you have about half an hour before he's in here breathing down your neck about the launch. Consider yourself warned. Good luck today."

I glance at the time on my computer and then set a timer on my phone to be in the bullpen during his planned arrival. It's not that I want to avoid him. I just need to maintain a clear head, and having him in here fretting about the launch is the last thing I want.

Hiding away with the team ensures he'll keep it brief if he does enter like he did the other night. Some of the programmers will be in by then, and I want to go over the game plan before we kick off.

Knowing it will be a crazy day for me, I text Victoria.

> Last night keeps running through my mind. I'm looking forward to spending the wknd with you.

Given the early hour, I don't expect a reply, but I smile at her picture, now my phone's wallpaper. If Maddie saw it, she'd give me hell for sure. But seeing Victoria's beautiful face whenever I want is a gift. Taking a few more minutes to stare at her picture, I lock my phone and set it aside to resume working.

Twenty-five minutes fly by with finalizing the pre-launch documentation before the critical employees on my team stream in. By the time my avoid-Preston-alarm goes off, I'm sitting in a chair next to one of my programmers shooting the shit.

He's barely had a chance to log in when the light squeal of the double doors sounds, with all of us avoiding the person whose eyes are boring into the back of me. I don't bother turning, instead pointing to my employee's screen to ask a question. He gets the hint and plays along until the door sounds again, and the boss is gone.

"Uh . . ."

He glances over his shoulder, nervousness bouncing his knee. I lean away from the screen.

"Don't worry about him. He's just checking in."

With a finality in my tone, we both get to work. My laptop is set up next to his workstation so I can monitor issues the second they arise. The early morning slips away as the sun rises, casting golden light across the workstations by the windows.

The room slowly fills up until it almost feels like a typical workday. Someone brings donuts, and another brings in bags of candy to ensure a slow drip of sugar and adrenaline to get us through the day.

As the launch time nears, someone in the room starts the

countdown clock on the big screen at the front. There's a high vibration of nerves, excitement, and panic as the number reduces.

All eyes stare at the screen while they chant the numbers in unison until a bang goes off at the end, signaling we're live. To my surprise, streamers shoot from little machines at the front and multi-color confetti peppers the room.

I glance over to see Maddie and Preston barely shoved into the room, watching all the excitement, and I mouth a silent "thank you" to her, knowing the shooting streamer and confetti was her doing.

She gives me a thumbs up before pulling on Preston's shirt sleeve as if to drag him out with her. I couldn't be more grateful to focus on the task at hand and catch up with him later.

A collective breath holds the room in tense anticipation as everyone's gaze locks onto the big screen displaying live metrics. Then, numbers climb rapidly on the display, and user accounts populate with each passing second.

Hoots and hollers fill the air as we celebrate the successful translation of our hard work into our real-world application.

The room buzzes with activity as the team tackles the influx of data and user feedback. Keyboards clack, conversations hum, and laughter breaks through occasionally—all signs of the well-synced team we are.

Lunchtime blurs into the afternoon, unnoticed amidst the continuous work. Tables are cluttered with pizza, wings, and soda, pushing aside the remaining hours old documents and candy.

My focus remains unbroken as I update, fix, and confirm every detail is documented. I collaborate with various teams and surf shoulder as support cases roll in to be solved and sent back out. The hours race by, my back aches from hunching over, and my eyes burn from staring at screens all day.

Late afternoon sneaks up on me when I glance at the clock

next to the big screen and realize it's after 4 p.m. I haven't checked my phone all day. Everyone in my life knows how important this day is, but should something have happened, and I don't have it—that's not good.

Hurrying back to my office, I see the missed text and call notifications across the room. In quick strides, I snatch my phone from my desk, unlock it, and see one missed text from my mom wishing me good luck.

But my eyes zero in on all the missed communication from Victoria. My heart rate spikes as I call her, and I am unwilling to waste time going through the message when I need to hear her voice.

"Marco, thank God . . . called . . . "

"Vic? Are you okay?"

Panic tinges my voice as she answers. Background noise muffles her response, and I strain to hear her.

"Where are you?"

"On my way to a meeting. In Miami."

Her voice comes through, tinged with panic and urgency.

"What? You're in Miami? Like right now?"

I'm stunned, looking at my wristwatch and working backward on the time it takes to get there from Houston. A couple of hours is all, but this is still a shock.

"My boss showed up first thing this morning and said they need me there ASAP for a planning commission meeting. Turns out the commissioner is a friend of my family, and my boss thought I could help smooth things over."

The disappointment sinks like a stone in my stomach. She'll miss tonight and possibly our first weekend together. All the plans we discussed are going up in flames because she's been called out of town with virtually no notice.

Is this what it will be like? What will we become? The thoughts strike fear into my chest, but I clamp down on it, keeping my voice even for her sake.

"Oh, wow, that's sudden. Are you okay with this?"

She exhales sharply, the sound filled with stress. The fast click of her heels makes it seem like she's running through the airport.

"I mean, I have to be, right? This is what I agreed to. This is my project now, and being out of state while it's in the planning stages is not going to work."

There's a hesitancy in her tone that I don't like. Is she holding something back? Having more to tell and choosing not to.

"I understand that, but are you okay with this?"

Are we okay?

That's another question I don't voice when I need to. The launch has me on an exhausting high, going successfully just one room away. Yet here I am facing a genuine threat that what I want more is slowly slipping through my fingers, and there's not a damn thing I can do about it.

My gut tightens more.

Sitting suddenly feels too passive.

I need to stand, pace, and think about how to close the sudden gap between us. One foot planted on solid footing from last night, with echoes of her screaming my name and her pussy clamping down on my dick. A crack in the ground beneath me widens with every second that passes. My other foot is on crumbling Miami ground, eroding beneath it as the crevice grows.

"Vic?"

The noisy airport fades away. The closing of the door and a brief instruction to her meeting place are communicated to someone before she resumes our call.

"It's more complicated than I thought it would be."

Neutral response. I hate how this fucking feels, I need more assurance for her, and they are slow to come.

"Mamita, talk to me."

A long sigh rumbles through the phone, sending my hand plunging into my hair as I pace the five steps it takes to cross my 12 x 12 office.

"I feel awful, Marco. Awful about canceling our plans for this weekend. I'm so sorry. Awful for being anxious about this trip. Nervous about meeting with a family friend that I haven't seen in years and knowing he'll bring up my family tragedy, possibly in front of a team of people. I know we talked this all out, and I thought I'd have a little more time to prepare my answers for questions I'm sure to be asked, but I didn't, and I don't. It's just a lot of things, and honestly, I'm getting tired of myself talking about them."

Relief ripples through my body. These are things I can help with. *Will* help her with. It's not the end of us. It's confronting her past without the support she has here, *in me.*

"One, don't apologize to me. I fully understand, so let's take that off the table."

Another sigh.

"I appreciate that and promise to make it up to you."

She has no clue how much she'll be making this up to me. Flashes of her bent over, at my mercy, as I lick her from hole to hole, dance in my mind.

"Don't worry about that. And yeah, he might do that if he's not a professional or a gentleman. Some guys are idiots. No, let me correct that. Some *people* are idiots, thinking they are entitled to know your personal life, but they aren't. So practiced a canned response, like you said, and then delivered it with a smile. Honestly, mamita, this is good practice for all the interviews and engagements where nosey people will ask questions they don't need to ask."

"Yes, that is true."

I can almost hear the wheels turning in that beautiful head of hers. If she were here, I'd hug the shit out of her. I suppress the groan rising from the disappointment of not seeing her this weekend.

"Like part of media training. You did have that, right?"

"I did," she admits, confirming we're moving out of the emotions and into the logic side of the conversation where I work best. "You're right. I just need to use my training, regardless of who it is—family friend or not.

"But Marco, I'm not sure how often these types of emergencies will come up, you know? Especially until I move here, which seems like it will be sooner rather than later. I thought we'd have more time. But now I'm not so sure."

Her words offer a semblance of resolve, but her lingering note catches my attention. A slight falter that doesn't entirely hide the uncertainty beneath my calm demeanor.

My pacing halts.

I lean against the cool glass window, looking out but not seeing anything. Her admission renews my fear and frustration.

"What exactly are you saying, Vic?"

"I don't know, Marco. I really don't."

She hesitates. In that pause, a chill sweeps through me.

"Are you ending things?"

My palm presses against the glass, needing something rigid and stable to ground me as my fear of losing her grows.

My brain chants no.

My cock chants no.

My fucking heart is being slowly and meticulously ripped from my chest, too weak to protest.

"No, I don't know. Maybe?"

The raw honesty in her voice pierces me, throwing my still-beating heart on the floor and trampling it. My breath comes out in pants, like hers, when she ran across the airport. The chill that swept over me is settling into the corners of my body, freezing me from the inside out.

I struggle with what to say.

My mind breaks into different directions, wanting her to fight for me as I've been fighting for her. This seems too easy to give up, too fleeting, having known her less than a week.

What happened to fate bringing us together? Would she be such a cruel mistress to have our worlds collide and then explode, never to be the same again? I'm sounding so fucking pathetic. But aren't all poets sad?

"I have to go."

Her voice lacks its usual warmth, clouded with stress and hurriedness, demonstrating she's not lying.

It's challenging to keep my tone level, not scream into the phone how unfair this is to her, me, and to us, not demand that she say we're okay and that we'll figure this out. All the promises we made last night were already broken the first day she was sent to Miami.

"Good luck, Victoria. You got this."

My words lack conviction, not in her ability to do the job but in my ability to pep talk her up as it doesn't matter anymore. I've seemingly overplayed my hand with her.

"Call me after, okay? Just to tell me how it went."

"Will do. And Marco, thanks for everything."

That stings—sharper than I expect.

Not goodbye but fucking gratitude.

It can't get much worse.

As the line disconnects, the silence of my office is loud. Almost blaring in my ears as I walk to my chair and collapse into it.

What the fuck just happened? How do two people feel what we feel and just end it? How do I walk back all the feelings I started having for her? What the hell do I do now?

So many damn questions without answers. And the one that has them is now several states away, stepping into her new life in a new city without me.

"Chinga madre."

16

VICTORIA

The early morning mist hangs low over the cemetery, cloaking the gravestones in an eerie calm as I navigate the familiar paths until I find him. The grass is softer than I remember, springing back against my heels as I stand here, staring at the stone that bears his name.

It's been years since I've allowed myself to be here, in this quiet corner of Miami that houses more than just his body but a chunk of my soul. The sky is a sweeping canvas of grays, and it is as if even the heavens can't decide whether to rain or shine today.

"Hey, Vic."

The words are foreign, falling clumsily out of my mouth in the sereneness of the cemetery. My voice is a lone sound amidst the whispers of the swaying trees above and the distant city sounds.

"It's been a while."

I drop to my knees, not caring about the dew soaking through my black pants. My fingers trace his name's cold, hard letters, sweeping away the dust and grime collected over the years, indicating that my parents don't visit him. Mama would never let his stone look this aged and filthy.

"I guess Mama and Papi don't come here either."

The words are bitter on my tongue. A statement I shouldn't have made aloud, yet bringing an odd awareness of a truth they cannot hide. They've abandoned him too.

The vase at the bottom of his tombstone was a special order. A custom add-on the cemetery sold them when making burial arrangements, reaching toward the sky and waiting for a bouquet of plastic flowers that will never come.

"I'm back in Miami. Back home. For good."

My confession stabs at my mouth, shards of glass slicing my tongue with too much damn meaning.

"Can you believe it?"

A bitter, hollow laugh escapes me. The irony of life and fate is a fickle bitch. Dragging me back to where it all started, forcing me to face my demons all at once.

"I guess you might have seen it coming before I did."

My hand presses into the cold granite, needing to feel him even though he's always with me.

"I have a secret, Vic. I'm seeing someone. His name is Marco."

My throat tightens around his name.

"He calls me by your nickname. He doesn't know that, though. It caught me by surprise when he first said it. I was going to correct him, but then . . . I liked it."

I shrug, my hand falling away. Tears well out of nowhere as I sit at the private confessional of my brother, the closest I'll ever come to speaking with an angel.

"He's wonderful. You'd like him. But I think I ruined it. I sort of ended things with him. I didn't call him last night. He called and texted me this morning, but I wasn't ready. I needed to talk to you. Did you bring us together? Is he right that it was fate? Or was it you? You and I share a nickname, whispered from the man you brought to me. Is that it? Is that how I'd know? And his last name is Delgado, like our old elementary school. Isn't that more than a coincidence? How can that not be fate? Or is it you? I don't know. I'm beyond confused."

The tears careen down my cheeks in steady streams, trying to deal with the heavy weight sitting on my chest ever since the plane's wheels touched down yesterday.

"I was thinking you could send me a sign, but maybe you already have. Maybe he's the sign."

I dig into my bag for tissues, pulling out several to wipe my face and blow my nose.

"He really good to me. Good for me. He's strong, kind, calm, and peaceful, especially for his age."

I chuckle with a strange lightness when I think about our first meeting.

"He's even close to his family. He helps his mama on Saturdays at my farmer's market. They are so cute together, and she's how a mama should be. . . . but I guess you see all that."

The wind picks up, sending a cascade of leaves to fall around me. It's like he can hear me, sending me the sign I requested a moment ago, confirming he's with me.

"But Marco's not the secret."

I clear my throat, feeling a lump forming as my true confession balances on the tip of my tongue. There's no going back when I say what I've come to say. Yet, it's exactly what's holding me back. What is contributing to the feelings I'm struggling with.

"I'm scared, Vic."

I inch closer to his headstone, laying my forehead against the cold stone. I need to touch something other than the wet ground to prepare for what I will say next.

"I'm angry. Furious at you. You left me alone. You promised you'd always be here, but then you weren't. You're not. And I hate you for it. I hate being an only child. I hate living your dream. And I hate that I hate you."

My voice cracks, overwhelmed by years of unspoken truths bearing down on me.

Anguish-filled tears fall into the grass, mixing with the morning dew to become indistinguishable. I lick my cracked lips, needing to unload everything that is eating me alive.

"If I don't keep this anger and hold onto my hatred, then what will I have left? Acceptance? Peace? Happiness? How can I feel all those things when you can't? How can I find peace in this void you left behind? Happiness feels like a betrayal to your memory. If I move on and let myself feel joy again, it feels like I'm forgetting you, like I'm saying it's okay that you left me here. But it's not okay. It never will be. How can I embrace life when you can't? It's cruel, Vic. It's tearing me apart."

I sob into the used tissues, absolutely gutted by my truthful admission. The guilt and torment suffocating the air from my lungs. The sky decides to weep with me, sending misty rain over my huddled figure, curling closer to the only thing left of my brother—a stone bearing his name.

"My anger and hatred have been a shield, a part of me for so long, protecting me from the pain, but I don't want to be this way anymore. I can't be. But I don't know how to change. How to let go and how to forgive."

I reach for my purse, which is damp from the falling rain. With it now protected from the elements on my lap, I pull out more tissues. With my head bent and my face toward the ground, I wipe the tears and mist from my skin.

"How do I forgive them? And their well-intentioned hopes that I could somehow replace you. Be you."

Silence settles around me, heavy and suffocating, as the rain intensifies, blurring the world into indistinct shapes. My clothes cling coldly to my skin, but the chill is nothing compared to the ice in my veins as my therapy session continues.

"I've treated them so poorly over the years. I mean. . ."

It was as hard as a confession as telling him of my hatred.

"Vic, don't you see how much damage I've done?"

Their loss was compounded. First, losing Vic and then me. I didn't see it until now. The revelation is crushing. The clarity brought by this visit is devastating, stealing my breath away.

"How much pain I've caused? Will they even forgive me?"

I breathe in the earthy scent of fresh, fallen rain—a balm of connectivity, anchoring me to him at the very place I've avoided for years. The wind blows harder, carrying my questions up to the heavens and whisking away the deep-seated emotions that have grown veins around my heart, decaying them in the earth around me.

"Can you forgive me?

Fresh tears threaten to fall as my whispered words join my guilt, which is floating up to him. His answer is immediate. A sudden chirping of birds fills my ears, drawing my attention toward the sky.

Raindrops fall in a steady stream onto my face as a flock of feathered friends swoop low to gather on the tree above his gravestone. Their loud singing is almost rejoicing in the dreary weather across the quiet graveyard.

Their chorus is joyful, almost ethereal—a distinct sign that there is life in the face of darkness, light on a gloomy day. Their melodies pierce the heaviness of my heart, nudging me to see the world as it is—a gift to experience.

Fully and deeply.

Pain and grief, mourning and despair.

Forgiveness and healing.

It's all available to me if I want it. In choosing forgiveness, I can find the freedom to live fully, not as Vic's replacement, but as myself—Victoria, whoever she is and wants to be.

In awe, my gaze fixes on his carved name, tracing the letters and releasing a choked sob.

"Thank you."

We drive down the familiar street, the one I left so long ago, towards the house that's a vault of memories and buried tensions. As my driver creeps past childhood friend's homes, my pulse picks up, and waves of anxiety crash over me. Keeping the divine download and internal peace from Vic's forgiveness at the cemetery is hard to hold onto.

My fight-or-flight instinct kicks in faster than I can comprehend. The old way of keeping myself protected, reinforcing the walls around my heart with my misplaced blame, seems easier and more comfortable to navigate. Managing the new terrain of vulnerability and forgiveness for my parents has my skin crawling, wishing I could ask the driver to turn around and take me far, far away from here.

The fragility of the new and undoubtedly awkward encounter ahead threatens to crack under the weight of my fears. What if this is all a mistake? What if they won't listen or, even worse, forgive me?

It's been years, easily more than a decade, since I've been home and stepped foot in this vault of my childhood.

What if everything is the same? Same décor, same furniture, same everything? Would it send me back to the day we got the news of his passing? What if they changed it all? How would I feel then? Would I blame them? Wouldn't I want to wipe away the past if it were me? Haven't I essentially done that by moving away and never coming back?

I'd clear out the rooms of my lost children—one to the grim reaper, the other to the other deadly sins—wrath and pride.

When the car stops at the curb, the driver knows to wait,

and I stare up at the building that holds it all. Sunny memories of playing in the fort in the backyard where my brother broke his arm, many Halloweens racing from house to house to see who could collect the most candy. Christmases filled with presents my parents couldn't always afford.

From the outside, the house looks the same as it always did. The shutters flanking both sides of every window look like cheerful eyes, with the sunlight suddenly breaking through the stormy clouds, painting the old bricks in warm hues.

It's as if Vic is sending a comforting light to guide me on my mission, pausing the rain long enough for me to slip inside.

I exit the car and reach the front gate before my eyes begin to well up again—the ghosts of the past whisper through the well-tended bushes and manicured lawn. Memories of my parents doing yard work and gardening hit me with a fierceness that makes my chest ache.

With a deep breath, I push the gate open. Its familiar creak is a sound from a lifelong pause. Each step up the walkway tightens the knot in my stomach. The familiarity is a comfort and a curse. I'm almost at the front door when it swings open unexpectedly.

My mama stands there, frozen, her hand still on the door. Her eyes widen in shock, taking in my soaked appearance, the clinging, damp clothes, and the hair plastered to my face. For a moment, she's speechless. Her mouth opens slightly at the ghost of her daughter coming to visit.

Soft curls of salt-and-pepper hair frame her face, shorter than she used to wear it, more of a bob now. The years of sun and stress have settled into fine lines that crinkle around her eyes and cluster around her lips.

Her skin, once the deep olive of our Cuban heritage, has faded slightly, looking paler as if she's been avoiding the sun. At just over five feet, she's always been diminutive, but her presence fills the doorway. Her posture is straight and unyielding, as if wielded in armor.

Her dress is simple—a patterned house dress she's likely worn to do her morning chores. Yet it's immaculate, ironed to a crispness that speaks to her perennial pride in appearance. Some things are the same, others are slightly different, and both disturb me equally.

My heart thunders against my ribs. My hand tightens over my purse strap, and I fight the urge to run, as I have always done. But this time, I must be brave and make long-overdue amends.

Armed with the strength of Victor's forgiveness and the beautiful experience at his tombstone, I step forward.

"Hi, Mama."

My tone is shaky, matching the shaking of my body beneath the layers of wet clothes. She blinks away her surprise, snapping out of her shock to close the distance and envelop me in a tight embrace.

"Victoria?"

Her voice cracks over my name, disbelief coating each syllable and making it almost painful to utter aloud. Her light fragrance fills my senses, bringing sharp, crisp, bittersweet, and overwhelming memories. Her arms tighten as if I'm a figment of her imagination that will disappear if she doesn't hold on.

"Victoria," she repeats as a sob loosens from her body.

My hands lightly cup her back, more instinct than intention, holding her as she cries. Years of hurt and pain I caused are flooding out of her, shaking her small frame.

I clutch her tighter, comforting her with a back rub. She pulls back, catching my hands and holding me at arm's length, ignoring the wetness that seeped from me onto the front of her clothes.

Her eyes scan my face as if searching for the girl she once

knew. Concern furrows her eyebrows and deepens her frown. The air between us is thick with anticipation and hesitation.

I slowly raise my shoulder—not exactly a shrug, but more an admission of guilt for how I left things when we spoke earlier this week.

"I came . . . my company flew me out here. My, uh, project is being moved up."

Breaking the tension with talk of work brought a bit of relief. The topic is neutral enough to tamp down my anxiety. Tears streaked her cheeks, a fragile smile forming.

"Oh, my girl. Let's get you dried off and warmed up."

Her hand threads through mine, a gentle tug that has me numbly following behind as she leads me into the house. The details of the house are a blur as she ushers me through the familiar yet different interior.

The house smells fresh of polished wood and a faint hint of jasmine. This scent is comforting and gives the place a homey feel, but it is disorienting because I don't remember it smelling like this in my youth.

We reach the bathroom, where I catch sight of myself. My mascara is smeared, black tracks down my cheeks, and my lipstick is cakey, the color matching the splotches on my cheek. I look downright frightful.

She pulls a washcloth from the linen closet behind me, turns on the hot water, and hands it to me.

"Why don't I find you some dry clothes while you get cleaned? I'll make some tea."

Her voice is softer now, coated in a maternal warmth that I've suddenly missed despite resenting it on the telephone. She moves to the open doorway, pausing and looking back at me.

"Or would you prefer coffee?"

"Tea would be great, thanks."

I manage a weak smile as I watch her nod, seemingly satisfied with her ability to tend to me in some small way.

"I'll go find your father. He'll be so delighted to see you."

She leaves, and her retreating footsteps make me sigh harshly. Alone, I stare at my reflection in the bathroom mirror. The face looking back is mine, yet the eyes seem to belong to someone else—a girl who long ago grieved, mourned, and cried countless times, wishing everything was different.

After dropping the cloth into the water, I ring it out and scrub the remnants of the morning. Wet hair clings to my neck, adding to my physical discomfort of being in drenched clothes that didn't bother me until now.

The washcloth is stained from my black mascara and bright lipstick. A fleeting thought of hoping it's not for guest's use, as I have completely ruined it, passes through my mind when she appears in the doorway. Her arms are full of brightly colored fabrics, with a tentative smile.

"See if any of these work. If not, I'll search for something else."

"I'm sure they will be fine."

My assurance falls flat when her smile falters, but when she catches the door handle in her grip and closes it, I'm shut off from another awkward exchange.

The pile of clothes is unloaded onto the counter, and I toss the destroyed washcloth into the trash can by the toilet. A grunt loosens from my throat as I work to remove my wet clothes, which have become tighter and more restrictive.

Once I'm stripped, I grab a towel from the closet, dry off, wind it around my hair, and fasten it to the top of my head.

"You've got to be kidding me."

The clothes she brought were mine years and years ago when I went to school in town. Emblazoned with my alma mater, I tug on the snug sweatshirt and matching pants, wondering why in the world she still has them.

Having been washed about a thousand times, the cotton broke down in the process and is soft against my skin.

Something about seeing myself in the mirror, wearing clothes a size too small and from over a decade ago, transports me back to living in this house. Fighting over the bathroom when Vic hogged it to get ready for a date flood back to me.

The intensity hits me in the chest, whisking my breath away until I'm gripping the counter to stop the wave of tears threatening to fall again.

"*Mija* did those work or . . ."

She knocks on the door before slowly opening it as I turn away, pretending to fumble with the pants leg to avoid her seeing my glistening eyes.

"They still fit. What I wouldn't give for my old clothes to fit."

The wistfulness in her voice is surprising, as if that's her greatest wish rather than having her beloved son back. I breathe through my mouth, unwilling to sniffle and let her know I'm overcome with emotion and struggling to keep it together.

"Yeah, they're good."

I sneakily wipe my eyes and turn to address her.

"Why do you still have them?"

Her features wrinkle with a confused look until my papi pops into the doorway. Taller than my mom, with a perpetual tan and longer, more white-than-black hair, he looks happy to see me.

Deep lines shoot from the sides of his dark eyes, and more age spots dot his skin, but otherwise, his warm expression is of love and delight.

"There's my girl! Come hug your old papi."

I can't help but smile, relief coating my insides. Things with Papi were always easier. He held the same expectations for me as my mama, but they were more silent. A glance, a nod, or simply a murmured hum of agreement. He didn't push, prod, or raise his voice like she had. Then again, maybe that was the way with fathers and daughters.

"Hi, Papi."

The words rush out with the air from my body. My mama dutifully steps aside in the small bathroom, forcing me to squeeze by and step into his welcoming arms.

"This is a wonderful surprise. Your mama told me the good news. Congratulations."

He kisses the top of my head. Temporarily setting aside my worry, I close my eyes and breathe in the safety and security he's always represented. I knew he loved me, although he rarely said it.

"Thanks."

I slowly untangle myself from him, standing between them, which makes me uncomfortable. Being boxed in within the small space, I sidestep into the hallway beside him.

"It's the culmination of everything I've been working for."

His face softens, pride filling his weathered features.

"I know you'll do great things, Victoria. Always have."

His compliment falls short by about several years. I fidget on my feet, once again fighting the desire to run out the front door. The air is thick with unspoken words until my mama breaks the tension and busily gathers my rain-soaked clothes.

"Let me take these. We'll get them washed and dried. Are these grass stains?"

My lips roll together, unwilling to tell them where I was—at least not yet. When my gaze moves past Papi, down the hallway to my old bedroom, she pushes past me, murmuring under her breath.

His hand catches under my elbow, turning my attention away from my old sanctuary to guide me toward the kitchen. As we move through the rooms, I survey everything and note the changes—a new set of curtains, photographs I don't recognize, and fresh paint in what used to be a dingy corner. Everything feels both intimately known and unsettlingly different.

A ripple of dislike tears through me. How dare they change

anything at all. As quickly as I have that thought, logic prevails. It's their house to do as they see fit. How many times have I overhauled my life over the years? Why shouldn't they?

We settle at the kitchen table, surrounded by the same floral wallpaper and plastic green plants that are typical décor from twenty years ago. It eases my anxiety that this room has remained the most unchanged.

Mama places the tea kettle and a tray of cookies on the table with a slightly too loud clatter, her hands trembling slightly.

She's as unhinged by my sudden appearance as I am. Then she disappears to the laundry room, working on the grass stains until the washing machine begins.

Waiting for her, I pour the tea into the awaiting cup and snag a cookie, my first food of the day. My stomach has been in knots since I touched down.

It started with the rushed conversation with Marco, who was unsure where we stood, visiting with the family friend who wanted to reminisce about my brother, and then this morning. It's been one continuous bout of anxiety and nauseousness simmering under the surface.

"Tell me about the project."

Leaning forward, setting his elbows on the table, Papi breaks the ice.

"What's this big development going to be?"

"It's a high-rise in Brickell. Mixed-use. Residential units and some commercial spaces. Sustainable building materials, green spaces . . . "

My voice trails off when Mama walks into the kitchen, a reflective look in her eyes—cautious, maybe worried. My focus drifts to the real reason I'm here.

"Brickell, huh?"

His whistle comes with a raise in his eyebrows.

"That's an expensive area."

My fingers curl around my cup as I take a sip. The bitterness is strong and grounding, seeping into the chill of my soul as I mentally prepare for what I need to say.

Worn, weary, and with a flickering hope, I start.

"I went to see Victor this morning."

My mama gasps, leaning heavily against the counter on the far side of the kitchen. Papi sits back in his chair, dragging his arms from the table to disappear in his lap. My nerves flutter, and my hands remain around the warm ceramic seeping into my chilled fingers.

"It's how I got the grass stains."

Building a bridge back to them over years of distance and pain, they remain silent and curious. Our grief wasn't openly shared amongst us. Each of us went about it our own way. We didn't talk about Victor much or mention his name despite him being the most important person in our family.

"I didn't bring him flowers."

Why does that seem important?

I have no idea.

Then again, they hadn't either. Not for a long time, judging by what I saw today.

"I talked to him about you two."

My tongue slides across my dry lips, waiting for either to react as my gaze darts between them. Papi is the first to respond —a throat clearing and then a shared look with my mom.

"Oh?"

I nod, grateful for his attempt to join me on the bridge I'm building, even if this is starting terribly.

"To be honest, I told him I hated him."

Mama makes a choking sound, her hand flying up to cover her mouth.

Papi grimaces.

Both remain quiet.

"I did. I finally admitted it to him. But honestly, he must

have already known. I mean, in Heaven, don't they see and know all?"

"I suppose so."

It's not a question I need answered, but I understand when Papi does. He adjusts in his chair, clearly uneasy with my bluntness, as I am.

"I told, or rather explained, that if I stopped hating him. Stopped being angry for him leaving and me having to take his place—"

"Mija."

Mama finally contributes to the conversation by saying my name, which is spoken with disappointment and surprise. I hold up my hand, needing to get everything out before their questions—or, in this case, their emotions—get messier.

"Please let me explain."

I gaze up at the ceiling, fighting the tears that are trying to flood my eyes. Thankfully, they wait a few moments until I regain control.

"It was easier on me to carry this rage for him, *at him* and the both of you."

My gaze drops back to them, finding a strength I didn't know lingered in the roots of my pain.

"Being angry at Victor made it easier to bear the pain of losing him. If I was angry, filled my heart with hatred, then I didn't have to bear the burden of my grief and guilt. I didn't have to fully mourn him, feel gutted by the anguish. I used that burning fury to stay away, blaming you both as easily as I blamed him. It's what drove me away and kept me away, thinking I was right and avoiding the pain and the mourning that comes with a loss of this magnitude."

Papi's eyes glisten, a sheen of unshed tears making them brighter. Mama wipes her cheek with the back of her hand, visibly struggling to maintain her composure.

"But in that anger."

My voice cracks on the tears not yet streaming down my face.

He pulls a napkin from the holder and hands it to me. Mama moves closer, not to sit at the table with us but to stand beside him. Her hand falls to his shoulder, and he covers it to comfort her.

"I pushed you both away. I took on his dreams and ambitions, not because I wanted to but because I thought that was what was expected of me. To replace him. And I resented you for it."

The room is so quiet you can hear the soft ticking of the kitchen clock. Outside, a gentle rain begins to tap rhythmically against the window, darkening the once-sunny room. I dab the napkin against my cheeks, collecting more tears.

"We never wanted you to feel like you had to replace him, Mija."

Mama's soft voice breaks the silence. Tightening the knots of regret in my stomach.

"But I did feel that way. Every achievement, every step forward in his field . . . it felt like I was erasing myself and drawing him in my place."

Papi's hand slips from hers when he leans forward. He rests his elbows on the edge of the table again, his posture slumping in sorrow and defeat.

"We were just trying to cope, Victoria. We lost him too. Parents aren't meant to bury their children. It's the worst kind of nightmare you can imagine."

Watery tracks caress smoothly down his face, unabashed at the grief that remains an unending well within him.

"And you . . . seeing you follow in his footsteps . . . it was comforting. I didn't realize then what you were doing and why you were doing it. Maybe I, or we, foolishly believed you changed your mind, and it became what you wanted. But we never stopped to think how heavy that burden might have been for you."

I nod, swallowing the lump in my throat and taking another sip of tea.

"We were proud. You were always so willful and a bit wild," she continues, pulling a chair beside him. "When you said you wanted to stay home for school, to become what he could not, we thought you were doing it for the right reasons. You were doing it for yourself. Maybe we were naïve to have believed you."

I had forgotten that part, having rewritten history in my mind to fit my narrative over the years. But hearing my words now transports me back to that day, years and years ago when I proclaimed in the living room that I wasn't going out of state for school and was staying close to home.

It strikes me like a thunderbolt.

"You're right. I did say that, but I don't think I meant it. I thought you'd protest and talk me out of it. But when you didn't, I stubbornly wanted to prove you wrong. That I could become him, a better version of him, and finally earn your love."

Her sob is muffled by her hands covering her face. Papi's arm encircles her shoulders, pulling her close.

"You've always had our love. You're our little girl. You don't have to do anything to have it."

Now, I'm sobbing into the napkin, pulling more from the container as their realization hits home. Carves through the thick stone walls around my heart and shatters them into pieces—the emotions I've avoided feeling for so long spewing forth and burning me from the inside out.

I want to vomit, disgusted with myself for holding onto this unnecessary reservoir for too many damn years. It didn't serve me at all, didn't protect me from anything, and only caused deeper and greater pain to all three of us.

"I'm so sorry."

Hot tears blur my vision, streaking down my face so quickly that they pool at my chin and collect on the wood-grain table. When she strokes my arm up and down, Mama's gentle touch burns understanding and comfort into it.

"Victoria."

I shake my head at my papi's singular word, holding up a finger to indicate that I need a minute. The room falls silent, the voices in my head screaming even louder.

It's suffocating and taxing, physically and emotionally, albeit necessary. I wad up my used napkins, grabbing more to blow my nose and wipe my face.

"I told him . . . Victor, today. That's why I went to the cemetery. To talk to him. Ask him for help. To tell him . . . and to tell you both . . . that I want to forgive him. And I want to forgive you. And I need your forgiveness, too."

My nose burns with snot, my throat is raw with emotions, and the tears continue to fall.

"Forgiveness for the years I stayed away, for the pain I caused, for how I treated you, and for adding to our loss. You lost him and then me. It wasn't fair."

"We don't have anything to forgive, Mija."

Sadness clogs her words, but her hand continues to soothe me.

"You were coping, just like us. We all handle grief differently."

The kitchen feels smaller somehow, as if our shared grief and confessions have drawn us closer, shrinking the distance created by years of miscommunication and silent suffering. A rumble of thunder echoes in the distance, the weather playing its part here, too, as it did at the cemetery.

It is as if Mother Nature is grumbling her unhappiness alongside ours as if fate is intervening and bringing all this together.

Fate.

My heart clenches for another reason—Marco.

He would believe in how this is evolving, even call it fate, and convince me that this situation with my parents was meant to play out this way.

"Victoria, whatever you need to heal, whatever steps you need to take . . . we're here for you. Always."

I meet his gaze, seeing the sincerity and hurt that mirror my own. The words are a salve, yet they reopen wounds of missed opportunities and unspoken words. Mama's hand slides down my arm, reaching for my hand and squeezing it tightly.

"We've made mistakes, Mija. Maybe we wanted to keep a piece of him alive so badly that we pushed you into his shadow. We never meant to."

"I know, Mama. I know you didn't mean to. And I pushed myself there, too. I thought it would hurt less if I could just be more like him . . . But it only made the pain different, distant but deep."

Her admission cracks something open in me—a dam holding back years of resentment and longing for acknowledgment.

"We understand that now," Papi clarifies, nodding slowly and wiping his eyes with the back of his hand. "I'm glad you went to see Victor. It's been far too long since we were out there ourselves."

My mama nods, withdrawing her hand.

"It's tough, Mija. We try to stay strong and visit his grave, but the days are short and the months even shorter until we realize it's been too long. As with you, we feel the guilt of our neglect at attending to his gravesite. It's not always easy to clear the stone of the one you love and miss."

Not that they needed to admit their long overdue absence that I witnessed firsthand earlier this morning. Yet her explanation clarifies things. I never thought it was easy, having seen it more as their duty. Also, I never considered the emotional toll it takes on them. The misunderstandings are too numerous to count.

Holding on to the past and its hurtful memories is suffocating the life out of us. This reunion is heavy and laden with grief for the present standing of our relationships, as much as it is a fault of the past hurt and blame.

I sigh, the weight of everything making me feel absolutely exhausted.

"Can we . . . is there any way we can move forward? I don't know how, but I think that's what he would've wanted—for us to be a family again."

Papi nods, his smile sparking genuine happiness. Mama's face falls in relief, collecting napkins to clean her cheeks from all the fallen tears.

"Yes, he would."

His hand stretches across the table in search of mine. I slip my palm against his, the love and acceptance I've craved for years seeping into my flesh and deeper into my being. Mama collects my other hand, then Papi's, until we are clasped hands and form a unity circle around the table.

Then, from my mama's lips come words I haven't heard in over two decades, echoing from a time long before my departure. She begins the unity prayer, meaning more profound than any sermon I remember from my youth.

The prayer transcends the space between us, a bridge to memories, lost time, and Victor himself. As she speaks, wispy raindrops tap against the kitchen windows, tears from my brother in Heaven layered in a reunion of forgiveness, love, and faith.

Now, I want to ask another for forgiveness for everything I've put him through in the last couple of days.

Marco.

17

MARCO

Saturday morning finds me hauntingly alert, my gaze fixed on my phone, half-expecting it to spring to life with Victoria's name. She had promised to call after her meeting, but the night passed in silence.

I spent the evening far longer in the office than necessary, monitoring our app's successful metrics from the programmers' pit. Officially, it was the data keeping my ass planted in the seat, but in truth, I was waiting for her—hoping for a text, a call, any indication that I crossed her mind.

Maddie occasionally checked in to see if the team needed anything, then wandered out when she was mostly ignored by those too entrenched in the work to respond.

Preston hovered over me at the end of the evening, anxious for the final numbers to relay to Dawson, who, according to Maddie, was surprisingly pleased with our success. As he should be, his investment and, more specifically, this app paid off in spades for his firm.

As the programmers trickled out, the office slowly emptied, leaving me in a dark, quiet room that was anything but peaceful. By midnight, my eyes burned from the relentless glow of screens, and I had not heard from Victoria. Reality set in.

I drove home clinging to feeble hope that maybe she had fallen asleep, overwhelmed by the day. Such an excuse felt hollow, making me feel even hollower. Victoria isn't one to simply forget, especially not with the seriousness of our recent conversations hanging between us. Now, barely five hours later, I'm up, unrested and unsettled.

My emotions are all over the place, from worried something tragic happened to her to anger for being so love-sick and foolish about her to sadness when thinking we're over. Even the long run along the bayou did little to calm my racing thoughts.

With last night's success behind me, the future largely uncertain, I return to the familiar—Mom and the farmer's market. A week ago today, everything looked brighter and seemed more hopeful, especially when I stumbled upon beautiful Victoria and her pomegranate lesson.

We bloomed into something wonderful and wilted even faster. Now, with the market buzzing around me and Mom fluttering around the booth arranging various things, the numbness inside me grows.

"Mijo, you're quiet this morning."

She hands me pill bottles that double as mini first aid kids, filled with bandages, ointment, tweezers, and other stuff.

"Is everything okay?"

I have never been one to talk to my mom about my love life, so I hesitate. I could have talked to Maddie last night but was more preoccupied with hoping for Victoria's call or text. I failed to do so, so now I'm left with her—not ideal, but maybe it's worth a shot.

"I don't know, Mom."

She motions for me to stack the bottles in a little pyramid for the children to take as they pass by while I talk.

"How did you know Dad was serious about you or that you were even serious about him?"

She pauses, her wise eyes studying me as she cuts stickers from a roll to sprinkle over the tablecloth she's straightened a hundred times.

"Your father had me smitten the moment I saw him, scared me to death with how fast I liked him."

Her smile is soft and genuine as she looks down, thinking about that moment.

"It was just a feeling, strong and sturdy. He asked me out, and from that night, I didn't want to be apart."

Her eyes are rimmed with warmth when she looks at me, the love shining through after all these years.

"I still don't. Of course, we like our space. He has his hobbies, and I have mine."

She gestures to the market around us, conceding that it takes work to keep it going.

"But it works for us. That's important."

"But what if it's all one-sided?"

The bottles topple as I attempt a taller pyramid, revealing my inner turmoil through the clumsy stacking. Mom rounds the table, her chuckle lightening the mood. She steadies the pyramid with ease.

"Is this concerning a certain someone that you met right here?"

"I guess I just expected more," I admit, aligning pamphlets alongside the pyramid. "We talked about getting serious."

"Communications, especially in new relationships, can be tricky."

She tapes down a corner of the tablecloth, securing our setup.

"If she's dealing with a lot, it might just be bad timing."

I nod, absorbing her advice while smoothing out another

stack of pamphlets. An attempt to keep my mind from racing down the same roads last night by keeping my hands busy.

"But shouldn't she want to reach out, especially if things are tough?"

"That'd be ideal."

She finishes taping and steps back to assess the booth.

"But everyone handles stress differently. Maybe she needs space to sort things out alone. Some people talk about their problems, like we do in our family, mijo. Others bottle them up and wait till they explode to deal with them."

The night Victoria fell apart in my arms speaks to the latter. I'm a talker, and she's a bottle stuffer. Will that make this even harder to work out?

"That makes sense."

I pause, picking up a sticker of a cartoon tooth detailing why brushing is important, and put it back down.

"I just don't want to feel like I'm the only one trying."

"Then give it a little time."

She places her hands on my shoulder, giving it a reassuring squeeze.

"See if she comes around. If it's meant to be, it will find a way. Just don't lose yourself while you're waiting."

Patience isn't my strongest suit. Does not blowing up her phone count as patience? I mean, I only texted her twice last night and once this morning, just asking her to let me know she's safe. That's not too much, right?

"She's moving to Miami."

Having moved back to cutting the stickers, Mom pauses and looks straight at me. Her expression says it all.

"Tell me more."

Her tone is as cautious as her expression. Both make me more uneasy and flat-out worried, as if she's going to take back all she said as easily as Victoria's taking back all we were.

She sets her scissors on the table and drags a chair over to settle in for a longer story. I move to the other side of the table to join her and not be overheard by everyone walking by.

"She's being promoted, but it comes with a job transfer back to her hometown. It came as a complete shock, and it's too good for her to turn down."

I pick up the chair from the other side of her booth, setting it close as more of my love life spills out. The light aroma of freshly brewed coffee floats our way, making my stomach harder as that was the excuse I used last week to flee Mom.

Instead of sharing another smoothie with my girl and walking the rows of booths she obviously loves, I'm sitting in a cold folding chair seeking love advice. The irony is not lost on me.

"It's a huge opportunity for her, and I fully support her. We even discussed trying to long-distance date."

My mom's eyebrows pinch together in thought.

"I mean, we haven't worked out the logistics and all, but that's how we feel about each other. Or at least that's how I thought we both felt."

My knee starts bouncing with the same restless energy that caused my fitful sleep and fourteen-mile run before picking Mom up this morning.

"That's a big change, mijo. And an even bigger commitment."

She resumes her task, picking up the scissors but slower and more deliberate. Her movements seem to mirror her thoughts—measured and careful.

"Yeah."

My hand automatically reaches for a pill bottle stowed in a box under the table to fidget with it.

"We talked about getting serious, and now this."

She places more cut stickers on the table, making me wonder if she needs to keep her hands occupied too.

"It will be harder than finding someone local. And you both have to want it."

"I know."

She is not subtle in her words. I know she liked Victoria, but hearing her now, I get that she dislikes the distance as much as I do.

"That's what is messing me up. That's why she hasn't reached out. If this will not work, just be straight up with me."

"Maybe she's just overwhelmed," Mom counters, her tone softening while defending Victoria. She's getting me so mixed up that I don't know whose side she's on. "Trying to figure out her feelings about all this change."

I nod, though the gesture feels hollow. Her insight strikes a chord, though. Victoria has been overwhelmed by the promotion and the upheaval of moving back home—factors that had her spilling years of pent-up trauma the other night.

Trauma that isn't just a figment of my initial jests but a deep-seated reality that continues to haunt her. I've done everything I could to support her thus far, and I'd go even further if only she'd reach out.

"Could be. I don't want to push too hard, but I had half a mind to fly out there and track her down. Who knows, maybe I'd fall in love with Miami and move there."

I toss the pill bottle in the air, catching it without realizing she stopped cutting her strip of stickers to stare at me.

"You are not serious, are you?"

The emotion in her voice is heavy, laden with panic when I gaze over at her.

"Yes. No. I don't know."

I shrug and sigh.

Moving away is my mom's greatest fear, yet I want to live my life for me, possibly Victoria, if she'll have me.

"Eventually, I am moving out of Houston. I've never lived anywhere else and want to see the world. And not just two weeks a year when I can escape the office long enough to grab a vacation."

She sinks into her chair, defeated, with a quiet nod.

"I know we've kept you here, mijo. You should have been in Silicon Valley."

She still pronounces it "cone" after I've corrected her a dozen times.

"I needed you at the time. With your father's illness and the girls—"

"What?" I chuck the bottle in the box and shift her direction. "Dad's sick?"

Panic races over my body, seeping into my veins and vibrating them under my skin. The sounds of the market coming to life around us as the morning fog wears off are too loud and intrusive, cutting off her words.

"Say that again?"

I shake my head to clear my ears.

"*Was*, Marco. Was sick."

She leans closer, talking louder and I'm still shocked, trying to catch up.

"It's why we didn't want you to accept that job in California. If your father wouldn't have made it . . ."

Tears simmer at the rim of her eyes. I sit at the edge of my seat, taking her hand in mine to comfort her. She hesitates, squeezing my hand as if gathering strength from the contact.

"Your father had a serious heart condition, Marco. We found out right when you got offers, all out of state. It was a tough time, and we didn't know how to tell you. We thought—"

"Thought what?"

My voice rises, not out of anger but sheer bewilderment.

"That it was better if you didn't know. If you stayed focused on finding something local for your career. We didn't want to burden you more than we already had by asking you to stay in town."

She looks down, her voice a whisper.

"We thought it would help."

"Help?" I repeat, my mind racing. "Mom, I could have been here, I could have—"

"No, mijo."

She cuts me off, her gaze firm yet filled with regret.

"You already gave up your big life and dream job. If I could go back and do things differently, I would. I trapped you here by our fears."

A feather could knock me over. I lean back in my chair, the cold hard metal leaching into my ass as I process her confession. Resentment quickly fills my mind at the secrets kept from me.

"Do the girls know?"

"No, they don't. Please don't tell them."

Her request is valid. I don't want them to know, either. My head hangs lower, studying the concrete before me as thoughts run in and out of my mind in rapid succession.

What if I had gone? Would I have lived my dream life? Would I have advanced further in my career?

It would have been amazing. Then again.

Would they have made it without me? What would have happened if Dad's condition worsened and I wasn't here to support them? Would I have regretted not being closer to home? What if he did pass away and I wasn't there to say goodbye?

My stomach turns.

These questions twist inside me, churning up a storm of 'what-ifs' that I can't possibly answer. I glance up at my mom, who's watching me with a worried expression. Her own tears haven't fallen and been wiped away.

"And now? Is he okay?"

I need confirmation and assurance that despite the secrecy, everything is indeed alright. I look at her without really seeing her. My mind races through every interaction with Dad over the past few years, searching for any sign that he wasn't well.

Although he's always been the type to keep his struggles to himself, he's never one to complain or show weakness.

"Thankfully, your father responded well to treatment. It's been a long journey, but he's much better now. The risk isn't gone but manageable through medicine, exercise, and diet."

Remembering a joke I made once when I caught him eating a salad. He'd quipped that salads were for rabbits, yet there he was, fork in hand. When I teased him, he simply shrugged and said he'd gotten it wrong.

"That's good," I murmur more to myself than her.

"It was his request to me. He didn't want to bother you, yet he also needed you around to be the man of the house in case he couldn't. He wanted to protect you, all of you kids. We were wrong, but it was out of love that we didn't want you to see him as a shadow of his former self if the illness took hold and his heart gave out."

I blow out a harsh breath, interweaving my hands to place behind my head as the shock still sends me down bad roads I don't want to be on.

"I hope you can see it in your heart to forgive us, mijo."

She pats my knee, needing to connect with me as I'm turned away.

"We kept you from your dreams, and you made the best of it."

Had I?

Is living five miles from my home, sitting at a farmers' market with my mom, and working almost eighty hours a week the best of it? No, not by a long shot. If Dad is doing better, Mom and my sisters are okay, why am I here?

My mind is spinning over Victoria, but now I don't know what's up. Realizing she's still waiting for my response, I turn to look at her. The shock, resentment, and tension are easing away into confusion and discontentment. By sharing an old piece of earth-shattering news, she's managed to shatter it again.

"I get it, I guess. But if something's going on, I need to know. I deserve to know. No matter what."

She pats my knee again before withdrawing her hand as someone approaches the booth.

"Agree."

With that, she stands, greeting the lady with a child running full speed toward her, ready to talk about shots. I take it as an opportunity to slip away and text Victoria again, hoping she'll respond, even though my pragmatic part knows she won't.

Whatever's happening between us, I still want you.

Call me.

Please!

The clank of metal echoes through the gym, each clang punctuating the raging torrent of my thoughts. My hands grip the barbell with a ferocity that turns my knuckles white, channeling the swirling emotions into each lift. With every heave of the weights, I shove away the heaviness settling in my chest.

First Victoria.

Then my parents.

This is my last-ditch effort to calm my racing fucking thoughts under the strain of physical exertion. Each rep becomes a battle against the iron and the betrayal that festers like a wound in my heart. Victoria lied to me. My parents lied to me. Who the fuck can I trust then?

Deceived by both. My decisions were influenced by lies I

didn't tell nor consented to. The revelation that my father's illness, hidden from me to keep me close to home, taints every memory, every choice I thought was my own. The same as making all those plans with her, promising to try a long-distance relationship, all up in flames.

Although the events are years apart and have nothing to do with each other, they twist and turn until they form one massive betrayal, fueling my aggressive workout. As I push through the emotions burning a hole in my heart, every rep, set, and drop of sweat is an attempt to reclaim the truth I never knew.

The physical pain is straightforward and simple. Punishing my body when I want to be punishing them, hurting them as I hurt now. The thought makes me sick, and I instantly dismiss it. The last thing I want to do is hurt the people I care about. I'm just struggling with how easily they hurt me, trying to make up for the chaos in my mind.

Out of the corner of my eye, I spot Giovanni striding towards me. His presence is unmistakable. Even in his crowded gym, Giovanni, the owner and a bodybuilding champion, commands attention, nodding at fellow gymgoers he passes with familiar ease.

His muscular frame is not just sculpted but a testament to disciplined craftsmanship. Each muscle group is sharply defined by his various competitions.

"Marco, man, you're killing it today, huh?"

His deep voice booms over the music blaring from the sound system overhead. His good looks draw women's attention effortlessly here, yet he pays no mind—too wrapped up in his lawyer lady.

"Yeah, something like that."

I'm covered in sweat, running everywhere when I run a towel over my face. He offers his hand, and I clasp it in a firm handshake. He doesn't care that I'm drenched when he hugs me and claps my back.

"It's good to see you. I keep missing you," he mutters before releasing me.

His hands plant on his hips, forcing his lats to each side. In his compression tank, he appears wing-like.

"You've definitely not missed a workout."

My eyes roam all over him, seeing muscles bulging everywhere. Without needing encouragement, he's typical Gio—breaking out into different poses to showcase his hard work.

"You're just showing off now."

"Yeah, I am."

His smile is easy when he hits the last one. The veins in his neck bulge from strain, and his muscles pop out. He releases it and slaps my stomach with the back of his hand.

"Someone's been missing ab day."

I look down at my flat stomach, despite having a desk job and working a shit ton of hours, before meeting his gaze. A playful gleam in his lightens my bad mood a bit.

"Shut the fuck up," I grunt, loosening the straps on my gloves, debating if I should continue or be done for the day.

"The gym looks good. Packed for a Saturday afternoon."

His smiles brighten. His eyes sweeping the room and returning to mine.

"Yeah, it's all good. Helps that the owner is this hot stud that keeps winning competitions. You know I'm starting a bodybuilding competition of my own."

If I hadn't been staring at him, I'd have missed the sudden changing of his stance, his chest pushing out in pride. It's been remarkable what he's done for himself. Literally built this place from the ground up, adding more classes, specialized equipment, nutritionists, and trainers.

Every time I step in here, there is something or someone new. I'm proud of him and a tad bit jealous. I'd love to have something I call my own. From idea to installation, an app, business, or just something.

"I didn't know that. Congratulations."

He's practically levitating with how happy he is.

"Just local for now, but who knows, maybe one day it will be nationwide, "The Giovanni Classic."

He does air quotes around the words before they fall to his bulky sides.

"You should come out, prep with us, compete like you did earlier this year. All weight classes will be there."

I chuckle at his offer. Sure, I work out, run, meal prep, and prioritize my health, but I don't have the time for bodybuilding and competing right now.

"Nah, man. I'm good for now. But I'll come the day you have it. Support you and this place."

"Days," he corrects, causing me to nod. "Now you want to tell me why you're trying to break my shit? I heard the clanging from the other side of the gym."

His arms fold over his chest while he assesses me with a knowing look. I hesitate, but with everything bubbling up, it would be nice to get someone else's opinion—someone objective.

"Just . . . stuff, you know. Family, and . . ."

A second later, he's racking my barbells as if they weigh nothing and essentially ending my workout without my permission. Swooping down, he grabs my duffle and water bottle and raises his eyebrow at me.

"Let's talk in my office."

Without waiting for my reply, he's already strolling off with my bag thrown over his shoulder. Like the celebrity he is of this place, he shakes hands with people he knows, fixes the position of someone doing a lat pulldown, and yells for his employees to bring him two "Hulks."

Whatever that is, all while leaving me to follow in his

famous wake like a desperate entourage guy. By the time I get to his all-glass office with sight lines to the farthest corner of the gym, I've pulled off my gloves and see my bag sitting in a guest chair.

When looking in, his office isn't much more private than the gym floor, yet people can't overhear our conversation. I appreciate his discretion and thinking of me, as I was too preoccupied with the shit going on to worry about others listening to my problems.

"This is a sweet setup you have."

His technology rivals mine. Three monitors are on the corner of his desk, and a television behind him is permanently muted. The tv shows a slideshow of progress photos and testimonials.

"Yeah, it's good. Good for business too."

He's humble, about to say more when his eyes move past me to over my shoulder. His employee asks for us to pardon her interruption long enough to place two giant colorful drinks in front of each of us before catching the door for it to swing closed.

"Don't mind how they look."

They look like Slurpees in rotating green and purple. They twist around the inside of the clear cup, which has a piece of pineapple stuck to the edge.

"High protein, low sugar, good for post-workout."

He grabs the fruit and tosses it before drinking a quarter of it. It's not exactly what I usually do for post-workout, but I trust Gio to know what's best since this is his life and livelihood. I follow his lead, getting the fruit out of the way before drinking some of it.

"Wow, this is—"

"Amazing, right? I have this lady who has degrees in nutrition and public health, formulating drinks and supplements for us. This is her latest creation and our bestseller. I'd love to offer these as a line in stores, but you can only get them here right now."

That bit of envy is turning into full-blown jealousy with all his different endeavors. It's inspiring and irritating at the same time.

"That's great! If anyone can do it, it's you, Gio. Everything you touch is turning into gold."

His head is already shaking before I can finish, his brown hair rather messy, as if he's growing it out or something.

"Nah, man. It's all about having the right support. You know I'm locked in with my woman, and she has all these ideas. It's been great. Really good."

That genuine smile is back, and his expression softens when discussing Kacie. I've seen her around and them interacting, and their love is easy to see. She's more serious and reserved, seeming to balance him out. Another thing that makes me fucking envious about him—his relationship.

"That's awesome."

'Yeah, it is. But what's up with you?"

His chair squeaks under his weight as he leans back and repeatedly crushes a hand grip to build his forearm strength.

"I got some news about my dad that knocked me sideways."

His eyebrows raise in concern, and I'm quick to tap it back down.

"He's mostly fine now, but long story short. I could have worked for one of the tech firms in Silicon Valley a few years back, but my parents had asked me to find something local instead. They didn't tell me why at the time, but it turns out he was near dying."

Giovanni's reaction is immediate and intense. His hand drops from his grip, and a frown creases his forehead as he absorbs the information. He leans forward, resting his elbows on the desk, bridging the gap between us with his empathy.

"Man, that's rough. Parents can be protective, sometimes

too much. They think they know what's best for us when they don't."

His tone hints at something else, as if talking more about himself than my situation, leaving me to wonder if there is more to it.

"It sucks they didn't give you the full picture."

"I feel betrayed, but then it's in the past, so now what do I do? I've already started my career here, my apartment, my friends. . ."

I gesture to him, and he meets it with a nod.

"It's too late to start over."

"It's a hard pill to swallow, finding out things could have been different if you'd known the whole story. It makes you wonder about the 'what ifs,' doesn't it?"

Giovanni's eyes hold mine, ensuring I understand he's not just hearing me. He's listening and empathizing. It's a rare quality these days, which is probably why he's so popular here. He genuinely cares.

"You've got every right to be pissed. I would be too. But it's never too late to start over. I see people transform their lives every day here. It's the most inspiring place to be in this gym."

He points out his windows, and my gaze follows. I see people working out, not the transformative experience he's talking about. I'm missing something.

"Is he fine now? Your father?"

"Mostly."

I return to look at him, curious about where this is going.

"Why?"

"Well, knowing what you know now, could you still get on with one of those tech companies? Aren't they always hiring?"

He's providing perspective, but I'm not sure I'm ready for it, and it's hard to accept that the opportunity is still out there.

"I guess?"

He drums his fingers on the desk, the rhythm irritating.

"I guess? That's not the confidence I'm used to seeing from you, Marco. If you were advising someone in your shoes, what would you tell them?"

I pause, considering his question. It's easier to dispense advice than apply it to your life.

"I'd tell them to go for it, not to let the past dictate their future."

"Exactly."

Giovanni nods, his agreement punctuated by a decisive clap of his hands.

"Life's too short, man. Your dad's health scare, it's a wake-up call. Not just about him, but about living your life to the fullest, whatever that means to you."

It's not just about the missed job opportunities. It's about the choices I still have.

Choices I've been too hesitant, too fearful to consider.

Victoria comes to mind.

"You think it's not too late?" My voice is low, almost hopeful.

"It's never too late. Look, I started this gym with nothing but a leased corner of a warehouse. Now, look around."

He gestures expansively, pride evident in his posture.

"You make your own 'too late,' Marco."

The conversation shifts slightly as he stands, stretching his arms above his head, his muscles flexing under the fabric of his tank top.

"Besides, the tech world, man, it's always spinning. New startups, new opportunities. You've got the skills. You've got the drive. You need to decide if you're ready to jump back into that world or are content here."

I chew over his words, the gym's blaring music fading into the background as I ponder his outlook. It's a crossroads moment, and Giovanni has made it starkly clear with his straightforward wisdom.

He pops his back, sits down, and grabs his drink to polish it off, but mine is barely touched.

"But there's this woman I've been seeing. Her name is Victoria . . ."

I launch into the rest of the story, how we met, how I helped her company, how this week had been going, and that now she is out of town at her new project and not responding. Slowly losing my fucking mind when Gio suddenly smiles and tosses the empty cup in the trash.

"You're in love, man."

"No," I flat out deny it because love can't happen this quickly.

I strongly like her.

But love isn't even on the table.

Not after a week, even if fate brought us together, which I'm not sharing with him. That kind of talk goes against the bro code, although Gio's not the type of person to judge me anyway for believing in it.

Giovanni chuckles, studying me with a knowing look.

"You don't have to say it to be true, Marco. It's written all over your face whenever you say her name."

I scowl, brushing off his observation.

"It's complicated," I mutter, glancing away, annoyed.

"Isn't it always? But that's what makes it worth it, right? The ups, the downs, the crazy in-betweens. Makes you feel alive."

There is truth to it, a raw, messy truth about human connections that is terrifying and exhilarating.

"You need to figure out what you want, Marco. If she's as amazing as you say, then maybe she's worth the hassle of long distance. But you have to be clear about what you're jumping into, especially with everything else going on in your life. And if she's not responding, that's an answer itself."

I rub my chin, contemplating his advice.

"I guess I just wanted things to be simpler."

"Women are never simple."

Giovanni laughs, the sound echoing in his glass office.

"Simple is for counting macros and meal prepping, not love. Love is supposed to challenge, push, and make you question and fight for what you want. My woman brings out the best in me. She supports me in everything I do and try. She's my soft landing, the reason I love to come home after a long day. There's nothing wrong admitting that to yourself."

I grab my drink, frustrated by this entire day and yesterday, aside from my success at work, which is strongly overshadowed by Victoria.

"Yeah, I just wish she saw it that way."

I'm sulking now, and he's gracious enough to let me. My mind is so confused that I don't know what to do. Even if she called me now, after making me wait almost twenty-four hours, I don't know what I'd say.

"Go after her, man. Or at least clear the air. You don't want to live with 'what-ifs.' See that wall over there."

He points over my shoulder across the gym, and a cynical grunt escapes my throat when I look.

"What does it say?"

"No regrets," I mumble, looking away from the well-placed and ironic mural on the wall to set my cup on his desk.

"That's right. No regrets. You leave everything on the line when you step in here. It's no different with you. You don't want to live in Houston anymore. If you want to chase your tech dreams, and the woman you want is moving to Miami, then move with her. Everyone's working remotely nowadays, so work remotely for your company or those Silicon guys."

He's leaning forward again, his expression more serious than I've ever seen.

"Put it all on the line. That's living with no regrets."

My brows pull together as a flood of possibilities slams into the walls I've built around my life, chipping away at things I thought were fortified. I stare at Giovanni, feeling his words dig deep, stirring up this strange mix of hope and a pang of something else—maybe fear.

"Man, that's... I mean, uh, I don't know if I can..."

His idea isn't just casual talk. It's real and hitting me harder than I want to admit.

His gaze is unflinching, and his muscles flex instinctively when he leans further across the desk.

"Why not? You're single, with no kids, no mortgage, and no business you're running. If you're not going to do it now, then when? You're waiting till you're locked down with every reason to stay put like your parents?"

I open my mouth to counter, but nothing comes out. The truth is, I know he's right.

My reasons?

They're mostly self-imposed, unlike my parents. Mine are built more on a fear of what I don't know than any real obstacles. I blamed Mom and Dad for years for clipping my wings, but now that Gio is presenting me the chance to fly, I'm terrified with no one to blame but myself.

Giovanni nods as if he can see the wheels turning in my head.

"Think about it, man. What's holding you back? Houston's not going anywhere. Your family? They'll understand. And tech? You know it's everywhere, especially in a place like Miami. And me? You'll always have a home here in my gym."

I can feel something sprouting—the idea of living a life that's actually mine. The panic and doubt about disrupting my plans start to shrink, and a sharper fear—of looking back one day and wondering, *"What if?"*—takes its place.

"Yeah," I finally say, feeling hope breaking through. "You might be onto something. I need to think about this ... really think things over."

Giovanni claps his hands together and stands, rounding the

desk with his hand held out. Once our palms connect, he's yanking me out of my chair into a tight hug.

"That's the spirit. Don't rush it, but don't take forever, either. Chances like this? They don't come around every day. Don't miss it because you're too scared to jump."

He releases me slowly, keeping his arm draped over my shoulder. I grab my bag, and we walk out together. My eyes drift over to the mural on the wall.

No regrets.

I've seen that line a thousand times, but now, it feels like it's staring back at me, daring me to actually mean it.

"Thanks, man."

His arm falls from my shoulder to clap me on the back.

"Anytime."

Now that he's free, his staff calls his name, herding him onto other tasks that don't involve being a therapist to me. I leave the gym, and the air outside feels different—cleaner and brighter.

Each step feels lighter, and every breath is more deliberate. Maybe, just maybe, this is the wake-up call I need—a chance to make a life that's mine.

"No regrets."

18

VICTORIA

The familiar hum of the air conditioning battles against the continuing rain batting the windows of my old bedroom. I lie sprawled on my childhood bed, a relic covered in the same floral comforter I picked out when I was twelve.

The walls around me are plastered with my past. Faded posters of Enrique Iglesias, whom I was convinced I would marry, photographs of high school friends, and even some artwork and awards from when my brother was still alive.

When I swung open the door, a potent and poignant wave of nostalgia swept over me after our exhaustive yet transformative conversation. The reunion in the kitchen was long overdue, and the pain and grief were still acute in my heart, yet my flight response was tamed for now.

Seeing my bedroom frozen in time made sense of Mama's odd expression when I commented that she still had the sweatsuit. She had it all and hadn't changed a thing in the years I've been gone. She should have, but I am glad she didn't.

The only addition is a treadmill blocking off access to my desk and parked in front of the television I used to watch telenovelas on. I doubt the small screen even works with all the streaming platforms. It's the only hint of the passage of time and the changes in my family's lives since I moved away.

This room was a sanctuary where I lost myself to my art, designs, and all the wild ideas about my future. Coming back here, immersed in a life that is no longer mine, with the hopes and dreams of yesteryear swirling around me, leaves me breathless. It's suffocating to step back into a world I once envisioned as my reality.

I turn my head to stare at a family photo taken a few years before Victor died. In it, my parents take us to Disneyworld, and we are all smooshed into a ride, wearing mouse ears in various designs. That beautiful, naïve child thought the world was what she made it. She was bold and audacious, creating art that would never see the light of day beyond this house.

If she were here now, would I tell her the truth? Kill her dreams, and then hold her as she sobbed? Or would I let her continue living in her own world, a fantasy land of what-ifs that would never come to fruition?

I don't know. Would it be a fair and just thing to do to tell her what the future holds? Or would it be cruel to extinguish that bright light that would burn bright for a few years more?

"Doesn't matter now."

Reminiscing is getting me nowhere, holding on to the person I claim I don't want to be anymore. The person who cried at her brother's tombstone and then walked into her parent's house like a long-lost ghost. I push up from the bed, sitting on the edge after a long and unexpected nap to take one step toward the person I want to be. One free of bitterness, blame, and guilt.

I search for my phone, needing to call Marco to explain everything to him. I hope he still wants me after my self-imposed punishment derived from my illogical thoughts that I was unworthy of his affection. The hallway is dark, and the glow of the television is the only light at the end. When I see my brother's bedroom door open, it casts a blueish hue over the white walls.

Curiosity getting the better of me, I tip-toe down to his room, peeking inside to see the silhouette of his furniture. The finer details are lost to the shadows as the drapes are drawn and the lights are off.

It's an eerie scene that sweeps over me when I look into the room that my brother used to forbid me from entering. After his passing, you couldn't pay me to go into it. It was a place for Mama to cry and a place haunted by a reality too heinous to live.

The emptiness and silence in this once noisy room kept me up at night, blaring my stereo to fill the silence with my parent's bedroom on the other side of the house. He was studious, his bedroom lamp always burning late into the night, poring over his books or building sketches.

When it became permanently dark, I avoided going down this side of the hallway every day until I didn't even look that way.

I pause at the threshold, the old fear gripping me momentarily before I shake it off and step inside. The room smells faintly of dust and old books, a scent that used to be synonymous with him—studious, quiet, filled with thoughts of his future that would never be.

My hand trembles as I reach for the lamp switch, which clicks loudly in the stillness. The light is dim and hesitant, flickering slightly as if unsure of its purpose after years of disuse. It illuminates the room, showing every dust particle and every faded corner where he once existed, welcoming all the same.

His desk is exactly as he left it. Pens aligned by color, blueprints yellowed and curled at the edges, and his sketchbook lies open, a pencil resting across the last page he worked on—a design for a house, simple yet elegant, perhaps a future family home he would never build.

His handwriting is meticulous, and the margins are doodled with notes and corrections, a physical imprint of his thoughts and dreams.

A lump blocks my throat, tears collect at my lower lids, and a deep sadness carves into my chest. The shadows in the room seem to deepen, echoing the sorrow that fills every corner of my heart until every drop of pain falls into a vast pit of blackness.

It never fills up and never stops collecting my grief, always searching for more mourning and heartbreak to leach from me. The useless sense of loss grips me, refusing to let go until the ache is so palpable that the pain radiates into my limbs.

I sit down in his chair, the leather is cold and unwelcoming. Here, in his sacred space, I feel closer to him than I have in years as if touching the things he touched could bridge the gap death has carved between us.

"Thank you, Vic."

My words are but a rasp in the stagnant air.

Yet he's here with me.

His presence is more known than felt.

"For today, for the hard truths to everyone, and for all the forgiveness you orchestrated."

My hands tremble, and my fingertips brush over his sketch, careful not to smudge the lines and ruin the last piece of work he ever created in this room.

My warmth against the cold surface sends a shudder through my body, choking back a silent sob in his forgotten room.

"I know you're always with us. But I felt you more today than I have in a long time. Is that because of me or you?"

My gaze roams over the familiarity of his things. The bed is made, the covers taut and untouched, a museum exhibit displaying the life of a young adult who will never grow old.

On the walls are posters of architectural marvels he dreamed of someday visiting or building himself. Everything is preserved, a snapshot of hope and ambition frozen in time, untouched by the years of grief that followed his departure.

"Did you plan this all along?"

The enormity of my career changes and how fast they developed could only be heaven-sent.

"Did I get that promotion, or were you bringing me back here to bring us back together as a family again?"

Tears slip down my warm cheeks, and I dash them away with the sleeve of my sweatshirt, careful not to ruin anything of his. But one gets away, a fat teardrop falling onto his sketch, evidence of my existence in his space.

Forever entombed as the dried-out old paper quickly absorbs the wetness.

For a moment, I sit stunned, staring at the grief I hold for him converging with the dreams of his past, collapsing the timelines until they are one.

His sketch, my teardrop—a physical merging of worlds. It's a fusion of my emotional journey with his halted one, a vow that his aspirations won't languish in the shadows of this untouched room.

Instantly, I'm flooded with warmth, my eyes closing as comfort is poured into me. Love fills every fiber of my being and nestles answers to all my questions in my mind until contentment overtakes sorrow.

It wipes away the pit of my pain and guilt until peace and a sprig of hope bloom in the charred ash around it. It's breathtaking and beautiful.

The light transference converting the darkness in me is brilliantly dazzling until it's gone, leaving me in the rapture of a new vision. A ribbon-cutting ceremony in hard hats, standing in front of a stunning sustainable skyscraper with media flashbulbs capturing the event.

In the corner of the building, a bronze plaque affixed to the stone surfacing leading into the lobby, "In Honor of Victor Alejandro Vega. Visionaries perceive beyond sight, guiding with heart and soul."

It's so utterly perfect.

My hands leave his sketch to cover my face as I start to cry. My shoulders shake, the sharp ache unclenching the stronghold loss and sadness have had on my heart.

Relief cuts through my emotions as the illuminated world he showed me fades. The lingering vision is imprinted in my mind and soul forever.

Using my sweatshirt to dab my eyes, I open them to the dim room before me, the grandeur of the skyscraper evaporating.

"It would be my honor, Vic."

Taking the best of what he was and the best of who I am, I make this vow to both of us.

With a deep, shuddering breath, I stand, leaving the lamp on as a silent promise to him and the last gift he gave me.

A vision forward.

My attempts to reach Marco by phone and text have not been answered. Panic and worry gnaw at my gut, eating away at the same area my family's forgiveness just healed.

The urgency to resolve our differences propels me onto a red-eye flight back to Houston. Armed with nothing but my purse and cell phone, I leave my family home and belongings in my hotel room.

The flight is a blur, fueled by tasteless airport coffee and anxious thoughts churning through my mind. As soon as we land, I barely wait for the seatbelt sign to dim before I grab my purse from under the seat and dash down the aisle, soliciting obnoxious comments that I would holler at selfish travelers like me.

They don't comprehend that I'm having a movie-worthy moment, the grand gesture every great love story deserves as I dash through the vast place to the awaiting exit.

The early morning chill hits me as I run out of the terminal, catching the ride I ordered and rehearsing what I'll say to Marco as I wait. The car pulls up, and I immediately give the driver directions to my place, urging him to take the quickest route.

I make several phone calls, apologizing and lying in equal parts until I secure the necessary information. Passing it on to the driver, he changes routes and heads to Marco's apartment.

As we arrive, dawn breaks out over the horizon, the sky painted in dusty pinks and light purples. It's stunning, something I'll appreciate more another day as I yank on the door, and it's locked up tight.

My heart pounds in my chest, and worry in my mind, trying to figure out how to get in. I try his phone again, my stomach plummeting with the endless ringing until his voicemail picks up for the zillionth time.

I mill about the fancy entrance, my mind flipping through various scenarios and settling on waiting for someone, anyone, to exit so I can slip in. Gripping my phone tighter, my purse barely slung over my shoulder, and I begin to pace.

Typing, deleting, and re-typing another text message until the door unexpectedly opens. I'm about to run to catch it when I skid to a stop, my borrowed sneakers from my mama slipping on the pavement in time to lock eyes with Marco.

There he is, looking as though he's been wrestled from sleep, his hair tousled and eyes bleary but widening in surprise at the sight of me.

Earbuds blare music loud enough for me to hear, his

athletic shirt and shorts hinting at him heading out for a workout. Yet, fate intervened, stopping him and bringing me to this exact moment for our lives to intersect again.

He called it fate.

I'm now convinced it's my brother.

With all the last-minute travel, the slightly delayed flight, and somehow arriving earlier than the posted arrival time and racing here, I could have been two minutes late, and I would have missed him. There's no reasonable explanation other than Victor.

"Victoria?"

He pulls the buds from his ears, clicking the button to shut them off before dropping them in his pocket.

"What—how—?"

"I couldn't wait," I cut in, the urgency in my voice matching the racing of my thoughts. Everything I had practiced now flies out of my brain, leaving an empty, wordless mind.

"I had to see you, to talk, to apologize to . . . I don't know where to start."

"You're here?"

He's stunned.

I am too.

This is the most impulsive thing I've ever done—a throwback to the girl who would dream of a whimsical life as an artist is my motivation.

"I am."

I step towards him, and he steps back.

Not a good start.

We're more miles apart now than when I was in Miami.

"How do you know where I live?"

His bewildered look moves from me to his building and back as if physically asking the same question. I clench my teeth, panic-stricken, to admit to my wild behavior that got me here, in front of him. Having enough troubles between us, lying isn't helping, so I shoot him straight.

"I may have called Ross."

"Ross?"

His head shakes, adding more confusion, but at least he's entertaining me on the sidewalk in his quiet neighborhood.

"Who's that?"

"Ross from the farmer's market? The guy who I was talking to when we met."

"Ah, the one checking you out while discussing pomegranates."

My eyes narrow when I detect a hint of jealousy, which I usually detest. In this situation, I realize he's saying that because of how he feels about me. This rash decision to come here is not a total loss, from the sound of it.

"He wasn't checking me out," I protest, and he grunts in disagreement, his arms crossing over his chest to gaze down his nose at me.

"He's married! Whatever, it doesn't matter. I called him, saying I needed your mama's number, and he—"

"You called my mom?"

His eyebrows dart up, his voice clouding with disbelief and something else. It's getting thorny between us already. I haven't even gotten to the tough stuff yet.

"Okay, in my defense, you weren't picking up or answering your text messages . . . I was desperate."

His jaw shifts, clenching and unclenching, and I decided to tell him the rest. Put it all out there and see how he reacts.

"I called and said I needed to see you in person because the fix for my company failed, and it was an emergency. She may or may not be calling you worried because she couldn't reach you either. And I may or may not need to report that you're alive when I get to your apartment. Which I should do now..."

I point my finger at him and flash an apologetic smile to his stoic face.

"You got my mom involved?"

His tone is so incredulous that I cringe, fidgeting in the neon pink and green New Balances that clash with my Hurricanes sweatsuit. His mind seems stuck on the fact I called his mom when I have so much more to tell him.

"You're unbelievable. This is . . ."

He turns away, his hands entwining behind his head as he gazes at the morning sky. If Victor could give me a solid from Heaven, now is the time.

I wait a few seconds to see if angels will swoop down and help me. When that doesn't happen, I follow him as he mumbles to himself something about no regrets.

"Marco, I'm sorry."

I touch his back, and he stills but doesn't turn around. Something about this makes it easier to face him without facing him.

"I messed up. *I was* messed up."

Long seconds pass, filled with the sounds of the city waking to life around us. My fingertips remain on him, feeling the breath move in and out of his body, the only indication he's alive and hearing me.

"I went to see Victor."

That gets him to turn around, and my fingers fall away with the heat from his body still penetrating them. His expression locks in sympathy when he rubs his forehead, struggling with what to say or not say.

"I saw . . . saw my parents too."

His gaze roams over me, taking in my appearance as if looking for something until he finally speaks.

"Are you okay?"

Three little words break the dam holding everything in. The last twenty-four hours burst and tears form and fall so fast that it shocks me. Without hesitation, he pulls me into a tight embrace. The impact is so heartfelt and comforting that I let loose, bawling. I've gone years without crying, and now it seems to be all I can do around him.

"Vic."

His words are thick with compassion, causing me to sob harder. Three letters I share with my brother, passing from Marco's lips after everything that's happened, are too many.

"Let's get inside. No one needs to see you like this."

The last thing I care about is how I look. Yet Marco's protective nature is kicking in, and I don't fight it. Even bad bitches need to be cuddled. He shuffles me to the side of his body, tucks me under his arm, and walks us to the door I was magically wishing and wanting to open.

With a touch of his fob, it clicks, and he ushers me through. Wrapped in his protective care and not wanting to make a scene in front of his neighbors, my crying slows.

Once in the privacy of the elevator, he jabs the button to the fifth floor and remains quiet, allowing me time to compose myself. More tears are swiped away on the sleeves of this sweatshirt, which will need to be washed or burned after all the weeping, snot, and airport germs on it.

The ride is quick, opening onto an interior hallway with doors as far as the eye can see and welcoming mats in front of most of them. His presence, so near yet still emotionally distant, loosens from me to let me into his apartment.

Stepping through is a peek into his inner world, his sanctuary, and it's almost as I imagined it would be.

Modern and masculine, decorated in minimal browns and tans. A whiteboard scribbled with his notes, coding, and ideas is pushed against the wall of his dining area.

The upscale kitchen is off to the left, and a balcony opens to the east. The morning sunrise crests over the treetops, filling the space with soft, hazy light. Stacks of books about engineering, coding, and calculus are scattered on almost every surface.

He moves me to the L-shaped couch with a fantastic view of the downtown skyline, a skyline so different from the one I'm about to contribute to in Miami. As I sink into the comfortable cushions, I pluck tissues from the box on the coffee table and blow my nose.

He retrieves a couple of bottles of water from the fridge, sets them on coasters, and sits next to me—not touching, but close enough to hold me if he wants to.

"I must admit, I'm still surprised to see you."

I ball up the tissues, keeping them in my clenched hand so as not to mess up his pristine place. Dealing with the mess of me is already enough.

"I'm surprised I'm here. I left everything in Miami and just got on the first flight I could."

Once again, I'm going off script, not starting the million different ways I rehearsed on the plane. Then again, everything with Marco has been off-script and unplanned.

His eyebrows raise again, a slight tilt of his head to understand. Honestly, I don't understand it myself beyond needing to ask for his forgiveness.

"Marco, I'm sorry for not calling, not responding, and everything from Friday until now."

The last two days have felt like two years. I have packed in so much therapy and life-changing events that I almost don't know where to begin.

He licks his lips, an uneasiness creeping into his posture as he sits more upright.

"I know I messed up. I did this to you at the beginning of the week and did it again. It's not how I normally am or how I want to be with you. Especially after everything we said on Thursday."

His hand moves to cup the back of his neck.

"Yeah, I was confused. I thought we were building on something, but then you just shut me out."

My stomach tightens with guilt. Not the years-old guilt that had grown tentacles and wrapped around my ribcage to suffocate my breathing when Victor or my family came up. This guilt is fresh and alive, bloodthirsty and seeking a host to leach from.

I place my hand on his knee, needing to touch and convince him that this time will be different. If there is a next time. His muscles flinch, tightening but not moving away, which I had expected.

"Stepping off the plane, I thought I could handle it. Thought no big deal all the way to meeting my parent's friend, but when he started talking about Victor as if he really knew him. It freaked me out. He brought up things I had forgotten, and I thought, how dare he. You don't talk about him with reverence when you don't even know him. I had forgotten that he was Victor's soccer coach. How could I forget that?"

Marco's hand covers mine, seeking to comfort me when I should be comforting him for hurting him as I did.

"We forget things as we get older. Maybe it wasn't important enough to remember then. But, in a way, it had to be nice to hear about your brother through the eyes of another."

His voice is gentle and soft in his approach, and tiptoeing into dangerous areas when he doesn't have to. He could have thrown me out, yet he's sitting here in pain with me, as he did earlier this week. Every time I've needed his help, even from the first day we met, he's been doing that. It's so damn rare, and I took it entirely for granted.

"Yes and no. It stirred up a lot of unresolved feelings. The meeting led into dinner and then drinks, which was complete misery, but it had to be done."

He squeezes and releases my hand, withdrawing the connection I thought I was bridging. My hand remains, still stealing heat from him and warming my heart, which only serves to endear him to me more.

"I understand. I've been to plenty of client dinners that take on a life of their own."

"By the time I got to my hotel, showered, and got into bed, I was too wound up. I should have called you then, but it was after midnight, and my mind was a wreck. I tossed and turned and had horrible nightmares of death and being murdered when I finally did fall asleep."

He inches closer, ready to scoop me up when I hold up my hand, needing to get through all this before he decides what happens to us.

"Please don't. I need to tell you everything because it's a lot."

I drop my hand, pull another from the tissue box, and cover my clenched booger rags before setting them neatly on the table next to the unopened water. His expression is serious empathy as he shifts on the couch, leaning more toward me.

"I hadn't been back to my brother's grave, not since we buried him. It was quiet and serene. It wasn't as scary as I had made it seem in my mind. But I felt him there. I told him things . . ."

An emotional sigh loosens from my chest, and my eyes brighten with fresh tears. Marco grabs the tissue box and offers me more, which I take. I wipe my tears back, and my throat is dry and hoarse as I choke back my emotions.

"Things buried in dark places I never wanted to see the light of day. But then, I had to tell him to get them out so I could ask for his forgiveness."

It's useless. They silently fall, rolling down my cheeks and collecting under my chin.

"He was there. So many signs . . . he sent me signs. I've never really believed in that, but then it happened and kept happening."

"Fate."

The word falls from his full lips, deep and affirming. Believing in forces beyond our control from the very first day.

"Yeah. Or Victor?"

His jaw clenches, mulling over my viewpoint on how we've come together.

"Next thing I know, I'm pulling up to my parent's house, daisy-chaining one act of forgiveness with another until I'm here, asking you to forgive me for being all over the place. I know it's not fair to you. For that, I'm sorry. Sorry for dragging you into all this old mess from the past that has nothing to do with you but affects you in every way possible."

"Victoria, life is messy. And you didn't drag me into anything I didn't ask to be a part of."

That affirming statement sparks hope within me that even after ghosting him, we might be okay. I dab my face, the tissue wetting more and more as tears of gratitude replace the grief-stricken ones.

"How did it go with your parents?"

"Surprisingly well. I had so many things wrong, and they did too. I took away their daughter when I didn't have to—choosing to preserve myself over them. That wasn't right, and I think I'll always regret it. But at least I have a way back to them. It will take time, and there could be more hurt feelings to work through, which we're all onboard to do."

I blow out a loud breath, sending the bad memories of hurt and pain out and bringing in fresh oxygen and relief that I'm starting anew.

"That's great, Vic. I'm happy for you."

He pats my arm, platonic and grandmother-like, not the touch of passionate lovers.

"Speaking of no regrets, my mom dropped a bomb on me yesterday."

My entire demeanor shifts from wallowing in my stuff to heightened alert.

"What happened?"

Maybe this is why his guard is up. Maybe he's got a one-two punch like I did this weekend. From the bitterness on his face, it sure seems like it.

"She told me my dad had been seriously ill a few years back —right when I was getting job offers from big tech companies in California."

Marco's voice is thick with suppressed emotion, and the betrayal is evident in the tight set of his shoulders.

I sit up straighter, my problems momentarily forgotten as I tune into his pain.

"They never told me, but they also asked me to stay in town and explore local opportunities instead of moving away. It turns out that if my dad had passed, my mom and sisters would have needed me. They were hedging their bets using my career."

I gasp, my hand leaving his leg to clutch my chest where a sudden pain hit it. The weight of our parent's expectations affects both of us deeply, and we share in our burden to live a life that isn't what we wanted. His betrayal is raw and fresh, an ugly gash wounding him deeply.

"The job you mentioned?" I probe gently, remembering our conversations about his dreams of working in Silicon Valley.

"Yeah, the very same."

He rubs his forehead, the strain of the revelation still fresh.

"I could have been part of something big, Vic. But they kept it from me because of his health. Said they didn't want to burden me with the decision, but didn't they burden me all the same?"

I reach out, touching his hand tentatively this time.

"Oh, Marco, I'm so sorry. If anyone understands, it's me. I'd never wish this feeling on anyone, least of all such a good person like yourself."

He nods, threading our hands together.

"I know. That's why I brought it up. I understand how you are feeling more and more as I grapple with this. Logically, I get why they did what they did. Mom even apologized, saying she wouldn't have done it in hindsight. But it's hard not to feel manipulated like my life wasn't mine."

That last part stabs me right in the heart.

My wounds are just as fresh as his, both fragile and susceptible to becoming an infectious cancer if left unattended. I move closer, seeing myself in him, watching the myriad of emotions play out in real time as mine did all that time ago.

"I get it. That is me, was me. And I have to say, as much as it hurts to be betrayed by those we trust the most, it's no life if you don't work through this with them. Don't be like me, Marco. Don't go over a decade with this eating you alive before you talk to them."

My voice is soft, trying not to push too hard but needing him to know how to process this healthily and not self-destruct as I did.

"I did, briefly. I said I understood, but the longer it dwells with me, the more questions I have. Especially from my father. Was it his idea or hers? I don't know who to be more upset with. And I need to sort things out in my head before going back to them."

His dark eyes bore into mine, seeking answers I don't have beyond the wisdom I can impart from my mistakes. Anger and sadness swirl in his expression as he struggles with this recent revelation.

"Part of me wonders what would have happened if I had gone. What would my life have become if I were there and not here? Would things have gotten worse with my dad if I wasn't here? Did my presence make that much difference that I couldn't have been a plane ride away?"

He shakes out of my hold, suddenly standing and pacing

between the coffee table and the entertainment stand. Now it's his turn to get it all out. If he doesn't, he'll explode.

"I can't figure out if I resent them more for holding me back or for not telling me or for letting them influence me so greatly that I'm to blame. It's a terrible feeling. I've always taken responsibility for my actions, even my bad decisions, but this is different. It's as if I'm suffering the actions of others, and that's extremely unfair."

The pain is so raw and foreign to him that it tremors through his hands. He's so wound up, so affected by this, I go to him. Pushing into his body, my arms wrap around him, and my cheek rests against his chest.

It's what he did for me when I was so worked up, and it helped me calm down, breathe, and make sense of things.

It's only fair that I return the favor, having vast experience in his feelings. Yet, moving to the other side of my pain and hurt, on the path of forgiveness and peace, I see both sides more clearly.

However, when he's in the midst of the storm, it's hard to see clearly and find the way out in the swirling winds and torrential downpours.

Initially, he tenses, his body fighting against the understanding I'm providing. He wants to hold onto his position of being right while also choosing the most destructive road I just abandoned as fruitless.

"What did you tell me? I have a right to feel that way?" I murmur into his soft cotton tee, his heartbreaking wildly in my ear.

His hands cup my back loosely, not the lustful embrace from downstairs.

"I guess."

"Then feel that way. Take as long as you need to wrap your brain around this, but don't take too long and shut them out. It would be a horrible mistake, especially if your dad is ill."

His hand slides up my back, rounding my shoulder and returning my embrace. The other remains clutching my waist, anchoring me to him and the only place I want to be. I close my eyes, breathing in his masculine cologne and praying that he doesn't let this eat him alive like it did me.

If Victor did bring us together, perhaps it was to walk this journey with him as an expert, leading a novice through pain, hurt, betrayal, and sadness.

Our embrace deepens, his body breaking from the lies to curl over mine. He needs this as much as I do. I still have no idea where we stand, but I set aside that conversation to be what he needs—a compassionate friend with a listening ear.

"Victoria?"

"Hmm?"

"I'm glad you talked to your family. I didn't understand why you didn't call or text, but I get it if this is a tenth of what you've been battling."

I squeeze him closer and open my eyes, shifting my face to look up at him. My chin is buried between the muscles of his defined chest. There's a dampness around his eyes, crying that I didn't hear or feel. A vulnerability edges his words, mirroring his expression. He's wrecked, and it's brutal to see him like this.

"I handled it badly, Marco. I shouldn't have done that to you. I shouldn't have left you wondering and waiting. At the time, I was overwhelmed and ashamed to show you the depths of my resentment. I'm sorry. You've been the only good thing in my life in a very long time. I don't want to lose that. I don't want to lose *you*."

Bearing my soul to him yet again seems so natural.

I realize the beauty in tragedy.

The right person will share in it and extend a hand to pull me from the pits of despair. That's what he did for me. That's what I'll do for him.

"You're not losing me, Vic. Quite the opposite."

He moves me out of his body, still holding my hand, but the space allows us to see each other better.

"I don't understand."

A soft smile teases at his lips, the first one since I arrived. It breaks the tension from across his face, causing my pulse to spike in sudden worry. I'm not sure either of us can handle dropping any more shoes.

"What if I came to Miami with you?"

My mouth falls open.

Shock surges through my system.

My mind reels at this revelation.

What does he mean? What about his career, his company, and his family and their problems?

"Is this because of your family? Are you trying to get back to them for what they did? Revenge or something?"

"No, nothing like that."

He pauses, searching my face for any sign of my inner turmoil.

"It's about us, mamita. About taking a chance on something that might turn out to be great."

I blink, still trying to process what he's saying. The idea of him uprooting his life to start over with me in Miami seems wildly romantic and intensely terrifying. His gaze is steady, his hand squeezing mine reassuringly.

"I've been thinking about it a lot, especially after what happened with my dad. Life's too short, and I don't want to spend it wondering what if. I don't want to do long distance. Risk having you slip away because of conflicting schedules and last minute trips."

I swallow hard, the reality of his words sinking in. He's considering a massive change for me and us. Putting me first in a world that has never put me first. It's a reality I never thought would happen. Yet this remarkable man is ready to do just that. Asking me if he can do that for me.

"But your job is here, your new app, your family and life . . ."

My voice trails off, thinking of everything he's giving up to come with me. The scales are unbalanced, with his entire life on one side and little old me on the other.

"I can work remotely or find something new there. It's not about the job. It's about where I want to be, and that's with you."

His determination makes my heart race with excitement. That's why I flew out here—my grand gesture, even though his is grander, and he is gesturing the hell out of me.

I bit my lower lip, gazing into his dark eyes and seeing his resolve. It's deeply moving.

"You really mean this?"

"I do. I wouldn't say it otherwise."

His thumb strokes the back of my hand, a small gesture that sends warmth spiraling through me.

A thousand thoughts race through my mind. Scenarios of what our life could be like, introducing him to my family and taking him to meet Victor, showing him where I grew up, my favorite places, and my alma mater.

It's overwhelming, happening so fast, but in the best way. I couldn't have predicted or rehearsed on the plane coming here.

"If you're sure," I finally say, my voice soft but steady. "If you're really sure . . . then yeah, let's do it."

His smile widens, relief and joy mingling in his expression.

"I promise you won't regret it."

"No regrets, Marco."

His eyes widen suddenly, his mouth falling open in disbelief. An odd sensation runs through me by the way he looks at me until he cups my face and sinks his lip into mine. The kiss is tender, almost hesitant at first, as if he's affirming that this is real, that I'm here with him and we're stepping into this future together.

His lips move against mine with a gentle insistence,

weaving promises into the air between us. I melt into him, and the anxiety and uncertainties that have plagued me dissolve under his touch.

I'll live with many regrets by the time they buried my body next to my brother's, but Marco will never be one of them.

He pulls away slightly, his minty taste lingering on my lips.

"Tell me the story behind this colorful outfit, Vic."

His gaze racks down my body, lingering on all the places I yearn for his touch. I chuckle, as the obviousness of deep forest green against the orange and white logos paired with my mama's old shoes is quite the opposite of my usually sophisticated attire.

I laugh, the sound as light and airy as I feel, releasing the old demons that haunted me when I cleaned out the skeletons in my closet back home.

"Funny you should call me Vic. I have a story about that."

EPILOGUE
MARCO

From our mid-rise apartment's vast sheet of windows, I see the Miami skyline before me—a vibrant mosaic of life, light, and love from a city bursting with so much culture and passion that I feel right at home.

As I stand gazing at the view, the outline of a massive crane soars into the dusky night sky. The red light winks at me, a beacon to symbolize Victoria's project coming to life. A grateful smile hangs on my lips.

The memory of that pivotal morning hits me with a force that tightens my chest. The fear that I might lose Victoria, the silent torture of waiting for her text or call, was like a shadow settling around my heart, ready to rip it in two. Then she appeared on my doorstep at dawn, out of breath, out of sorts, and utterly perfect in her disarray.

Dark bags hung from her puffy eyes, remnants of makeup caked around her eyelids, and a dab of lip gloss on her cracked lips. Her hair was a tangled mess, wound up in a bun that barely held it on the top of her head. And that ridiculously bright and a tad too tight sweatsuit with U Miami overly branded on it. I never told her that day, but she looked prettier than ever—feminine, vulnerable, and begging to be mine.

I remember the turmoil of emotions that surged through me—the relief that she was back mixed with remnants of frustration, swirling into a cocktail of intense heaviness. Her arrival wasn't just timely—it was necessary.

It pulled me from the edge of a precipice where I teetered between hope and resignation. The sight of her there, the raw apology in her eyes, cracked something open in me. I gave her my heart that day. I never want it back.

The risk of moving to Miami, of throwing my lot in with hers, was immense. My emotions had already made the decision before logic caught up, fueled by the visceral need to be near her and be with her in every sense. That decision, made in the throes of our reconciliation, felt like the most honest action I'd ever taken. The intensity of that morning presses against my ribs, a reminder of how close I came to losing her. The fear of that loss lingers, a shadowy backdrop to the vibrant life we're building. But more potent than fear is the gratitude that washes over me—gratitude for her courage to confront me, to bridge the gap with her presence and her apologies.

Her touch that morning was a lifeline. When she reached out, her hands shaky and unsure, it wasn't just physical contact but a connection that pulled us back from the brink. That touch said more than her words could—it spoke of need, desperation, and a tangled future we were still unraveling.

As I prepare for our gathering tonight, those emotions blend into a profound sense of rightness. Following her was a leap into the unknown we took together. As I look out at the construction site, the physical manifestation of her dreams and our shared future, I'm struck by a deep, resonating peace.

However, not everyone had the same opinion about my decision. Mom and my family were the loudest protestors, especially with a much-needed reminder of what I sacrificed for them. Her protests died on her tongue, a look of guilt replacing it.

The day I said goodbye, she cried. Dad clapped me on the back, saying we go where life takes us. His more silent way of saying he understood and supported me. My relationship with them is a work in progress, not whole, not burned to the ground. A pendulum in the middle, I'm satisfied with enough to move away.

I've seen firsthand the destruction caused by carrying the weight of a parent's expectations—the deep-rooted resentment and pain of being forced to abandon my dreams to fulfill someone else's. Even though she's made remarkable progress in reconciling with her parents, I refuse to let the same thing happen to me. Her brother's cancer forced her away. My dad's illness forced me to stay. Both decisions were made for us by force, without our consent, leaving us to live with the consequences. But not anymore. This time, it's about us—our dreams and goals, individually and as a couple. As we carve out our new life, we're happy to block unsolicited parental advice and forge our own paths.

Preston's disgust was immense. The idea of moving for a woman is foreign to him despite juggling two. As if my decision to follow Victoria was an affront to his masculinity. Challenging me to stay focused on my career and not get "sidetracked" by relationships, especially ones that demanded significant changes like relocation. His reaction only fueled my resolve.

A glaring reminder of the differing values we held. Preston saw it as a potential career misstep, whereas I saw it as aligning my life with what truly mattered to me. Needless to say, I quit and am working freelance, making more money than I ever did.

Ironically, he's become a client, almost groveling for my expertise. Despite his deep bench of talent, he still considered me the best engineer for his projects.

A gentle touch warms my back, her hand sliding over my

shoulder to get my attention. I turn my head, my eyes greedily drinking her in with the luxurious red dress hugging every curve. Her thick hair in waves down her back, getting lower when I wondered aloud how it would look, hitting the top of her ass.

"Don't you look handsome."

Her tone is teasing and sensual, my cock jumping to attention with all my senses firing. A visceral reaction to how I always feel about her. She eyes my black suit, a cut she picked out for his night, and insists on a red tie to match her dress, although I have yet to put it on. The black shirt with the black suit makes enough of a statement while blending into the backdrop of showcasing her in her beautiful dress.

I don't need to match or stand out. Don't need any attention pulled away from her. She's the spotlight and the star. I'm content to be her arm candy, knowing I'm securely her partner in every aspect of the world.

"Red lipstick."

My balls tighten, the huskiness in my voice transporting both of us to that night when I smeared it before she sucked me. Her beautiful eyes darken, knowing precisely what I want to do.

"No, Marco. My makeup is too perfect to make a mess of it."

Her hand presses into my chest as I clutch her waist, pulling her against my body to feel my hard cock. He's already leaking with anticipation of slipping past her small slit and soaking in her juices. I attempt to kiss her, willing her to submit, but she turns her head, presenting me with her cheek—an unhappy groan releases from me as I dutifully deposit a light peck against her soft skin.

"Good boy."

She pats my chest, patronizing and teasing at the same time. A delicious idea wiggles its way out from the depth of my mind, and my body stiffens in response.

"One day, I'm going to cover your body in red fucking lipstick and have you on your knees sucking my cock."

"Oh, I'd love that. Then stain your body with it too."

Chinga madre.

This woman.

We're doing all that and more with her fucking lipstick.

"Can I kiss you? I won't mess it up."

My mind is reeling, spinning through all the different ways I can have her, kiss her, and lick her without making a mess of her like last time. Here, eyebrows pull together in confusion before thinking and then slowly answering.

"Sure."

A smooth smile graces my lips, my hands loosening as I step back and then kneel. I'm already raising the silky fabric to her dress, starting at the mid-thigh slit displaying miles of smooth, flawless skin.

"What are you doing?"

She squirms under my touch, trying to wiggle away, but my fingers have already looped into the tiny panties she's wearing to pull them down her thighs.

"You know exactly what I'm doing. I'm kissing you without touching your makeup. Besides, I haven't kissed her all day."

I tilt my head as a slight smirk spreads on my lips. I place a gentle kiss on her inner thigh, slowly inching closer to my desired target. My eyes never leave hers, watching the gradual transformation of her face from confusion to acceptance.

"You kissed her last night and the night before that."

Her hands settle on my shoulders, stepping out of her panties even though she's protesting a bit too much. Her actions do not align with her words. Something I find she often does—playing coy before turning into a desirable siren.

"Then I'm past due," I murmur against her flesh, breaking out in goosebumps as my lips brush up her thigh. "You're so beautiful, mamita."

My fingers keep her dress draped away from her pussy, now glistening with her arousal. The smell rips a growl from my throat as I latch onto her. She gasps, losing her footing until her back is pressed against the window, her hands splayed against the glass for balance.

"We don't have enough time."

Reaching my destination, I generously munch on her clit, flicking, licking, and eating it as she pants above me. My palms stroke the back of her leg, soothing the chills settling there.

I don't respond intentionally, waiting and wanting to see how far she'll let me go. If I get my way, I'll have her strip, fuck her against this glass which suits our shared voyeur appetite while no one can actually see, suiting my possessive, protective nature.

Her hips move, grinding into my face and sending a wave of satisfaction through my mind that she's not saying no and not pushing me away. My cock is blistering hard, ready to fuck the shit out of her. It will be quick enough to get us both a bit of relief before her party. An appetizer before the main event happening much later tonight when I can smear that red lipstick with the tip of my cock.

With slow deliberation, I lick along the exposed slit of her pussy, tasting the sweetness that awaits me there. Her moans only encourage me further as I dip deeper into her core, lapping at the tender folds. Her hands clasp into my hair, tugging me into her body and burying my nose in her wetness.

"Marco."

She moans my name, a plea for more, and I oblige. Her pussy drags against my mouth, needing more friction. My hand slides up her thigh, around the globe of her ass, and teases at her drenched entrance. I pull away, and she whimpers. My fingers stroke through her folds, swirling her clit and then plunging into her pussy.

"Do you need me to fuck you? Fuck that pretty slit against this window for the world to see?"

Her dress drapes her from view. It won't be for long if she says yes. I'll keep my promise of not messing up her hair or makeup. I'll fuck the shit out of her tight body and bring us both to completion in a matter of minutes, knowing the car is already waiting downstairs. All I need is to slip her out of this dress and pull my cock out. The power play of her being naked and me being fully clothed is a favorite between us.

"Yes," she purrs, her hand loosening from my hair.

As if reading my mind, she turns, presenting the back of her dress to me to unclasp and help her out of. She steps out of the fabric circle at her feet, careful not to snag it on her stilettos, and I quickly drape it over the couch.

She's already turned to face me, her perfect tits with hard nipples welcoming my mouth as her wet slit is engorged and ready. Desire floods her face, her eyelids half hooded when she sees my cock pulled from my pants, just as eager to please her.

"You're so fucking hot, Marco."

She doesn't compliment me often. It's not her way nor something I need. But *chinga madre*, when she does . . .

Her upper back braces against the glass, her hips and pussy jutting out in invitation, and her legs widen to hold herself upright. If I had my phone, I'd take a picture to make my fucking wallpaper on all my devices and jerk my junk to it every damn day, especially the long ones when she's off working twelve hours.

"Not as hot as this. Fuck, I'm lucky."

I reach her, my hands seizing her roughly, pulling her from the window and spinning her around. Her tits press into the glass with a yelp at the coldness, her body outlined with the soft interior lights showing every inch of her delectable skin.

"You're going to watch the world while I fuck you."

I smack her ass, the sound echoing across our modern

apartment. She mewls, wedging her hips out and wiggling that hot ass against my leaking pipe. Knowing we must be fast, I spread her ass cheeks, my finger dragging through her pussy to collect wetness to caress her puckered hole. She moans, squirming against my finger and grinding against my cock.

"Mar—"

I plunge into her dripping pussy without much notice to her. My name getting lost in her loud groans. The pleasure I've been teasing her with is becoming a reality that has me closing my eyes, trying not to nut before she does. When she's this hot, pliable, and ready, it's hard not to be selfish and fuck her rough and fast to get off. She's so tempting and irresistible that I have to fight against my cock, wanting to spray her pussy with my seed. I thrust into her repeatedly, showing her no mercy as this is what we both need right now. She begins to pant loudly now.

Her hands brace on either side of her body, withstanding the force of my blows and matching them haphazardly with her own. I urge myself on, not stopping until she has reached the edge of ecstasy.

"Look at your project, Vic. That blinking red light in the distance."

I shift back, pulling her with me to allow her space to move. Her face turns, her eyes transfixed on the crane. I smile at our reflection in the mirror, gripping her flesh, watching her get fucked in person and in the glass sends satisfaction through my body.

"Do you see it?"

"Y-yesss."

Her words are a slur of panting and lust, holding on and listening all at once.

"That's your building. You're the badass who's building it, aren't you?"

I punctuate my question with my hips, not needing an answer. This is for her, complimenting and praising her for the fierce and determined executive she is, the passionate woman I'm so lucky to call mine.

"Walking around in those tight fucking skirts and high heels. The men lusting after what is mine. That want to fuck like this. Don't they?"

She moans, adjusting her lower body against my hard thrust, the force making her wetter, and squishing sounds begin to emerge. Once again, she doesn't respond, letting the feelings I'm giving overtake her.

Doesn't matter.

I see the side glances they cast her when she's not looking the few times I've visited her at the site. With her professional silk blouses and long waves buried under a hard hat, it's difficult for them not to stare. When their gaze slides to me, her boyfriend and protector, their eyes dart away with a guilty flush to their cheeks.

Men look, it's natural.

But no gaze lingers around me.

If they dared try, it would be a raised eyebrow, followed by a couple of steps in their direction. Most guys get the hint that the behavior isn't respectful. Not that I doubt Vic's ability to put them in their place. It's just that she's so busy talking to the foreman or engineers that some glances escape her attention but not mine.

I'm careful not to cross the line at her workplace. Careful of hand placement and not overly affectionate, my lips linger longer than they should when planting a parting kiss on her luscious lips, followed by a murmured promise to continue this at home.

It always gets a reaction out of her, sometimes a shy, simmering look, other times a lick of her lips. It doesn't go unnoticed by anyone around us but possibly her, innocently thinking she's hidden her reactions well. She doesn't, and I'll never tell her otherwise.

Her hand clutches my wrist, squeezing it with less ferocity, her pussy clenching down on my dick as she comes.

"Fuck, I'm . . . coming."

She doesn't have to tell me.

My grip slips on her sweaty skin as I almost blackout, with my release threatening to spill out. I love to coat her walls and wait for it to drip out of her. Every once in a while, she'll let me take a picture of it—adding to my private collection of her.

Images I use to fuck my fist on long nights when she's working late or off at a dinner meeting. I even have a handful of private videos, the sounds she makes fucking my ears as I fuck her. It's glorious and always gets me off quickly. I'd record all our sex if she'd let me.

She is gorgeous, and I want to see her getting pleasure from all angles. Usually, she laughs, pats my chest, and remarks I'll make it without a porn library. If she only knew how wrong she was. I want a porn library of only her and us.

"Come all over my cock, mamita. Feel how good this is in your sweet little slit."

My voice is hoarse with lust and love. An emotion I have yet to tell her as I'm still grappling with how fast it's developing. Moving here to be with her—the best fucking idea of my life.

No regrets.

Her body tenses in my hold, her pussy spasming around my thick shaft when another orgasm drenches me. It's fantastic and bittersweet, wanting to come, needing to come, yet never wanting this to end.

Her hand loosens from my arm, planting a sweaty handprint on the glass that fogs up the window from our heat. A smokey glance over her shoulder, a bite of her lips, and I'm bursting into her.

"My queen of construction."

It's cheesy as fuck.

I offset my sudden onset of corniness with a slap to her ass, causing her to jump. Those stunning eyes never leave mine as sensations spread over my body. My balls tingle as they send hot ropes of cum up my shaft and shoot out my hole into hers. My panting, my breath fanning over her slick back, now glistening in the dim light from the lamp to my right. It makes her skin shimmer, too irresistible for a few sucking kisses.

Her lip pops from her teeth, a bright smile replacing her lustful look.

"Queen, huh?"

Standing naked in her sparkly stilettos, her hair still perfectly styled, her makeup with a bit of a sheen now, and that damn red lipstick.

Fuck yes, she's a queen.

My queen.

"Always."

Turn the page to read Chapter One of Diego and Isabella's in *Full Throttle!*

FULL THROTTLE: CHAPTER 1

DIEGO AND ISABELLA STORY

The streetlights flicker above me as the city of Boston hums with the distant echo of nightlife and the closer growl of motorcycles lining up along the Seaport district. My heart is pounding in sync with the rhythmic thumping of the engines. It's Saturday night, and the air smells like freedom and burnt rubber—our usual cocktail.

The air is crisp now that it's fall and the start of my final semester—the beginning of my last class. One credit short from graduating with a degree in chemistry, having miscalculated the load I took my sophomore year and still trying to catch up.

Makes no difference as I'll roll right into my Master's program, then Ph.D., before working for big pharma or a biotech company. At twenty-two years old, the blueprint of my life is already laid out for me, so I don't worry.

The extra semester gives me time to fuck around with my boys and lap up this last semester before shit gets real next spring. MIT for two years. Harvard for another four. Then I'll be making bank.

It's not about the money.

I come from money.

My parents came from money.

But this is about making my own. A personal challenge to step out of the long shadows my last name casts to carve my path. To make a name separate and apart from those of my grandfather's. I'd say I was the richest, except for Holli.

Hollister Prescott Morgan Harrington III. Dude sounds like a law firm. But yeah, Morgan—from those Morgans—the American dynasty that created banking as we know it. The other knuckleheads are from new money, something their families are proud of even if old-money families at the club look down on them for it.

Another thing I don't give a shit about. Social status, economic, and political crap. Holli is trapped in the middle of it, having to go to galas and fundraisers, unlike my family, who abstains from all the bullshit while summers are spent in the Hamptons.

The twins blast past me, signaling to something up ahead that catches their eye. They are the newest nouveau riche. Too loud, too ostentatious, and too wild for almost everyone I know. Their first-generation wealth affords them all the toys they ever wanted, all the ones I've already had. The newness wears off faster than one might think.

Bringing up the rear is Dominic.

The smartest of us all.

That's saying shit, considering we all attend some of the most prestigious schools in the nation. Dom already graduated from MIT, finishing in under three years, and has moved on to Harvard after finding "Princeton too liberal." He's also the most calculating, his wheels constantly spinning and analyzing every aspect of his life.

"Man, this strip never gets old, huh?" I yell over the roar to Holli when I catch up to him.

My grip tightens on the handlebars of my BMW S 1000 RR,

a sleek black beast that's gotten me through more street races than I can count. Growing up racing bikes, I've taken my share of spills and broken bones and laid down my bikes too many times to count. Had to give all that up after the last competition where I came down wrong and heard my spine crunch. Several weeks in the hospital convinced me to become a leisure rider.

"Gets better every time," Holli shouts back, flashing his trademark grin that is catnip for the chicks.

He's the best-looking of us.

His confident smirk and charismatic personality get him laid far too much. A revolving door of chicks to his apartment, sometimes two at a time, and getting noise complaints from his neighbors. He's idling next to me at the stoplight, astride his cherry-red Ducati Panigale that practically glows under the streetlights.

Of the five of us, Holli is the golden boy with a sharp jawline, dirty blond hair, and tatted sleeves. He lands more phone numbers than any of us can bother counting when we hang out at our local bar.

And then there's Dominic, pulled up next to me, leaning against his black with sick red accent Aston Martin AMB at the end of our lineup, arms crossed, surveying the scene with a casual indifference.

"Look at those idiots."

When his head jolts up, the edges of his lips twitch upward. His intense gaze casts straight ahead to the twins that blast through the light, leaving us behind. Unable to tell which is which from this distance, their black, red, and neon green Aprilia are clown colors and identical—the same as their looks, haircuts, and all-black riding clothes.

One of them is standing on the saddle of his bike as it careens down the street. Arms are thrown out to the side, and he looks like a live cross with every bit of a death wish. They are the jokesters of our group, never taking anything seriously and always doing stupid shit.

Without leather and helmets, they're risking it all. The knuckleheads act as though they are invincible and give me shit for having an "old man back" despite my young age. They don't know shit about the dangers of these bikes.

"Fucking fools."

My words are lost in the idling of our three engines.

Holli shakes his head and rolls his eyes. He knows the risk, having lost a cousin a few years back to a motorcycle accident. The guy was sideswiped by an eighteen-wheeler running a red light. They had to scrape pieces of him off the front of the grill.

"Let's save them from themselves."

The light barely changes to green before he shoots off, his bike almost the fastest among us. Dominic blasts after him, taking my position in the formation we always drive in. I follow slower, unable to deal with the twins's bullshit again. I had to babysit their ass last weekend when they pissed off some guys at a new bar we stopped at to grab a beer.

Emilio or Massimo, one of the fuckers shot off their mouth to a group of frat boys. Despite their gym obsession and having a solid thirty pounds of muscles on me, we were outnumbered. I wasn't looking to get my ass kicked right before school started again.

I've shown up too many times to class with bloody knuckles and bruises to know teachers make one judgment and seal your fate for the rest of the semester.

With Hollister willing to pull babysitting duty this time and Dominic flanking him, I ease into the ride—the loop. Our favorite route, a winding stretch along the Charles River, offers the best view and the perfect curve that tests precision and speed—the two things I live for. It's where we lose ourselves in the blur of the city rushing past and the adrenaline of the chase.

The cool night air hits my face, and I inhale deeply, feeling calm. Riding has always been my therapy, my church, and my meditation. When shit gets real or deep, I escape to my bike.

Always loyal and always available.

There's nothing like speeding down this historic stretch, with the modern skyscrapers on one side and the timeless flow of the Charles on the other—an odd contrast that never fails to amaze.

When I catch up with them, the twin forming the cross is now straddling his bike. Holli and Dom, having talked some sense into them, force them back into the riding formation. As we weave through the lesser-known back streets, I take the rear, tires gripping the occasionally slick cobblestones.

The only sounds on these narrow streets are the rush of wind and the symphony of our revving engines. It seems we're not the only ones drawn to the thrill tonight.

That's when I see her.

A new figure on the scene.

She's astride a MV Augusta. So bold it could only belong to someone who knows how to handle it. Hot pink with a glossy finish that catches the shimmering lights of the city and a distinctive sticker—If You're Gonna Ride My Ass At Least Pull My Hair.

I chuckle, drawn to her like a moth to a flame. She's dressed in all leather, her knee-high, heeled boots tucked tightly against the bike are things dreams are made of. Images of those boots hiked over my hips flash before my eyes.

Her helmet extends my laugh—all black with a bright pink braid coming from the top, making good on her sticker to pull it and offering no clue about who she might be.

"Whoa, check out that color!" Emilio yells, his eyes rippling with excitement when he drops back toward me. "What does her bike say?"

Without a word, Holli accelerates, his competitive edge

flaring as he aims to catch up with the mysterious rider. We all fall into formation behind him, curiosity piqued, and spirits ignited by the unexpected visitor who must be new to the bike scene. We've ridden these roads for years, knowing even the most casual riders.

But she is new bait.

Fresh game for any of us.

Except Dominic, who already has a thing going that he's pretty tight-lipped about. Holli is the last person who needs to add another notch to his belt. He had a half-naked girl walking out of his place when I went by to pick him up for this ride.

The pink bike is fast, really fast.

The rider's form is perfect, tucked low over the handlebars, every move is fluid and precise. Completely unaware or uninterested in us, she white lines through some cars, darting between lanes with the ease of a seasoned pro.

We all speed up, keeping pace with Holli, who's trying to catch her. Emilio laughs, yelling over the scream of the wind and the roar of our bikes.

"She's smoking us."

The thrill in his voice, the challenge in his face, and the rev of his bike let me know he's enjoying every bit of this. Reckless as it is, racing through these side streets, I push my bike harder to its limits as she is with hers.

It's fascinating watching her lean into the curve, her gloved fingers caressing the black concrete that could end her life in seconds.

It's the sexiest fucking thing ever.

"Did you see that?"

Em's voice is hyper at witnessing her smooth stunt.

He's the lover of stupid shit.

Probably the twin doing the cross on his bike, although his brother can be just as foolish and reckless.

I don't respond, leaning into the curve and fighting the

temptation to touch the concrete as she had done. Emilio does, his hand tearing from the asphalt, ripping away his skin at this high rate of speed. He's a grinning fool when he shows me the blood and grit of his fingertips.

It's a stunt trick often seen in racing.

Something I used to do for show and rarely for balance, the physics of a well-positioned body doing the work instead. That small gesture tells me more about her.

She races or has raced.

Something we have in common, and common ground is all I need to win her over from Hollister. Does she prefer lean-built, dark-featured Pacific Islanders or a tattooed golden boy with a penchant for cheating? Maybe she's a freak, desperate to be sandwiched between the twins that share every women they meet?

We're a blur along the river, the city lights streaking past like stars racing across the sky. The mysterious rider glances back just once, surprised at the sight of us chasing after her. She throws us a low V sign, a brief greeting amongst bikers.

Her fingers pointed to the ground for a split second, too fast to be longer than a blink of an eye, before adjusting her posture and radiating confidence. Then, with a burst of speed that seems to come from nowhere, she pulls ahead, leaving us trailing in the wake of her audacity.

"She's got guts," I mutter through gritted teeth.

The engine growls beneath me like some great beast straining at the leash. I pull ahead, overtaking Holli, who flashes me a knowing grin. The smile of a competitor, as the wind sucks the tears from my eyes and sends my shirt flapping high up my back.

As we approach the final stretch, the one with the sharpest turn along the river, she shows no sign of slowing. Instead, she leans deeply into the curve with a grace that's almost infuriating, her bike's tires kissing the asphalt in a perfect arc.

I blast ahead, my racing experience shining through as the guys slow, and I accelerate. Every time I race like this, my dick hardens. The velocity and adrenaline pumping blood straight into my crotch while my heart throbs with excitement. Rarely have I struggled to overtake, much less keep up with a female rider.

They just don't have the experience, hours on the bike, and stamina to push themselves this hard for this long. Yet, there she is—me in female form, gaining distance as her tires eat up the road between us.

My forearm strains against the throttle.

The ache is familiar and welcome.

A throwback to my younger years when my body ached all the time due to racing injuries. She releases her handle to toss the pink braid over her shoulder, catching the wind and flying behind her helmet. The casualness is shocking as I glance down at my bike, seeing we're well past 120 mph. A speed in which no one should release their hand to fool with their fake hair.

Then she blasts forward, forcing her bike beyond its capacity until she's gone, disappearing into the shadows she emerged from. Her taillights, a pair of red eyes winking out of existence, taking the sticker and her helmet hair with her.

We slow down, gathering at the usual end of our loop, hearts pounding and breaths coming in short, heavy bursts. Holli runs a hand through his sweat-dampened hair, a rare look of defeat etched across his features despite the wide grin he has for me.

"You in love, Diego?"

He tosses his head in her direction.

Dominic sides up on my right, dragging from his vape with his usual disinterest. Both sets of eyes land on me with his question. They know I don't chase women. There are too many options for that, given all the schools in this city. I'm not the player that Hollister is, nor the quietly committed Dominic, but somewhere in between.

"Who was that?" Massi asks, both hands on his upper thighs as he catches his breath. "If she likes it that fast, she'll definitely love a few rounds with me."

"You mean us," Em adds, shoving his brother while pumping his hips, replicating what they'd do to her.

"Why settle for Diego's micro dick when you can have two real dicks. One down her throat while the other is shoved up her—"

"Shut the fuck up, Emilio."

Dominic's words mix with the exhalation of his latest vape. He's never one to get vulgar with us out of respect for his mystery woman. Or that's what Holli says. I think it's because the dude is a fucking genius, and the twins' idiocrasy gets on his nerves.

I used to wonder why he hung with us mere mortals, but then I realized all the intelligence needs an outlet. Bikes, vaping, and lifting are his only social things outside his studies and labs.

Holli's gaze bores into me as he sits astride his bike, his forearms crossed with a casualness that exudes more confidence than anything.

"What are you going to do, Diego?"

"I have no idea, Holli, but I need to figure out something."

The image of that hot pink bike and its fearless rider burns bright in my mind as I look down the dark street she blazed down.

"She got you all bricked up, huh?"

Massi knows since he used to be in competitive sports and understands what increased testosterone does to a guy. Emilio tries to reach for my cock, wanting a feel, and I shove his ass away.

"What the fuck, brother? Diego doesn't want you touching his junk."

He shoots his brother a bloody bird after almost falling over his bike.

"He knows I don't like cocks. I just wanted to cop a feel of his tiny dick," he defends, which gets an annoyed snort out of Dom.

The whole micro dick debate started at a party a couple of years ago when Emilio was drunk off his ass, showing everyone his cock and wanting to compare. With his pants around his ankles, he kept tugging at this guy's pants and almost got his ass beat before Massimo and I got across the crowded house party to get to him.

He sagged heavily against his brother. His hand fumbled for my pants when I slapped his face and said I have a micro dick to get him to knock it off. Something I thought he'd forget in his drunken haze, yet somehow, that seemed to stick in his brain.

"What the fuck, Em? What happened to your hand?" Massi asks, his eyes wide with surprise, reaching toward him.

Em wipes his gravel-coated digits across his shirt, leaving a bloody trail across his midsection, and whispers to his sibling.

"Good luck with that, man." Dominic ignores them, clapping me on the back in sympathy. "She's probably halfway to the Cape by now."

"Probably."

With that bike, that speed, and her undeniable confidence, I'm certain I'll see her again. If not by karma, then by my surveillance of popular bike groups. I'll ask around, as she is not someone I can easily forget.

"Are we going to keep standing around like a bunch of pussies, or are we going to ride and find some pussies?" Em whines, toying with his engine and revving it like an impatient child.

Dom casts him a death stare and tucks his vape away.

"I'm out," he says, reversing his bike and angling it in the opposite direction.

"Come on, Dom, don't be a pussy. You always bail. It's not fair."

Either Emilio doesn't hear the whininess in his voice or doesn't give a shit. Either way, he's successfully run Dominic off again, resulting in Dom texting me asking if we can ride out of town tomorrow.

It's almost like clockwork with these two.

"Hollister, Diego, I'll catch you guys later. See you, Massimo."

Dom scratches his beard, glares at the idiot twin, and rattles the accelerator before taking off, leaving Em shooting the finger at his back.

"What a little bitch," Em huffs, his immaturity almost too much for the group until Holli puts his hand on Em's forearm, telling him to chill. He doesn't listen, pulling his bike ahead, indicating he's leading the formation instead of the usual Hollister.

"Don't mind him. He's just antsy because his semester is shit due to late registration."

Massi constantly makes excuses for Emilio. I suppose it's a twin thing or maybe a brother thing. I wouldn't know as an only child, but he's got to get tired of it at some point. Being his brother's keeper is a full-time job with that idiot.

"Yeah."

Emilio rarely gets on my nerves.

Once I categorize people, their actions and emotions don't affect me. It's only when I can't figure them out or they don't act according to their assigned category that it irritates me. The twins are categorized as overgrown children that could kick my ass if they wanted to, although neither is really the fighting type.

I tried to share my philosophy with Dominic since he is hair-pinned triggered by everything the twins do, but he was asking for the science behind my theory. As if I sent it through a chem lab to draw these conclusions. Sometimes that motherfucker is just too smart for his own good.

Em and Holli take off, Massi follows and leaves me to ponder my thoughts as I take up the rear. It's been a while since I had a steady girl. I've got plenty of free time this semester, but with a heavy load in the spring, I'm not sure I can commit to a relationship. Friends with benefits would be ideal, particularly with someone who rides.

As the guys bullshit ahead, arguing about what bar we're headed to, I'm already plotting a return to the loop. Not just for the thrill of the ride but to find my mystery rider.

"Once I do, I'll ride her ass and pull her hair."

Read the rest of Diego and Isabella's in *Full Throttle!*

(The Bikers of Boston Series, Book 1)

She's teaching him about chemistry in and out of the classroom.

DIEGO KAHALE IS COASTING through his last semester at Boston College, ready to nail his advanced chemistry class and finally snag that hard-earned degree. But his carefully laid plans take a hairpin turn one night when a mysterious motorcyclist on a blazing hot pink bike blazes past him and his friends, leaving nothing but the roar of the engine and the sting of curiosity in their wake. Determined to uncover the identity of the adrenaline junkie rider, Diego's hunt leads to an explosive discovery —the daredevil is none other than his new, off-limits chemistry professor, Isabella Rossi.

Smart, sharp, and achingly untouchable, Isabella doesn't just teach chemistry—she is chemistry, igniting something in Diego he's never felt before. Their attraction crackles with forbidden tension, and soon, the walls of the lecture hall aren't the only thing between them. What starts as stolen glances and heated debates spirals into a connection too intense to ignore.

Will their undeniable bond be worth the risk of everything they've worked so hard for—or will their explosive chemistry leave them both in ruins?

Full Throttle blends the excitement of a biker romance with the reverse age gap, the forbidden love between a charismatic student and his captivating professor. It is the first book in The Bikers of Boston Series and is a connected standalone.

GET TWO FREE BOOKS

Sign up for my newsletter to ensure you are the first to know about new releases, sneak peek excerpts, cover reveals, book sales, and author giveaways!

The Cougars and Cubs Series
is steamy, naughty instalust
reverse age gap fun.

DOWNLOAD FOR FREE ON MY WEBSITE
www.gigimeier.com

Paolo and Taylor's story is a duel POV, meet cute,
reverse age gap, workplace romance.

The Cañon Series 🖤
is deliciously dark and intensely traumatic.

DOWNLOAD FOR FREE ON MY WEBSITE
www.gigimeier.com

Dani and Tomlin's story is a single POV, slow burn, enemies-to-lovers, forced proximity romance. Check my website for a list of content and trigger warnings.

BONUS CONTENT

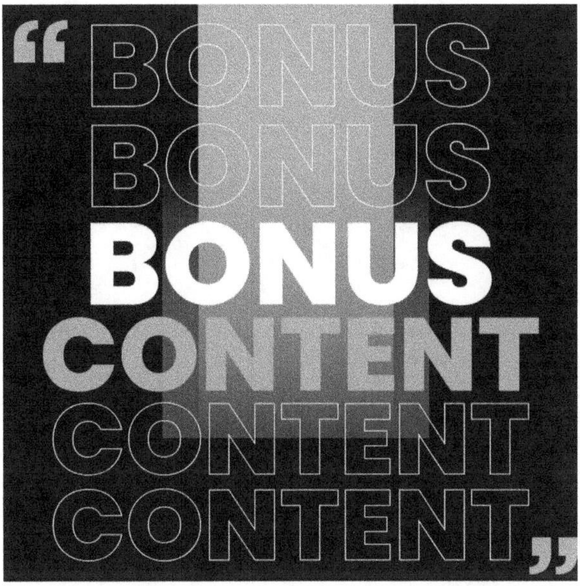

Want more?

I have exclusive bonus and deleted scenes for you on my website: www.gigimeier.com/freebies.

I'm always adding more for my loyal readers as a big THANK YOU for loving my books and supporting me as an author ❣

IF YOU ENJOYED THIS BOOK

Thank you for reading *Marco,* the fifth book in The Cougars and Cubs Series . Stick around for *Full Throttle*, the first book in The Bikers of Boston Series.

If you enjoyed *Marco*, please consider leaving a review on BookBub, Goodreads, or your favorite retailer to let others know about this steamy Latin couple, reverse age gap, fated soulmate, workplace romance.

Reviews are greatly appreciated. They help independent authors like myself get our books in front of more readers.

GiGi Meier

ALSO BY GIGI MEIER

Standalone Book

Coyote

Sammie and Carlos's forced proximity

cartel, kidnapped, Military hero, dark romance

The Cañon Series

Tomlin

The start of Dani and Tomlin's

slow burn, enemies-to-almost-lovers

Tomlin Takahashi Duet #1

The Cañon Series, Book #1

Takahashi

The conclusion of Dani and Tomlin's

friends-to-lovers, happily ever after

Tomlin Takahashi Duet #2

The Cañon Series, Book #2

Hamilton

Hamilton and Molli's second chance,

small town, police officer romance

The Cañon Series, Book #3

Isla

Isla and Gabe's opposites attract,

age gap, forbidden love romance

The Cañon Series, Book #4

The Cougars and Cubs Series

Paolo

Taylor and Paolo's reverse age gap,

forced proximity, office romance

The Cougars and Cubs Series, Book #1

Sebastian

Sebastian and Chloe's reverse age gap,

opposites attract, Christmas romance

The Cougars and Cubs Series, Book #2

Giovanni

Giovanni and Kacie's reverse age gap,

protector, Alpha male romance

The Cougars and Cubs Series, Book #3

Kadus

Kadus and Bex's reverse age gap,

best friend's brother, rockstar romance

The Cougars and Cubs Series, Book #4

Marco

Marco and Victoria's reverse age gap,

steamy Latin couple, fated soulmates romance

The Cougars and Cubs Series, Book #5

The Bikers of Boston Series

Full Throttle

Diego and Isabella's reverse age gap,

college professor and student, forced proximity romance

The Bikers of Boston Series, Book #1

Gods and Goddesses Anthology

Eternal Reign

Hades and Persephone Modern Retelling

Russian bratva, kidnapping, touch her and die, slow burn.

ABOUT THE AUTHOR

After retiring from a thirty-year career in corporate America, GiGi Meier is delighted to be writing romance novels about strong female characters and their complicated, swoon-worthy men.

She loves telling stories and figuring out why her characters do what they do. With heartbreaking angst, panty-dropping lust, and enviable love, her stories linger long after you close the book.

When GiGi is not eating over her laptop, she likes to spend time in the pool with her children, walk her furry babies, and film videos for Instagram and YouTube. Whether attending a book club or hosting a game night, she loves connecting with new people and making friends.

Sign up for my newsletter to ensure you are the first to know about new releases, sneak peek excerpts, cover reveals, book sales, and author giveaways!

www.gigimeier.com

www.ingramcontent.com/pod-product-compliance
Lightning Source LLC
Chambersburg PA
CBHW061130200626
46817CB00016B/541
* 9 7 8 1 9 6 3 6 2 5 0 7 3 *